Tales of the Feisty Druid: Book One

THE ARCADIAN DRUID

CANDY CRUM & MICHAEL ANDERLE

LMBPN Publishing

PMB 196, 2540 South Maryland Pkwy

Las Vegas, NV 89109

First US edition, July 2017

From Candy:

*To my boys, thank you for
being my reason for everything.
To my family who support me
no matter what.
To the fans and readers--thank you!*

From Michael:

*To Family, Friends and
Those Who Love
To Read.
May We All Enjoy Grace
To Live The Life We Are
Called.*

The Arcadian Druid Team

TEN YEARS AGO

Matriarch... Patriarch... Please don't let her die like this. She must survive.

Silent prayers filled Elayne's mind; her arms held her young daughter tightly on the horse as they raced through the woods. The Hunters weren't far behind, and death was sure to accompany them.

The druid said she was extraordinary. Arryn must *live.* Her mind focused on the promise, to the hope the druid provided.

Elayne pleaded to the old gods as she ducked under a tree branch. *Please accept my sacrifice and save her life. I believe she would serve you well.*

The sound of iron-clad hooves thundering against the damp ground echoed through the night air, assaulting their ears. The cool wind whipped the coarse mane of their spotted horse into Arryn's face. She closed her eyes tight as Elayne cradled her tighter.

The darkness scared Arryn, and she wasn't quite certain if it was the heavy fog that had settled in the woods or the pounding of the two horses in stride behind them that terrified her more. Things lurked in the darkness—large things with ferocious teeth—especially in the fog, but the greatest threat right then were the Hunters not far behind them. They may not have claws, but they had magitech.

Weapons far worse and *much* more lethal.

Now, riding on the back of a horse whose thundering hooves carried them further away from Arcadia and closer to freedom, Elayne and Arryn silently prayed that they be delivered to safety—to Elysia, the Druid they had met in the Dark Forest. Free from the Hunters who Elayne could now see were getting closer. Free from Adrien. Free from death.

"Arryn," Elayne said, her voice trembling with fear. She knew the words that she needed to say, but they killed her to speak them. Tears welled in her eyes, knowing what she was about to do. "I love you. I love you so much."

Arryn's entire body stiffened in Elayne's arms at the sound of her voice, and she knew that her daughter was far more aware of their situation than a small girl should have been.

"No! You can't! Please!" her daughter pleaded, somehow knowing exactly what was about to happen.

Elayne had heard that very same tone that she'd just taken in her husband's voice before he'd pulled them both to his chest. He'd hugged them and then forced them to run while he sacrificed himself to the Hunters to buy them time to escape. But it didn't take long for the Hunters to catch on, and now Elayne sounded just as desperate.

"It has to be this way, baby. I can't let you die when I can stop it." Her mother blinked the tears away. "Remember, you have greatness in you. One of these days, you will come back and save our people. Help them, guide them." Elayne squeezed her daughter's waist with the arm that held her in place. "You know where to go. You know what you must do. You'll be safe there."

Arryn began to cry. Elayne felt the tears drip from the girl's cheeks down onto the bare skin of the arm that she had wrapped around her waist. There was no way to know if Christopher had survived, and now Elayne planned to sacrifice herself as well.

It didn't matter as long as their daughter lived…

The sting in her eyes fought the pain in her chest as she continued instructing her only child. "Please. Do this for me. For your father. Don't let us die in vain. Let this be our victory—let your *full life* be our victory. One day, Arryn, one day you will make this right. Return to Arcadia when you're strong enough and take it back. Do what we *couldn't*."

Her daughter was too young to understand the love a parent carried for their child, but she certainly understood her love for her parents. Elayne hoped that it was enough to drive the girl forward and allow her never to look back.

"Arryn, *promise* me!" Elayne demanded, her own need to hear it come back coloring her request.

"I promise," Arryn said, her small arm lifting to wipe away her own tears.

Elayne pulled hard on the reins, the horse crying out into the murky darkness as she did. He slowed to a stop, and Elayne quickly dismounted.

She moved to the side and squeezed her daughter's hand.

She pointed down the path. "Hold tight to the reins and head west. That's all you need to know. Stay close to the water. She will find you and keep you safe. *I love you!*"

Arryn was barely able to choke out the words, "I love you," before her mother slapped the horse's rear, sending him into a full gallop.

Then, her mother turned from watching her daughter streak away, and settled herself in the middle of the path, waiting for those who would do her child wrong.

The girl wanted nothing more than to stop. She wanted to go back for her mother, but her instincts and the promise she made drove her forward.

The foggy darkness lit up bright orange behind her as the tortured screams of men echoed throughout the vast wooded land. Suddenly, a bright flash from a magitech weapon filled the sky, and the sound of her mother's pain-filled screams reached her ears.

Then—there was nothing.

No horses. No men on foot. No voices. No screams. Just the sound of her horse running through the night, the tiny branches and ground giving way with every stride. She said another prayer that the Matriarch and Patriarch would take care of her heroic mother, knowing she'd just given her life to protect her.

Blinking the tears away, Arryn focused on moving faster to get to safety. The Dark Forest was a long ride away. The horse would need to stop for water, and she would need to sleep, but fear and desperation pushed her. Her mother had told her to head west and stay close to the water, so she found the Kalt river and travelled along the edge.

Horse and rider traveled as long as they could before her horse couldn't go any farther.

Being outside of a city was new and scary. After a not-so-restful sleep from losing her mother and anything familiar she'd ever known, she and her misappropriated stallion carried on.

They traveled in search of the druid, Elysia, the woman who only a few months prior had vowed to care for Arryn in any emergency to repay a life debt. As Arryn approached the edge of the lush Dark Forest, Arryn saw people waiting for her.

Elysia was standing there with several other druids. Arryn saw another familiar face with those standing—Elysia's son, Cathillian.

Somehow, the druid Elder had known of her coming. How she knew wasn't important to Arryn at the moment, but the success of her parents' sacrifice, was.

Arryn pulled back on the reins and slowed her horse before slowly climbing off. Taking the reins in her hand and walking alongside him with tears in her eyes, she approached Elysia and the others.

"Oh, Arryn," Elysia said, opening her arms to the young one.

Elysia took in a deep breath. The young girl's presence without her mother could only mean both of her parents sacrificed all for their child. Elysia's expression was warm, but sad. It held the weight of young Arryn's reality.

Arryn dropped the reins some ten feet from the group and ran into Elysia's arms, the tears finally releasing in a torrent, overflowing. Cathillian stepped forward, placing a hand on her back. She turned her head over to see who was touching her, and he brushed the black hair from her face.

"I'm sorry about your parents," he said in a small, fragile voice. She watched with her eyes as he turned his face to the horse, and with a wave of his hand, her stallion approached. Cathillian took hold of the reins and turned to face her once again. "You have a home here now."

Arryn pulled back off of Elysia's shoulder and nodded to him. "Mourn tonight, child," Elysia told her, gently stroking Arryn's right cheek with her thumb. "Tomorrow is a new day, and we will go to the river to honor them. Tomorrow, you'll say your goodbyes. They will rest well knowing that you're safe."

The words pierced Arryn's heart.

Her mother had said as much. Arryn's life would be her mother's victory. If she wasted her life wishing for other outcomes, she would dishonor her. As Arryn turned and looked into the eyes of the beautiful, golden-haired druid, she knew that her parents' judgement had been well placed.

All Arryn could see was the kindness of her heart, and the smile of a mother.

All Arryn could think about was realizing the future that Elysia had seen for her the day they'd met. The power that Elysia had sensed in her.

Arryn nodded to the woman, promising herself she would become strong enough to return to Arcadia.

And she would avenge her parents.

ONE

PRESENT DAY
TEN YEARS LATER

T*he intense, morning sun was* bright enough to shine through the thick canopy of leaves overhead as Arryn prepared for the day.

She made her way outside of her small cabin that was expertly crafted out of live trees by magic, bending and shaping them into a thriving home. Walking down the steps made of stone, she stopped to take in the morning view.

The ground was particularly cool against Arryn's bare feet. It had rained the night before, and the sun hadn't yet risen enough to allow the dirt to completely dry. Still, it was dry enough for her to walk around without her boots, and that was good enough for her.

Like the druids she'd come to call family, she preferred to explore the area barefoot. In training, battle, and normal, everyday living, the druids below always kept them close to nature and allowed them to better access magic at all times.

Only when it rained or on journeys did they prefer to wear shoes.

Over the years, she'd grown to enjoy it just as much. It didn't matter to her that she'd been adopted into their ways instead of being naturally born there—she loved them. The druids' peaceful way of life allowed her to be free. Free in every way.

Several of her friends were up and wandering around, but she could easily sneak away. Those few moments alone always brought her joy.

Arryn had only made it a few hundred feet away from camp when she felt something slither around her left ankle. She gasped and jumped, trying to pull away, but it held strong.

Then, something wrapped around her right ankle, tugging a little as it did. Another gasp escaped her throat as her heart began to pound. She looked down to see thick, leafy vines encircling her legs.

Her face fell, and her eyes narrowed as a heavy sigh escaped her. "Oh, *hell*," she said to herself just before her feet were pulled out from under her.

She landed hard on the ground, the air rushing out of her lungs in a loud *oof!* She silently thanked whatever gods could hear her that it had rained, and the firm ground beneath her was softer that morning.

Arryn sighed in defeat, lying there, ankles tied together. She defiantly crossed her arms over her chest like an angry child. "Who the hell needs enemies when I have the two of you?"

Wild laughter at her expense echoed through the immediate area, only irritating her further.

"Come, now," Elysia giggled. "You can't blame us *entirely,* now can you?"

Arryn looked to her right to see Elysia and Cathillian standing there, both with mischievous grins on their faces.

The elusive and mythical druids… Arryn had heard tales about them as a child, but no one really believed they existed.

Oh, they existed alright.

And they were assholes.

But they were only assholes if they *liked* you, and only if they cared enough to teach you to always be on guard and never lose focus. Otherwise, they were just piss-your-pants terrifying.

Arryn, however, was not amused.

Still wearing her smile, Elysia looked around the forest as she inhaled deeply, no doubt taking in the scent of the early morning air. Cathillian locked eyes with Arryn, the smirk on his face telling her he was very pleased with his prank.

"It never fails!" he said. "You have to do better than that. Always keep your senses up! If you don't close yourself off to nature, it'll warn you of impending dangers. How do you think we know when something wanders into the Forest?" He tapped on the side of his head. "Guard's always up."

Arryn kept her position on the ground as she let him lecture her about the usual. Her mind always wandered a bit. Being in tune with nature one hundred percent of the time didn't come easy for her. It was something a druid was taught from day one to do, but she had to work hard.

Elysia always played little harmless pranks on her to remind her to open up. Cathillian, was just as bad. He was a damn good warrior, but his magic was a bit weaker in comparison.

Though, that wasn't saying much as he was one of the strongest warriors that they had, and he was also the grandson of the Chieftain which meant his magic was nothing shy of strong. Unfortunately for him, he was always a total scatterbrain. Not much better than Arryn in that department.

And she planned to remind him of that.

As he prattled on, a large bird landed in the tree next to them. It was a golden eagle, not unlike Cathillian's own familiar, Echo, though much smaller by comparison.

More specifically, the eagle landed on a thick branch just overhead of Cathillian. Arryn furrowed her brows and nodded her head, feigning sincere interest in his lecture.

He was so sure of himself that he didn't notice the slight shift in the position of her eyes as she focused on the bird. She felt the connection to the eagle, allowing her to communicate wordlessly through her magic. It looked down at Arryn, and the corner of her mouth turned up as she pointedly looked over to Cathillian.

With a familiar—animals that have a much deeper, magical connection to their druid—the communication happens seamlessly. The effects are unpredictable with random wildlife, though the bird seemed happy enough to entertain her.

The bird unfurled its large wings for a moment before settling in, shaking its tail feathers a little, and shitting directly on top of Cathillian's head.

Arryn laughed hard—almost too hard.

"Oh, my," Elysia said, sharing in the laughter as well. "I suppose you should take your own advice, son."

"You're no better!" Cathillian argued, wiping the mess from the front of his face where it had run down his forehead. "You didn't even notice she was casting!"

Elysia shrugged. "I was taking in the morning. Perhaps we should all take lessons on keeping our guard up." She looked over to Arryn, smile still on her face and winked. "Nice one."

"Thanks. So, uh… You guys planning to let me go any time today? Or should I plan to forage on—" she looked to each side of her "—these lovely ferns here? I'm sure they're delicious."

With only a wave of Elysia's hand, the vines unraveled, and Arryn was freed. Cathillian made his way over, and Arryn put her finger in the air.

"No! No, you just stay right there, sir."

Cathillian gave a devious smile. "Aw, but I just wanted to help you up."

Arryn knew better. She shook her head. "Nope. Not with *that* on your hands. You just stay right over there, shit head." She looked up, thinking over her witty retort for a moment before laughing hard all over again. "*Oh*, damn. You're *not* living that one down."

"Jerk," Cathillian said, waving his hand a bit. A few clumps of mud lifted from the ground and hit her directly in the side of the head, sticking to her hair and rolling down onto her shoulder.

Arryn sat there, shocked for a moment before jumping to her feet. "Oh, you're gonna die now, bitch!"

The two had grown up together as best friends. Always arguing.

Always sparring. Always playing pranks. It wasn't unheard of for one to attack the other, especially when there was a single step taken too far.

"Arryn!" Elysia said, stepping between the two. "It's such a beautiful morning. You should walk with me to the river. We'll clean that mess outta your hair."

"Can I come? Because I have *far* worse than a little *dirt* in mine," Cathillian said, looking to Arryn. "Besides, she wants to kill me, and I can't pass up the opportunity to show her up."

He winked, earning an eye roll from Arryn.

"After that speech you gave, I assumed you were one with *all* of your surroundings, son. Right? I'm sure you'll figure it out," Elysia said with an exaggerated smile before turning to walk away.

Arryn bit her lip to keep from laughing or slinging another insult his way.

She loved Elysia like a mother, though she'd never been raised to think of her that way. Elysia showed Arryn the love and affection that any mother shows her children, but Arryn was more like a friend of the family, and Elysia was her godmother.

"That wasn't the first time I've caught you wandering off alone," Elysia said. Though her words might have suggested that she was irritated or upset, her voice was as warm as it usually was. "You know how I feel about that."

Arryn didn't answer right away. They walked in silence as Arryn tried to pull larger globs of mud from her hair, but instead only pressed them in further. Her nose scrunched as she pulled her hand away and saw just how dirty it was, knowing her hair was even worse. She wiped it on her brown, leather pants.

"I know how you feel about it, and I'm sorry," Arryn finally responded.

"I don't need to tell you that large beasts lurk in the woods, even in the peaceful Dark Forest. They, too, find their way in. They aren't quite as deterred by thick walls of thorns and brush as humans. There's never a shortage of food sources here because of our people. It attracts animals of all kinds. You know better than most why I fear anyone wandering off alone. Everyone travels in pairs."

Arryn absolutely knew why Elysia had such an issue with traveling in solitude.

Her son, Cathillian, was always quite the rebel when he was a child—from what she'd been told anyway. He liked to wander off alone and be an adventurer.

One day, ten years ago, that didn't work out so well for him. If it hadn't been for Arryn's mother, Elayne, Cathillian would have been killed by a large lycanthrope. It was because of that day that Elysia owed Arryn's parents a life debt.

"I never go far," Arryn said. "Sometimes, I just need to be alone, ya know? I connect with nature way differently than all of you. You wake up, and you're bonded. You're bonded while you eat, while you play, while you sleep. For me, I have to walk through nature. It's hard to do that while so many eyes are on me."

"You underestimate yourself. You always have," Elysia said, reaching for Arryn's hand and giving it a light squeeze.

Arryn returned the gesture, working up the courage to speak candidly. "There's something I've always wanted to ask, but never did because I didn't want you to think I was an ungrateful brat."

Elysia turned to look at Arryn for a moment. "Never be afraid to talk to me. Ask away." Elysia smiled, and it was warm, motherly.

Arryn sighed.

She could feel the energy pulsing through Elysia's hand. It was something her godmother had taught her to do. Sense energy in all living things: plants, animals, and people alike. Once a person could do that, they can sense the magic of others.

They can also sense their true nature.

Arryn nodded, taking a breath before beginning. "Why'd you do it? Take me in, I mean. You owed them a life debt. That only meant you needed to save my life. Hell, you could've sheltered me for a few days, maybe even a week or two, and then set me loose like we'd never met. You didn't have to take me in and raise me to adulthood. You definitely didn't have to teach me your magic or your ways."

Arryn absentmindedly kicked at a rock as they walked, narrowly missing it. Having forgotten she was barefoot, she was grateful her depth perception was shitty that early in the morning.

When Elysia said nothing right away, Arryn continued. "You guys hide nothing from me. I've seen things you don't let outsiders see. Even other visiting druids don't get to know those things. So—why did you take me in the way you did? Why take in an outsider if you hate the outside so much?"

There was a pause as Elysia contemplated her words. "It's not that we hate the outside world. In fact, we used to trade with the people of Arcadia. But Adrien became an insatiable, twisted human being. There was no real reason for us to trade with them because we were self-sufficient. So, we don't hate them. We just have no respect for people that are ungrateful to the land, animals, and even the other people that they take from in order to have the lives that they do."

Arryn nodded. "I guess that makes sense. Still, why'd you take me in?"

"You were so young then. Do you remember the day we met for the first time?"

At only the mention of it, Arryn's mind immediately began to swim with the memories of that day. Her parents had taken her on a trip to find a place to hide her if the worst were to happen.

In other words—if Adrien, the tyrannical Chancellor of Arcadia, happened to catch on to their plan to liberate the Arcadian people and order them to be killed.

Christopher, Elayne, and Arryn had traveled over the course of a couple of days and had wandered close to the edge of the Dark Forest when they heard a scream followed by a terrible growl.

They turned their horses and were fast to rush to the aid of the person that was in trouble. That person turned out to be a young boy that Arryn would later come to call her best friend.

It was Cathillian.

He ran from a terrible beast. A large, brown lycanthrope. Half wolf, half man, yet larger and far more powerful than both combined. Its elongated face was pulled back in a terrible snarl, and its long teeth were covered in slimy, foul drool that glistened in the sunlight poking through the canopy of trees above. The monster sprinted at impossible speeds on its thick, hind legs, rushing forward with his long, powerful arms outstretched, and its claws ready to tear the boy apart.

"Stay here. Christopher, protect Arryn," Elayne said before running to the boy. "Run past me! Get to the horses!" she called out while still moving toward him.

They met in the middle, and he continued past as she'd told him to do. Arryn waved him over, but was terrified to speak. She didn't want to break her mother's concentration.

"That thing'll kill her!" the boy said as he finally made it to the horses. "We need to help her!"

Christopher shook his head. "You've never seen her throw a fireball."

Arryn's heart filled with pride, and she ignored the boy's worries as she focused on her mom.

Elayne had stopped in her tracks, taking a quick breath as she circled the beast. Arryn could see her mother's eyes turn pitch black just before she placed her hands in the center of her chest, focusing her power as she pulled them down to her sides.

Arryn had seen her mother's fire during training. It was stronger than any she'd ever seen, and now was no different.

A large ball of fire then appeared in each hand, bright red with a hot, blue spark in the center. She let loose one of the fireballs, and it hit him in the chest.

Arryn watched as the lycanthrope howled in pain as the flames exploded, burning his skin and fur all across his shoulders, chest, and torso. As he was distracted, she threw the other and hit him in the same spot.

The lycanthrope hit the ground, rolling around and flailing at his burning fur in an attempt to put it out. The damp ground would soon extinguish the flames if Elayne didn't react soon enough.

Fortunately, she was an incredible magician. She'd studied long and hard, and she'd even taught Arryn well.

The boy tried to voice his worries several times, but Arryn couldn't be bothered. She was completely hypnotized by the event. She'd never seen anything so terrifying, yet exciting in all her life. It had never occurred to her that magic could be used in such a way.

She studied her mother's movement as her flat hand extended in front of her while she gathered water from under the surface of the ground. Then she closed her fist, several ice shards bursting from the wet ground and piercing the body of the lycanthrope.

The beast howled as the painful ice ripped through him, his blood soaking into the ground below him, but the cries quickly stopped as his life faded out.

Arryn smiled and cheered as her mom began to turn back toward her captive audience, but the sound of quick footsteps filled the area and interrupted the celebration.

A beautiful woman clad in deep brown, leather clothing with a bow and quiver on her back was riding toward them on an unnaturally large, black, Shire horse. It had been Elysia.

"Mom!" Cathillian had yelled as he darted past Elayne.

The woman stopped her horse, the large animal kneeling to let her climb off. She examined the body of the lycanthrope before coming to stand before Elayne.

The woman had flawless, porcelain skin and ears that were slightly pointed at the top. Her blonde hair was long and hung in a braid slung over her left shoulder that nearly reached her stomach.

Words were spoken, but Arryn couldn't hear anything from where she sat. Soon, the woman looked directly at Arryn before smiling and making her way over.

Elysia watched as Arryn lost herself in thought. It wasn't uncommon, but that memory was a particularly hard one, or so she imagined. It was the day her parents sought out asylum for the girl in case they died.

Not something easily forgotten, though Elysia had certainly done her best to teach Arryn healthier ways to deal with it—use the past as a way to push forward.

"Do you remember that day?" Elysia asked again. Her words brought Arryn back to the present.

Arryn nodded. "Sorry. It's impressive just how clear I can still remember that day. I remember seeing everything that happened, but I was too far away to hear anything you guys said. So, this whole time, I've never known why you took me in."

Elysia smiled, remembering the moment she'd laid eyes on Arryn. It was the first time she'd seen an outsider in quite some time, let alone three of them, and she held hope that the world away from the Dark Forest wasn't *all* bad.

"At first, I thanked her. I knew she wasn't like the others I'd met in the past, so I told her if you were ever injured, poisoned, sick, or in any other danger, you were welcome into the Dark Forest. Mother to mother, I told her I'd protect you with my life as payment for her risking hers for my only child."

Arryn continued. "But that only explains why you didn't turn me in to the Arcadians. Not why you kept me with you for ten years after," Arryn said. "I don't know if you personally knew Adrien or not, but your father did. You know how awful he was. He could've hunted me down and come to the Dark Forest. You risked a lot to keep me here."

Elysia shrugged. "I wouldn't have had it any other way. Your mother told me what had happened in Arcadia, and that you might be in danger. She was strong, and it made me curious. I turned my attention to you, curious to see if you had the same potential. When I came to stand near you, I reached for your hand."

Arryn stopped walking. "You were searching for my potential for magic."

Elysia nodded and smiled. "I wanted to know how powerful you were and, more importantly, what kind of person you were. I don't know a damn thing about physical magic, other than what it can do, but I wanted to know if you'd be tainted by it like Adrien had. Your mother hadn't been."

A howl in the distance followed by several others caught their attention for a moment. Elysia knew the first one well. It had been Luna, the wolf familiar of one of the warriors, Nika, followed by some of her pack.

She ignored them and turned back to the conversation. "It's just Luna playing with the others," she said, reassuring Arryn. "Anyway, nature spoke to you, even though I knew at the time you had no idea that was happening. If the worst happened to your family in Arcadia, I didn't want you to be adopted and raised by some asshole Arcadian only to let your pure heart be tainted. I wasn't about to let you die. *That* is why I permanently took you in. Because I saw a great life for you here. A life your parents would be proud of and would rest in peace knowing you had."

Elysia saw the look on Arryn's face and knew what was about to happen. She opened her arms as Arryn rushed forward. She held the girl tight and ran her fingers through a clean section of her hair, smiling as she thought of the earlier dispute her son and the Arcadian girl had and the others they had on a daily basis.

They never allowed for boredom, that was for sure.

Elysia was about to speak when she felt a shift in the energy around her. Her body stiffened, and Arryn pulled back.

"What is it?" she asked.

Elysia closed her eyes before whispering the name of her horse, her familiar, "*Chaos.*"

Within moments, the rapid fall of hooves echoed through the trees. Chaos was a solid, obsidian-black Shire. His mane and tail were incredibly long, as was the long hair around his ankles that hung like bells around his hooves. His gallop slowed before coming to a complete stop next to Elysia.

"Get on," Elysia told Arryn. Chaos knelt and allowed both women to climb on before he stood.

"What's happening?" Arryn asked.

"We're going to the river. Someone's passed the border and is inside the Dark Forest."

TWO

Talia took her time as she made her way through the Academy, looking over every square inch as Amelia, the former Dean of Students and current Chancellor of Arcadia, showed her around and gave her a bit of the history on the building.

She'd heard about the great Academy her entire life, but she'd never been there. All she had to go on were stories and descriptions, but it was obvious everything had changed.

She narrowed her eyes as she looked to where a large statue of the past Chancellor had once stood.

"Is everything alright?" Amelia asked as she looked Talia over.

"What used to stand here?" Talia asked. Most of the rubble had been cleared, but there were still scars from where the damage had taken place.

"Ah," Amelia said, her sweet voice suddenly turning cold. "A statue. The former Chancellor, Adrien, had it erected in *his* honor." She shook her head then added, "He was a real son of a bitch. Anyway, now that he's gone, the sculpture is, too."

Talia stared at the area for a moment longer before looking to Amelia. "Now that you're Chancellor, will you put another in place? One of you perhaps?"

Amelia laughed. "Oh, no. I'd never do something like that. I always hated looking at it. The monstrosity was a gigantic reminder of whose thumb I was constantly under, that *everyone* was under. It wasn't a good life to live. Fear and insecurity don't have a place in the Academy—not anymore! I'm sure we'll put something there in time, but for now, it sure as hell won't be anything quite so selfish and pathetic."

Talia forced a smile as she continued following her tour guide. She'd heard terrible things about the Chancellor from several people, but she wanted to know how Amelia felt in particular. "Was the Chancellor really *that* bad?"

Amelia stopped, clearly thinking of a proper response before turning back to Talia. "I've never seen or met anyone like him. He was charismatic and intelligent, well-spoken and powerful."

"Well, that doesn't sound so bad," Talia sighed. "In fact, it sounds like everything a Chancellor should be."

Amelia gave a sad smile, her eyes telling Talia just how much she was holding back. "You're *very* right. That's everything a person in power *should* be. However, he was also cold, cruel. He was a vengeful man, and he killed a *lot* of innocent people. Children even!"

"It sounds like Arcadia went through terrible times with him," Talia said.

Amelia nodded down the corridor. "Let's move on," she said, obviously wanting to leave the old site of the statue. After a few steps, she spoke again. "I still have trouble sleeping because I know I helped him—even if I had no idea what he was doing, what he was trying to accomplish."

"Well, it seems like the city has a brand-new chance. If things go right, this city will get everything it deserves," Talia said. "I can assure you of that."

Stopping, Amelia placed a hand on Talia's shoulder. "That's why I was so happy when you applied. Someone from far away that had no experience with him or even knew much about him. Believe me, Talia. You'll have a *great* start here at the *new* Academy. You'll be in the position that I held for so long. As Dean, you have the opportunity to do wonderful things for this school, and unlike my predecessor, I can use my new position to help you see those through."

Talia nodded. "So, you believe you can lead the Academy back from the darkness he left behind, Chancellor Amelia?"

"Even with things so strained, this city has more hope than ever," Amelia said, "and it's all because of a teenage girl from the Boulevard. It's all because the people of this city came together and fought for what's right, for what's theirs. It's so inspiring. Please, let me show you to your office. You're gonna love it. Trust me!"

Amelia began ascending the stairs, Talia close behind. Talia paused, taking one last look down the hallway to where the statue of

Adrien once stood.

No... You will certainly be the last *person that I trust,* she thought before faking an excited smile and following the newest Chancellor to the Dean's office.

Elysia held tight to Chaos' mane as Arryn held on to Elysia's waist. The horse moved quickly, taking every silent direction that Elysia gave him as they navigated through the lush woods to the river.

"Ya think it's something bad?" Arryn asked.

"Not long now. We'll see once we get there."

Chaos slowed to a stop before they crossed over the edge of the woods by the Kalt river. "Stay here with Chaos," Elysia said. "I'll call for you if it's safe."

"But you might need help," Arryn replied.

Elysia smiled. "Trust me; I'll be fine, child. Stay."

With every step she took, Elysia pushed away her thoughts and worries about what she might find. She only focused on her connection with the forest around her.

She could feel the life flowing through every tree and every flower around her. Their power would be needed if she met with danger.

Once she came to the tree line, her eyes widened as she saw a man lying face down on the river's edge. He'd washed down stream, more than likely from somewhere close to Cella, a town to the northeast.

Most of his body was in the water, but his head and arms managed to find enough land to hold him, though that would change if he were left there for long. The winter had passed, and spring had approached, but she knew the water would still be frigid.

If the current didn't carry him away and kill him, the temperatures might.

Elysia approached, slowly at first, as she attempted to sense any danger. There was a moan that escaped him as he tried to move onto his back, but he immediately fell again.

"Arryn!" Elysia yelled as she ran to his side.

She rolled the rearick to his back. He strained to open his eyes, but was unable to manage even that. The sound of Arryn's footsteps caught Elysia's ears.

"Whoa. What's a rearick doing here?"

He groaned as he tried to move.

"Don't worry about that," Elysia said. "Help me pull him to the grass. We can heal him there."

Arryn did as she was asked, grabbing hold of his arm and helping her pull him from the river. Rearick were shorter than most people, but they were built like small, brick shit houses. They could drink a man under the table or kick his ass if the occasion called for it. They could even do both at the same time.

The men were feisty, and the women were worse. Still, they were good, honest people. If a rearick made a promise, they fought to the death to keep it.

Arryn remembered the rearick from her time in Arcadia. They came and went, bringing shipments of the mystics' brew, the amphorald gems and magitech crystals that fueled the magical devices, and whatever other items the city might have need for from the highlands.

They always traveled together. Safety in numbers and all that. That's why she found it so odd for him to be so far north—and alone.

"Place your hand over his heart and one on his forehead," Elysia ordered.

"You should do this. You know I'm not the best healer," Arryn protested.

"Well, I guess this is probably a good time to learn, now isn't it?" she asked. "Now, do as I say." Her eyes narrowed, showing Arryn she meant it.

Arryn looked down at the injured rearick. It was obvious he was on death's door. His breaths were shallow, and his color was some mix between blue, purple, and white. It scared her to think he might taste death for the sake of her education.

"Arryn," Elysia said sternly, snapping Arryn out of her thoughts.

Arryn nodded and took a deep breath, realizing Elysia was right. What better time to learn how to save a life than in an emergency? Or she hoped so anyway—for the rearick.

She made sure the placement of her hands was correct, then watched as Elysia placed her hands over Arryn's.

"Push everything out of your mind and focus on the nature around you. It's full of life and energy. Harness that energy and push inward, toward him. Fill him with it."

Arryn didn't reply as she followed Elysia's instructions. She pushed everything away. The only thing allowed in her mind was the sound of the river, the feel of the wind on her skin, and the feel of the damp ground beneath her.

Soon, her hands felt warm as energy filled them. As she felt it grow, she released it, pushing it toward the rearick. Within moments, his eyes opened as he took a deep breath, coughing and rolling to his side.

Arryn's face lit up as the rush of saving his life filled her. "I did it!"

Elysia flashed a quick smile in her direction before helping the rearick on his side. He coughed a few more times before groaning.

He had brown hair, but a large beard that had a copper tint to it; both were streaked with silver. His light brown eyes were bloodshot, and the freckles on his cheeks stuck out in stark contrast to his bluish-white pallor.

As he continued to cough and breathe, his cheeks turned rosier as their normal color slowly returned.

"How are you feeling?" Arryn asked.

"About as good as I am pretty, lass."

Arryn tried not to laugh at the rearick's joke. "Can you sit?"

He nodded as he struggled to get into position. Arryn and Elysia tried to help, but he grumbled something unintelligible about not being helpless, and they backed off.

"Thank ye, lass, but I doubt yer gonna wanna spend the night watchin' over my old arse. I'd better start tryin' ta get back on me own two feet."

"What happened to you—" Elysia started.

"Samuel," he answered after she paused, silently asking for his name. "As fer what happened—I got quite a hit on the head a little over a month ago in a battle. Well worth it, I tell ye. Still, it chaps me arse that I let meself get dizzy and tumble over like that."

"You fell into the river?" Arryn asked. "You must've been pretty far north from what you're used to."

"Aye," he said. "We had a delivery fer brew goin' north to a noble's house near Cella. Lord Girard is long gone, but the lady of the house likes ta treat the servants there ta the drink. On ol' Girard's coin, I'd say. Anyway—I ain't one fer fancy dinners. I decided to kill mine. I went fishin' when that damned bump ta the head came back ta pay a visit. Vision went cloudy, and I fell in."

"You cracked it again from the looks of it," Arryn said, pointing to a place just below his hairline.

He raised his hand and hissed as he touched the sensitive area. "Seems so," he snorted. "Maybe that'll knock some sense into me, and I can get back ta normal."

"I should be able to help with that," Elysia said, placing a hand on his head.

He pulled back for a moment, clearly unsure about letting someone directly cast magic on him. It was no secret that rearick were extremely cautious about magic. They didn't trust it at all.

"Relax, rearick. I mean no harm. Quite the opposite," Elysia said.

"Have ta forgive me," Samuel smiled. "Old habits die hard, I suppose."

Her jade green eyes flashed an even darker green as she channeled magic through Samuel. The wound on his head disappeared, and Arryn imagined whatever pain came along with it as well.

"There you are. Perhaps that'll help with the dizziness, too," Elysia said.

"Magic users. Never thought much of any of ye until that whole mess in Arcadia. Now, I have a bit more respect."

Elysia smiled. "I accept that as your way of saying thank you."

The rearick only nodded in her direction. Arryn wasn't certain exactly how much time Elysia or any of the other druids had spent around rearick, but Arryn remembered them to be kind, but brutish. Not much for apologies or praise.

"I do feel much better. Thank ya, druid."

"Elysia. And you're welcome." She softly smiled at him.

Arryn couldn't contain her excitement any longer. "So, you said something happened in Arcadia?"

It had been years since she'd thought about the city for more than a few minutes. She tried to ignore any intrusive thoughts unless they revolved around what she planned to do to overthrow Adrien at some point when she finally returned, or unless she was training.

Allowing that kind of sadness and rage to fuel her hatred really seemed to help her fight harder, both physically and magically.

She dreamed of going back and trying to find her father, but she was terrified of what she might find. Especially with Adrien still in control.

"Aye. There was quite a battle there. The people finally got off their pampered arses and did something about that shit stain Chancellor of theirs. He's long gone now."

Arryn's eyes widened, and it felt like her breath rushed out of her. She hadn't realized until that very moment just how much she'd wanted to go back.

It was all random thoughts and hollow plots of vengeance she never thought she'd have the resources for. But now, she felt conflicted. It should have been her that helped liberate the city.

She'd promised to go back.

Promised to save them.

He's really gone... she thought to herself. Hope filled her as she remembered her mother's words. She'd made Arryn promise to go back when she was strong enough. Well, she sure as hell wasn't strong enough to reclaim a city on her own, but maybe she didn't have to be the conquering hero to fulfill her vow.

Maybe she could help in other ways.

Arryn scooted a little closer, focusing on him like he might disappear at any moment. "Gone? As in dead?" A cautious smile spread on her face.

"Arryn," Elysia said, reaching for her hand.

She shook loose, once again focused hard on the rearick and any information he could give her. "Is it true? Is he?" Arryn asked again, continuing to ignore her adoptive mother completely.

"Aye, he is," Samuel said. "It was a revolution. Some girl from the Boulevard came through with a wizard and a mismatched group of rebels, riled up everyone in the city, and then took it back. Damnedest thing I ever saw. That stone-hearted son of a bitch got just what he deserved if ye ask me. No one better than his own people ta give it to him, too. I never thought I'd live ta see the day when Arcadia wasn't a shit ta get through. All those stuck up bastard guards with their magitech."

He shook his head, clearly recalling his hatred for the Capitol Guard.

"As far as I'm concerned, ye can't call yerself a man if ye can't even fight with yer own hands and a proper weapon." He spat on the ground next to himself and patted the hammer lashed to his belt.

"I don't believe it," Arryn said, her eyes still wide and glistening from the tears of happiness that threatened to form. "It's free. Everything they wanted... Everything my parents worked so hard for... It's been done. I wasn't the one to do it like I promised, but that doesn't mean I can't still save the city. Help them rebuild."

She couldn't help but smile as she thought about the possibilities of going to find her father.

"Arryn," Elysia said. "We need to talk about this."

Arryn looked to Elysia, her smile fading as she looked at the expression on the druid's face. She realized then that her excitement had caused her to completely forget about her home in the Dark Forest. Even about Elysia. She did her best to pull it back, but it was hard.

"What is it?" Arryn asked, reading the lines on Elysia's face. "I know you didn't know them well, but this means their lives weren't taken in vain. Hell, my father might still be alive! I can actually search for him! I can see the city the way they always prayed I would. Maybe I can even help now."

Elysia sighed, her brows furrowing further as Arryn's excitement mounted. "Before you go making too many plans and getting your hopes too high, there are some things that you *need* to know."

THREE

Arryn and Elysia escorted the rearick to the edge of the Dark Forest. Without their magic, he'd never have made it through the thick wall that barricaded it. He thanked them and went on his way, but not before giving Arryn a promise.

"Ya saved me life, lass. If ye ever do find yer way back ta Arcadia, and ye need help, I'm yers. I don't like owing debts, especially ta some Arcadian, but yer not one of 'em. The druid folk seem OK enough."

Arryn had tried to tell him he didn't have to owe her a life debt, but it had been her magic that saved him—with Elysia's help, of course—so it was her who received his promise. He refused to take no for an answer.

"Rearick are very strange, but noble creatures," Elysia told her as they turned and headed back to the village. "He'd still owe that debt to you even if you continued to say no. That's how they work. Besides, if you do decide to go back, it wouldn't hurt to have his loyalty."

Arryn tried to prod her for information about Arcadia and why they needed to talk, but Elysia was a steel trap. She wouldn't speak any more on the subject until they'd returned home.

By the time Arryn and Elysia made it back to their village, Arryn had become increasingly anxious. It was the tone that Elysia had taken with her that made her worry.

They soon crossed the threshold from the thick forest to the cleared section where the druid community was built. Above, the branches of the trees stretched overhead, struggling to shade them, but coming up short. It was where the sun shone through the forest the brightest, allowing the various plants to grow larger and stronger.

Only grass and smaller crops and flowers grew within the borders of the community—no larger trees grew for fear the lack of sun would stunt the growth of their food, which needed ample light.

Elysia turned to Arryn. She thought Elysia looked either guilty or concerned, only increasing her anxiety. "Wait here," Elysia said, giving Arryn's hand a light squeeze. She turned away then and walked toward the Chieftain's home.

"What happened?"

Arryn jumped when Cathillian came up behind her, once again taking her by surprise. His long blonde hair was pulled back in a loose bun, a sign that he'd been training in hand-to-hand combat, judging by the redness on his cheeks and the sweat on his forehead.

"Would you stop doing that? I don't know how you manage to get me *every* single time," Arryn scolded.

For once, Cathillian didn't seem to take delight in scaring her. "Sorry. I actually didn't mean to that time. I saw Chaos running in your direction, and I got worried, but knew Mom would be pissed if I came nosing around. I figured if it was important, she'd have sent Chaos to fetch me or one of the other warriors. Is everything OK?"

She shook her head, her hand still over her jumpy heart. "We were walking and talking when she sensed something in the Forest, so she called Chaos. We rode to the river and found a rearick in the water that had nearly drowned, but we pulled him out in time."

Cathillian looked at her, confusion on his face. "That's it? Then what's with her telling you to stay here? Did you piss her off or what?" His expression changed, a smile growing at her expense.

Arryn chose to ignore him. "Nothing like that—I don't think anyway. She started acting weird after the rearick told us there was a battle in Arcadia. There was a rebellion, and the Arcadian people rose against Adrien."

"Oh, yeah?" he asked. "That's pretty huge."

She paused, taking another moment to smile and enjoy the heroism of her people. "Yes! I still can't believe it. I think I may have overreacted— maybe that's why she's upset. Surely, she wouldn't expect me *not* to care about Arcadia, though. She shouldn't be angry with me about that, right?"

Arryn stopped to replay her reaction to Samuel's news in her mind, hoping she didn't seem too eager to leave the Forest. She shook her head. "Anyway… She said there were a few things I needed to know and hasn't spoken much since, which leads me to my current station. Standing here. Talking to you. Which—by the way—is *the* highlight of my day."

Her backhanded insult was suspiciously met with silence. She looked toward Cathillian when he didn't give a snarky response. His eyes were focused on the ground. He nodded his head without saying a word.

Arryn's eyes narrowed. "No smartass retort?" Silence. Her eyes narrowed. "You know something. Spit it out."

"I don't know anything," Cathillian said. His eyes dodged hers. Even when he faced her to respond, his eyes never met hers.

"You're lying!" she accused.

"I'm sorry!" he yelled. "She made me swear, or I'd have told you. Look, it's nothing bad. But I'm telling you this, if you're thinking of going back to Arcadia to search for your father—you need to think hard. It might be under new government, but it's no less dangerous. You have *no* idea what it's like there. Just because the almighty Chancellor is dead and gone doesn't mean there aren't others there like him. I'm sure most were identified and cleared out. Those assholes usually stick together, but it could still be dangerous. Don't let emotions control you. That's their way. Not ours. You might have been born there, but you're one of us. Anything she needs to tell you—well, it was done to make damn certain you were safe."

Arryn wasn't sure if she should be angry that something had been hidden from her, or if she should be touched by his rambling words.

"Arryn," Elysia said, walking toward them. "Don't be angry with him. He was only doing what I told him to do. Come with me. We're ready for you. Try to keep an open mind."

Cathillian grabbed her hand to stop her. Leaning down, he whispered, "Don't give 'em too much hell. They love you. We all do."

Arryn did her best to keep that in mind as she made her way toward the Chieftain's home with Elysia. *An open mind,* she told herself.

"Arryn," the Chieftain said, welcoming her over as she stepped inside.

The house was small, as was most of the dwellings. Druids weren't the flashiest people. They didn't care much about jewels, expensive things, or large homes. They only cut down what they needed and were quick to replant and nurture whatever life they took.

The walls and roofs were made of live trees. They planted small, strong trees or even bamboo and controlled how they grew, coaxing them to bend in certain ways to allow their inhabitants to be surrounded by life. The homes were unique to each druid and always beautiful.

"Have a seat," the Chieftain said. "I understand we have some important things to discuss."

Arryn nodded. "Yeah, I guess so. I kinda get the feeling there's a big secret everyone's been keeping from me."

"You trust us, yes?" he asked, the corners of his eyes wrinkling as he smiled.

Though he was almost eighty years old, he appeared to be closer to fifty. Druids aged very slowly because of their healing abilities and pure, stress-free way of life. It was nothing for a druid to live to be well over a hundred years.

While the Chieftain was the first to learn the magic, others in the tribe were much older and had proven just how much nature magic can work to heal its user.

Several of the older druids were several years past their first century, even though they'd first been wanderers and then Arcadian before finding their true place in the world with the Chieftain in the Dark Forest some forty years ago.

"I do. I always have. You kept a promise to an Arcadian couple you never met. You took me in and cared for me, and you taught me your magic and ways of life and much more. I've never been treated like an outsider. I've always been family here. So, yes. I trust you—which is why this is so confusing."

Elysia sat on a small blanket across from Arryn, shifting to get comfortable. "I know things seem confusing, but I promise, if you try to see things through our eyes, you'll come to understand."

Arryn took a deep breath, steeling herself for whatever was about to come. "Alright then. Let's have it. I'm ready."

There was a pause as Elysia gathered her thoughts. "A few weeks ago, an old man came here. Do you remember?"

"Yeah. He came late at night with a younger guy, and you went to meet them. I ended up training with Cathillian all night because he couldn't sleep. They were gone by morning, so I never got to meet them. When I asked Cathillian about them, he said it's not uncommon for people to wander through every so often—which now that I think about it is a damn lie. Unless they come through that raging river, they ain't getting through that barrier we have. Not unless they use magic."

The Chieftain took a drink of coffee from a clay cup he had sitting between his legs. It was his favorite. Tea had been their main drink of choice—minus the delicious sweet wine that they made—but they wanted something new.

They'd spent quite a bit of time growing and nurturing the Arabica beans so they could flourish in their area, and it was well worth the effort for the Chieftain, much to the dismay of his daughter.

It made him even more hyper than normal, and it drove Elysia crazy.

He sat the cup back down and nodded. "That's very true. We've had a few visitors throughout the years, but they mostly come by way of the river. It's far too strenuous of a task for a non-druid to cross the walls we've created to protect the Dark Forest. However, Ezekiel, the man that came to see me, was no ordinary man."

Arryn's brows furrowed as she saw a smile cross the Chieftain's face. "Then who was he? And why did Cathillian lie about that?"

"Cathillian was doing as he was told. I'm sorry. But it'll all make sense soon enough. As I said, the visitor's name is Ezekiel, though, I'm sure you probably heard him called by a much different name while in Arcadia. Ezekiel is the Founder," he answered.

Arryn's poor eyelids were getting a workout this morning. They lifted again in shock. "The *Founder*? No one thought it was pertinent information that the damn *Founder* was here?" She sat back then, reining in her excitement when she realized she'd accidentally cursed in front of the Chieftain. "Sorry, but that's huge!"

"Bigger than you know." He fidgeted with his coffee cup before sitting it on the floor next to him. "Magic was taught to Ezekiel, and he chose three students. Selah, the mystic, Adrien, and myself. We were all Arcadians then, but eventually went our separate ways. Each of us had our different ideas of what magic could be, and we each formed our own community. Well, with the exception of Adrien, of course. He had the help of the Founder, but ripped apart the spirit of everything Ezekiel had wanted. Ezekiel was the one who taught me how to use nature magic, and I used that knowledge to teach my people."

Arryn snorted. "I'm glad to see not *all* his students were ass—jerks." She cleared her throat, once again regretful of the slip. "Anyway… Why was he here?"

"He came to us for aid," Elysia said. "The rebellion was growing, and Adrien and his deranged followers had already killed a lot of people. Children even. Ezekiel came to us for assistance, but we couldn't risk it. They'd already lost so many as it was. There was no way we'd risk losing a large number of our own for a war that wasn't ours. That being said, even knowing how dangerous it was, not *everyone* felt the way we did."

Arryn caught the emphasis in Elysia's words. "No? Then who wanted to help? Besides me, of course. I would have in a heartbeat, which tells me that's what all the lies were for. To prevent that."

There was a brief pause before she remembered something she hadn't put much thought into until right then. Realization struck Arryn as things started falling into place.

Druids were very protective of one another. There were different bloodlines among the community, but everyone was considered family. They stuck close together, and almost no one left.

If someone *did* want to leave, be it for traveling to one of the other druid communities, hunting on their own, or even being as adventurous as traveling to a city, they had to pass a test called the Versuch.

The Versuch was a rite of passage that all druids were able to take advantage of, but very few did unless they wanted to marry—forcing them to travel to another tribe to find someone.

It wasn't something that was taken lightly.

The druid that wanted to leave was pitted against another older, stronger druid. A warrior. The leaving member must go through all three trials—hand-to-hand combat, weapons, and of course, magic—and come out the victor of all three. There is no room for error. All three are vital.

And a young druid had recently done this. *Privately.*

"Laurel," Arryn said. It was more of a statement than a question. She hadn't really considered the timeline, but it was too perfect to be inaccurate. "You sent Laurel with them."

"It wasn't our plan to *send* her," the Chieftain said. "She *wanted* to go. You know Laurel. She's very much like Cathillian was when he was a kid. Very adventurous and mischievous. It wasn't until he was attacked by the very lycanthrope your mother saved him from that he realized exactly why we have these rules in place. You have to understand—she was of age. She was old enough to take the Versuch. She spoke the words of her own volition. It would've been unlawful for me to deny her the opportunity."

Arryn laughed, but it was less amused and more sarcastic in nature. "But you would deny me, and I'm a full three years older? That's OK, right?"

"Arryn!" Elysia scolded. "You may be angry, but show some respect."

"Respect? Laurel *just* turned sixteen. That was *barely* old enough for the Versuch. Why was I not even given the option?" Arryn was pissed to say the least. It took all she had to keep her voice down, but she managed out of her love for the two Elders in front of her. "When I sat on the edge of the Kalt today, listening to that rearick tell us there was a battle that liberated Arcadia—I was so proud of them. Proud of *my* people."

Arryn regretted the use of those words when she saw the hurt look on Elysia's face, but her passion was high, and it stopped her from properly filtering her thoughts before speaking.

"What I mean by that," Arryn continued, "is that I felt pride. The people my parents fought for—and that my mother *died* for—finally took a stand. The resistance won. But now—now, that pride is overshadowed by regret. I could've been there. I *should* have been there. I'm old enough. I'm strong enough. *They* built an army! All I had to do was help! I *am* strong enough for that. To know that I could have aided them in their fight, that I could have finished what my parents started..." She paused, a tear sliding down her cheek. "You speak of respect, yet you thought it was OK to deny me the right to avenge my parents."

Arryn was shocked by her own bravery at that moment; speaking up for herself to the Elders was a big deal.

Elysia sighed. "I made a promise to your mother that I'd keep you safe. Mother to mother, no vow is more sacred than that."

There was a pregnant pause as Arryn locked eyes with Elysia, slowly shaking her head in disbelief.

"What of a vow from child to mother? What of the promises *I* made?

I swore I'd go back when I was strong enough. I promised her I would end Adrien and seek justice for her death and my father's disappearance. When it was a group of anonymous rebels—that was fine. No one could have predicted that, so I can't be blamed for not joining. But now that I know they came knocking on our door for help, and I was led away to be lied to..."

Arryn stopped, taking a deep breath to regain control. "I understand you love me. I love you, too. I will *always* love you. But this is the official notice. If you consider me family, then you consider me druid enough to follow your laws."

"We do," Elysia said, her voice almost seemed desperate. It was obvious to Arryn she was fighting back emotion of her own. "We do consider you family."

Arryn nodded. "Good. Then find your warrior."

Elysia shook her head, her eyes widening. "Please, no. Don't say the words. You're not ready yet. I told you that you underestimate yourself, but this wasn't what I meant for you to do."

Arryn gave a sad smile before reaching for Elysia's hand. "I know, but I *am* ready, and I'll prove it." She turned to the Chieftain, her shoulders square, and her head held high. "Chieftain—I request Versuch."

FOUR

The Dean's office was quite welcoming. So warm and beautifully decorated. Neutral colors on the walls mixed beautifully with the hand-crafted furniture with vibrant reds and golds in the fabric. The desk was quite beautiful with a large basket of fruit in the middle. It seemed there had been a lot of time and care taken to make the new Dean of Students feel at home.

And Talia hated it.

Even the smell annoyed her, but that was the least of her worries.

There would be a lot of work to be done to get the school back in order after all that happened. Though classes were back in session, everyone was taking it easy with some of the curriculum.

The faculty had been shaved down quite a bit due to so many of them being on Adrien's side or simply hating the idea of what they considered "Boulevard scum" joining in their classes.

Those professors still needed to be replaced—a job that Talia would have to do now that she had the Dean's position. The application process for staff would be far more tedious than that of the students—as it should have been all along, but wasn't.

Because of the lack of staff, the current teachers were overwhelmed with bringing in the new students from the Boulevard and teaching the basics. Those students' skills would have to be built from the ground up.

Quite a few had very little—if any—experience with magic due to Adrien's laws and the fear of the Guard marking them as Unlawful. The Prophet's deviant Disciples made it so much worse.

A lot of those from the Boulevard that actually had any talent were hunted and brutally murdered. That left a lot of people with no knowledge of magic that desperately wanted to learn. Luckily, several magic users emerged during the great battle which gave them enough of a foundation that it relieved *some* of the tension.

Previous students that were still enrolled had taken on more of a Teacher's Aide role, which was a bigger help to the teachers that were still employed than they could comprehend.

All that aside, Talia still had a stack of applications to go through. They were only a formality, as any student with a will to learn and a good conscience was accepted, but she wanted to learn every face and every name.

It was important to her to know anyone coming in or going out. She would need to if things were to go her way.

She slid a few papers across her desk, an annoyed groan escaping her when their edges met with the basket of fruit on the back edge. She wanted to throw the damn thing out, but forced herself to keep it for show.

Instead, she'd opened it and removed two pieces of fruit—immediately tossing them in the trash before throwing an application for employment in on top to hide them. It wasn't that she didn't like fruit; she just didn't exactly trust the Chancellor.

Amelia was nice. *Too* nice.

No one was that sweet without a motive. And seeing as there was recently a coup on the last Chancellor, and Amelia was suspiciously in his seat—well, that told Talia all she needed to know. Besides, she was convinced there was a lot more to the story that she wasn't being told, and she planned to find exactly what that was.

Talia sat back in her chair and massaged the bridge of her nose. Over the next few days, she would be expected to sit in on several classes as well as multiple interviews.

The oh-so lovely Amelia had asked her to sit in on the History classes to catch her up. She would need to learn the true history of Arcadia and of the Founder. Not only was Talia placed in the Dean position, but until there were enough teachers, she would play that part as well.

All this was her fault for showing her ass in the interview. Her magic was strong. Strong enough to make even Amelia raise her brows.

Talia had wanted to make sure that she would be the one chosen. That required skill, precision, undeniable confidence, and intelligence. All things she possessed in excess.

It was a balancing act to show her abilities without coming off cocky or rude. Lots of fake smiles helped with that one. Personal communications wasn't her strong point. Still… Talia had to have the job.

She *needed* it.

As she reminded herself of that fact—her necessity for the position that she held—she let out a heavy sigh. Leaning forward, she opened the bottom drawer of her desk. Inside was a small box sealed with a magitech lock. She placed the box on her desk before removing her necklace.

She held the elongated, silver pendant in her hand, running her thumb over the large, blue stone in the middle as she smiled. It had been a gift from her father—a man she'd spent limited hours with once a month or so until the year before his death—who she loved more than anything.

She understood why he'd made the decisions that he did. To do great things, there must be sacrifices. That was what he'd always told her, and she believed that. It was very true. She only wished she had more to remember him by than physical possessions. The necklace, the box, and the contents inside.

The silver chain connected in separate eyelets on both the left and right sides instead of the classic placement at the top. This, combined with its weight, insured that it never flipped over to show the back, which was important, given what it held.

She turned it over in her hand to reveal a small key secured inside the hollow back, connected by a tiny hinge. She gently pulled at the bottom of the key, unclipping the end and allowing it to lift at the hinge.

Placing it in the magitech lock, she twisted it and opened the box. She reached inside, shuffling a few items around so she could pull an envelope from the bottom. All that was written on the front was a large *T*.

Talia remembered the day that a rather sheepish man had brought it to her. He had no confidence. She knew this from several stories her father had told her in one of his very few visits.

Still, the man had faked it—especially when he saw exactly how beautiful she was, which she found amusing in an uninterested, yet funny kind of way, though she knew her father certainly wouldn't have.

He would've been pissed.

Doyle had no idea who she was, and he was forbidden to know. She knew he was given strict instruction to take the envelope to her, tell her it was urgent, and see that she read it right then.

She knew of the threats her father faced, and he'd told her early on that if he had to risk sending word to her, she had to check that the seal had not been broken.

Doyle was smart and hadn't broken the trust of the Chancellor. But she knew it was fear that kept him honest, not loyalty.

"I understand," were the last words she would ever speak to her father, and they were spoken through that pathetic bootlicker's mouth.

She opened the envelope, pulling the folded-over piece of paper from within. It had become slightly worn with as many times as she'd read it.

Whenever she felt exhausted or annoyed with her new life in the city—which had only just begun in the last few weeks—she pulled it from the box and read it. Over and over again, if necessary.

It was because of her father's paranoia and caution that she sat where she did—in a position to see that his life had not been lost in vain. They would pay for what they did to him.

My Dearest T,

　I never thought the day would come in which I would actually need to write this, but it is here. It has begun. If I should fail, you know what to do. -A

She read it five times before lowering it, looking across the room to the open window with the nauseating, red curtains.

Oh, I know exactly what to do, Father, she thought. *I won't allow anyone to forget the name Adrien.*

Cathillian stood with Elysia as they looked over several warriors from their tribe. They were the strongest the druids had to offer aside from Elysia and the Chieftain. Their magic was fierce, and their bodies were long and leaned out from constant sparring matches.

Druid warriors didn't spar like other soldiers. They hit full force and used weapons, careful to avoid piercing anything vital like the chest or head. When the final blow was made, the loser would be healed by those supervising, and they would begin again.

Druid warriors were the fiercest around, and that was what gave them the deadly reputation. A warrior that won't hold back on their own while training will never hold back on an enemy. This made their hand-to-hand combat skills unimaginable, and their expertise with long and close-range weapons made them unbeatable.

Cathillian was a damn good warrior, having begun training at eleven years old—just after the attack from the lycanthrope—but even he couldn't stand a chance next to any one of the five men and women standing before him.

"Is this really necessary?" he asked his mother. "Laurel didn't receive this level of abuse."

"Abuse?" Elysia asked, her expression revealing shock. "And what exactly is it you think she'll be met with if she runs into trouble going to Arcadia? Do you think the bandits she might meet are gentlemen? That they ask permission before raping, beating, and gutting a lady?"

Cathillian's eyes widened. "Holy fuck, Mom. That's a bit extreme, don't ya think?"

Elysia let out an exasperated sigh. "Laurel trained in magic from the time she was a toddler. Her physical training began at ten. She was born with a closeness to nature magic, and her parents and instructors have taken great care to harness that since she was very little. Same as you. Same as every druid here. Arryn was raised in Arcadia with destructive physical magic. She hasn't been trained in either form as thoroughly as we teach our children. Not even close. The Arcadians train for power. We train for survival. Protection. Honor."

Cathillian turned to face her, his arms crossing his chest. "You make it sound like we're always on the brink of war. While there are a lot of dangers lurking about, we train for the *possibility* of war. We don't face death on a daily basis. Arryn won't either. She's strong—way stronger than you give her credit for, apparently, which strikes me as strange given you're always telling her not to underestimate herself."

Elysia opened her mouth to speak, but Cathillian continued. "And what the hell are you thinking anyway? If you think she isn't strong enough, why give her the strongest of our tribe? Why not Jenna? Jenna fought in Laurel's Versuch. That's what would be fair. I'm not the best, but I'm good, and I doubt even I could beat any of these guys."

"If she's as strong as you say, then she'll have no problem going against one of them, now will she?" she asked, pointing to the men and women quietly standing by as mother and son argued. "Besides, was it not you who told her just yesterday if she planned to go back to the city, she needed to think hard about it? That she could still be in danger there, even with the change in government?"

Cathillian shook his head. "Holy shit. That head of yours is like a steel trap. *Yes*, Mother, I did. It's true. I have no problem at all with her requesting the Versuch. If she passes, then it's clear she's strong enough to go off on her own. That's what our laws say—the same laws I elected to uphold when I began warrior training. That's not a problem. What I *do* have a problem with is you doing your damnedest to make sure she fails. She's a fierce competitor. I know that because I train her every single day. She has a lot of heart, and you refuse to see it."

Cathillian didn't make a habit of challenging his mother. The biggest reason was because she was scary as hell.

The Chieftain was taught the magic directly from the Founder himself because he was the strongest, most capable, and had the purest heart. Elysia is next in line for the most powerful. Her small stature was nothing to scoff at.

She could beat the shit out of any man in their community and still have the energy to laugh them out of the Dark Forest afterward.

He knew he still had a long way to go before he could go head to head with her. Times like this, however, when her judgment was clouded by maternal instinct and the need to keep an oath, he had no choice but to step in.

"Cathillian, you know nothing. This has nothing to do with potential. It has everything to do with the *present*. I just see fact. As I said before—her parents didn't train her like we train our own. This left a lot to be desired in her physical magic, I'm sure. I've seen her fireballs. They're weak. Small. Add to that the fact her training abruptly stopped, her physical magic is all but useless. It took her nearly a year—"

Cathillian groaned as he arched his back and rolled his eyes. An exaggerated movement to vent his frustration. "Just *stop*. Seriously." He straightened and took a step closer to Elysia. "Yes, yes, I know. It took a year for her to understand nature magic and to start using it at all. I know she struggled with it, but she's getting good at it now. She was only slow because we never lit a fire under her ass to learn."

At a loss for words regarding his mother's stubbornness, Cathillian threw his hands up. "This is all pointless. I'm not gonna argue about this anymore. You're gonna do what you want to. You're gonna pick one of them to fight her so she *loses*. Not because you're worried she might fail outside our walls, but because you're worried she might *succeed*."

"What did you just say?" Elysia asked. Judging by the look on her face, Cathillian knew he'd messed up, but he didn't back down.

"You heard me. You're afraid she'll succeed. You're scared she'll go back to Arcadia and fall right back into the life she always should have had. More than that, I think you're afraid if she goes back, she might just find her father—if he's even alive after all this time and all the city has been through. But if she does that, she may never come back. You'd never see her again. *That's* why you're doing all this. Not because you're thinking from a logical standpoint or because of some damn oath. You're flat out worried that your once-wounded bird might leave the nest and never come home."

With that, Cathillian walked away, leaving a pissed off Elysia in his wake. He was sure his exit was perfect, but as soon as he was out of eyesight, he wiped the thin layer of anxiety-induced sweat from his forehead and sighed in relief he'd made it out of that alive.

Elysia couldn't believe the words Cathillian had spoken to her. She was so angry she could hardly see straight. Still, she had to admire his courage to stand up to her like he did. More than that, she wondered just how right he might have been.

Was she really just trying to protect Arryn and make sure she was ready before she did something as big as go back to Arcadia? Or was she being selfish for wanting to keep Arryn there?

"Elysia," one of the warriors, Nika, said. "What would you have us do?"

That boy doesn't know anything, she thought to herself before looking to the five men and women before her. Each one had different strengths, though they were trained to be powerful in all areas.

"Nika, I'd like for you to go against Arryn in close quarter combat." Elysia waited for the nod of acknowledgment from the woman before turning to one of the larger men. "Ryel, your magic is stronger than the rest. You'll go against her for that category."

"Two of us, Elysia?" Ryel asked. "That isn't customary."

"It's not against the rules, either," Elysia said.

"Perhaps Cathillian is right," Nika said. "Maybe you should think a bit more about this. You love her. We've all seen it. But you *don't* wanna break her trust. This is gonna seem like overkill. She knows our customs, and she knows what's expected. It'll be painfully obvious to her that you're trying to keep her here. That you want to see her fail."

Shit, Elysia thought. Nika had a point. She loved that girl as much as she loved her own son. She only wanted to keep her around a bit longer so she could train harder.

Maybe she could put her through the rigorous warrior training that Cathillian went through instead of having him train her in his down time for the basics. Then her physical strength would increase as well as her magical expertise.

That's all I want. To make sure she's strong enough.

No... I'm not wrong. She isn't their responsibility. They don't understand.

Elysia squared her shoulders. "Do you decline to participate in the Versuch?"

"No," Nika said. "I'll participate. I just want you to think about this. Unless the Chieftain says otherwise, there's time to change your mind. She'll be given three days to prepare unless she requests an expedited process as Laurel did. You have three days to change your mind on who challenges her. I've worked with her myself. She's very strong, but I'm damn sure she won't win. Not against me. However, *if* she does, you don't want her final memory of the Dark Forest—of *you*—to be that you tried to sabotage her."

Elysia swallowed, working hard to keep her confident posture. She nodded once. "Then it's settled for now. I'll think it over, but just so you know, everyone misunderstands my intentions."

Elysia turned and walked toward her home, eternally grateful that the sun had gone down enough that it was dark under the canopy of trees. No one could see the worry in her expression.

FIVE

Distant beating on the front door woke Arryn with a start, but it sounded strange. Too far away to be in her small home. If someone were to beat on her door, she would hear it very clearly. Instead, it sounded muffled. As her eyes adjusted to the darkness, she saw the nightstand beside her bed. Rich, oak wood stained a deep, red color with a beautiful decorative vase with flowers in it. Next to her, on the feather pillow, was her doll. It had been a very expensive gift from her father, Christopher.

Arryn wasn't awake at all.

In fact, she was stuck in a dream that she'd had for the past several nights, ever since she'd met Samuel. The story he'd told her brought back emotions and memories she'd long since pushed away. Things that she only pulled on during training.

Requesting the Versuch was an even larger added stress. She hoped that it was her mind's way of preparing her for the biggest day of her young life.

Her door flew open and dim light poured in from the magitech sconces on the walls in the hallway. "Arryn," her father whispered loudly. "Arryn, you need to get up. Now."

"What is it?" she asked, unable to control her body or her words in the dream. As was usual over the past few days, she was strictly along for the ride. "What's wrong?"

"Do you remember what we talked about? That we might have to leave Arcadia? That time is now," he said.

"Christopher," Elayne said from the door. "We have to hurry. I can hear them screaming outside. They'll kick the door in soon."

Arryn watched as her father nodded before picking her up and rushing her out of the room. They ran down the hallway to the upstairs office. There, her mother had two small bags packed.

"How did they find out so soon?" Elayne asked in a hushed whisper, tears threatening to spill, though she held them back. "We'd barely begun!"

Christopher shook his head, regret marring his handsome features. "I made a big mistake. I was snooping around somewhere where I shouldn't have been so soon. It was too big to ignore. I should've gotten you out as soon as I found out Saul was dead."

Arryn felt her stomach roll as she heard the front door downstairs bust open. She could hear the shouts of several men—Arcadian Guards and Hunters—rushing into the house to search for them.

"Go! Take Arryn and escape through the window. Don't go to our stables because they'll be waiting for you. Run. Find another stable and take what you have to!"

"What was it?" Elayne asked as she rushed to the window. "What did you find out? It can't be lost with you if it'll help us take him down."

Christopher quickly looked to the door before turning back to his wife, helping her out to the ledge. "Adrien… he has someone…"

Arryn didn't care to listen to what her father told her mother; it didn't matter to her. All that mattered was what she was about to lose.

She reached for her father as tears flowed down her cheeks. He quickly kissed her face as Elayne clung to the window, lying on her stomach, the top half of her inside the house as her legs hung outside over the ledge.

Arryn quickly followed suit right next to her mother as they hastily discussed whatever instructions he had for them. The plan was for Elayne to drop first and help Arryn when she dropped. It would be a long fall from the second story window, but they'd made careful preparations in case the worst happened.

Elayne hung there for a moment as Christopher said something, but Arryn couldn't hear the words over her sobs and the racing of her mind. She could only see his lips move as he finished telling her mother the secret he'd learned that had doomed them all.

She wanted to scream for him, but she was unable, knowing that if she made any loud sounds, they'd be found. Elayne nodded then, and Arryn watched as she pushed herself the rest of the way out the window, dropping straight down into the large pile of hay.

Now… it was her turn.

"Arryn," Elayne said, but her voice sounded different. Very different.

"Arryn!" Elayne said again, only this time her voice was more masculine.

Arryn's eyes opened, her lungs immediately filling with air as she readied herself to scream and punch the person next to her in the face.

Cathillian sat on the edge of her bed, smoothing back her hair, but he quickly snapped into action when he saw the fist coming for him.

He caught it and held it tight, his eyes wide. "Relax! It's just me!"

She looked around, taking in the familiar surroundings as she fell back on the bed. Cathillian released her hand, and it fell to her side as she struggled to catch her breath.

The sides of her face felt chilled. She reached up to touch her cheeks and found herself wiping away tears. Her dream had been a bit more realistic than she'd like to admit. She could even smell her father and feel the warmth of his hug.

"You were screaming. Are you OK?" he asked.

She nodded. "Yeah. I just need to get the hell out of this bed."

"That's probably for the best," he said.

As she was about to sit up, a large, bluish-grey wolf ran through her door and jumped on her, tackling her back down and smothering her face in sloppy kisses.

"Gah!" Arryn called out. "Luna! Nice to see you, too, girl."

Cathillian laughed and stood away from the bed as Luna continued to cheer Arryn up in her messy, slobbery way.

Like Chaos to Elysia, Luna was the familiar to another warrior, Nika. Not all familiars became so much larger with the bond, like Chaos, or the Chieftain's black bear, Zobig, or even Cathillian's golden eagle, Echo.

Only those sharing a bloodline with the Chieftain seemed to gain that trait. For all others, a small change in size *could* happen, but more than likely, it would show increased intelligence, differences in color, or other various characteristics.

Luna certainly had a unique blue tint to the dark grey in her fur, especially around the darker places on her neck and tail. The rest of her was light grey or snowy white.

Finding a familiar was yet another rite of passage, like the Versuch. And even though the Elders had tried to aid her in the connection, it was a step that Arryn wasn't so sure she would be able to have, at least not anytime soon.

Even without having a familiar of her own, she certainly had a gift with animals—including the familiars of others.

"I don't know why she likes me so much," Arryn said, using her blanket to wipe as much wolf saliva from her face as possible. "Most companions don't go crazy over other people. I'm the only person in the village that Zobig hasn't tripped, and Luna has attacked me the last three mornings when I wake up."

Cathillian laughed again. "Maybe Luna senses you're a loser, and she just wants to give you pity snuggles. Zobig, too. You know, something about not kickin' 'em while they're down and all that."

"You're a dick," Arryn said, punching him in the shoulder. "I'm going to have to wash my bedding now." There was a growl from the wolf, and Arryn smiled and finished with, "But I appreciate the love, Luna."

Luna barked once before jumping down and trotting over to the door, lying down like she'd done the last three mornings. It seemed the wolf had sensed her apprehension and came to her aid.

Arryn shook her head, clearing her thoughts as she once again attempted to sit up.

"You ready for this? Or do you need some time?" Cathillian asked.

Arryn shook her head. "Nope, I'm fine. I just want to put on some pants, which I could do if you weren't here." She flashed him an annoyed smile.

"Are you sure you're OK? You don't have to act all tough with me, you know. That dream seemed pretty terrible."

Arryn rolled her eyes. "How is it there are two vaginas in this room right now, neither of which are yours, and you're *still* the biggest girl in here? Stop asking if I'm OK. I'm fine. It was just a dream. I had that same dream for weeks after I first came here. I got over it—and now I'm having them again because of everything going on. It'll pass. I'll be fine."

Cathillian only nodded before standing and heading out of the room, Luna close behind. Arryn sighed, realizing she'd been a bit rude when all he'd wanted was to make sure that she was OK.

"Cathillian," she said. He turned, his jade green eyes meeting hers. "Thanks for worrying about me. I promise—I'll be alright. They're only dreams." She gave a genuine smile then. "You don't have to worry about me so much."

The corner of his mouth turned upward. "I'll never not worry about you." Arryn had almost been moved by that, until he finished with, "You're a loser, remember? Luna thinks so, so it must be true."

Before she could yell at him, he bolted out the door, laughing as he closed it behind him.

Amelia looked at the mile-long list of things to do sitting in front of her. The biggest of which was hunting down Doyle and the Governor. Doyle had escaped before the battle had ever happened, and Amelia needed to find him. Fast.

It had almost been a couple of months and there had been no luck. She was worried that Doyle would gather an army of all the pissed off people that had been exiled or fled and start another battle. Pathetic as he was, he was loyal to Adrien.

He needed to be found.

The second biggest thing to do was rebuild Queen's Boulevard. It was to be something much different than before. Something people could feel proud of, but most importantly feel *safe* to come home to. The problem was she had zero idea of where to start.

Adrien had hemorrhaged a lot more money than people thought. All those high taxes went to paying what was essentially hush money to the families back home when their men disappeared into the factory.

Not only that, but there was an *obscene* amount of coin going to the rearick for the increased amphorald shipments, which only increased as the time for the flying death machine to be completed drew nearer.

The only thing keeping the city afloat were the nobles and the way they spent money. But of course, many of those people refused to stay when they realized the Boulevard would no longer be the trash receptacle of their great city—that the *scum* of the city would no longer be segregated. They would be welcomed with open arms in any part of Arcadia they liked.

Good riddance.

Amelia couldn't give a shit about those people, what they liked, what they wanted, or even where they went. Their money, however, well—that was another story. She *would* regret losing that.

"Chancellor," Marie, her new assistant, said as she peeked through the door.

Amelia smiled at the woman. She had a lot of planning to do for the new Hunters—the Guard scouts responsible for hunting down the traitors as well as patrolling the valley for any threats—but she could use a small break.

"Yes, Marie. Please, come in. And you can call me Amelia."

Marie smiled, seemingly happy to have been given the option. The woman had never had positive experiences with Adrien before. Amelia wanted to keep her around for her knowledge of how things worked in the tower and also in the city building.

Most of the city's work went on in the city building, but Adrien had always stayed holed up in the tower of the Academy.

Amelia had no plans to do that.

She was the backbone of the city now, and she planned to be in the heart of it. Not in the Academy, sequestered away from everyone and everything. That was why she hired Talia, to deal with all things education, and she seemed more than capable.

Marie was kind and sweet, though a bit mousy. Amelia saw the fear in her eyes when Adrien's name was mentioned, so she trusted her. Amelia knew the woman was innocent.

"Yes, ma'am," Marie said in response. "I'm sorry. It's still so strange working for someone so kind." Her head shook, no doubt trying to clear her mind of the terrible memories. "Anyway, the reason I stopped in... I hope you don't mind. I came in here earlier to try to help organize, and I saw that list you're holding."

Amelia laughed. "Judging by the look on your face, you found it just as amusing as I did."

"That's an understatement. Again, I'm sorry for getting in the way, but I thought you could use some help. So, I rounded up some volunteers, and they're down there working on the cleanup on the Boulevard. Everything so far is burned or broken. I told them to dismantle everything down to the foundations, and if anything was salvageable, save it. It's not much, but I hope it helps."

Amelia stood and made her way over to the woman, slowing her pace when she saw the worry on her face. Amelia pulled her into a hug, and Marie stiffened at the contact.

"You're amazing, Marie," Amelia said, pulling away. "Thank you! There are lots of things on that list, but that one is closest to my heart. I wanna rebuild the Boulevard for Hannah. She and Parker came from there;

her family died there. So many people lost so much there. I want to see they're taken care of for once. If we can get volunteers for the demolition, maybe we can get some volunteers to get new wood and supplies. Then, we'd just have to rebuild."

Marie smiled, her posture straightening a little as she got a bit more comfortable. "I think I can help with that! Why don't you let me focus on the Boulevard? I know it's your special project, but I can handle the big work, and we can work on the details together." Her voice was high, and her words were fast. It seemed she was genuinely excited to do the work.

It made Amelia happy to see that lives were being changed, even with the mess around the city. "I think that sounds like a wonderful idea. It would allow me to focus on the Academy and doing the work I *actually* know how to do. I need to get some teachers and fast. We have a lot of students pouring in. I try to avoid getting in Talia's way, but this stuff I kind of need to help with. She's still a bit new."

"I understand! Please let me know whatever I can do! I'm gonna get to work," Marie said, her already impossibly bright smile somehow growing. She turned and left the room then, closing the door behind her.

Amelia made her way back to her desk, sitting down to look over her list again. "Doyle will have to wait for now, I suppose. Back to the Academy, it is. I'm sure Talia will need the help with the applicants anyway," she thought out loud.

Elysia leaned on a tree as she watched Cathillian sparring with Arryn. He was smart, not letting her expend any real energy while still showing her moves that would help in the battle. She knew that with Arryn having someone like Cathillian training her, she stood a chance.

Still, over the past few nights, the guilt began to wear on Elysia. Night after night she fell asleep, worried that her son may have been right, that her choices may not have been as noble as she believed.

As she stood there, watching Arryn putting aside her differences with Cathillian to ensure her victory, Elysia wondered just what else she'd underestimated.

"I can't do this," she said to herself.

She turned and headed toward the Chieftain's home. When she found him, he was sitting outside, enjoying the sun peeking through the canopy above.

"You look like a woman on a mission," he said as Elysia approached.

Zobig, his overly large, black bear, grumbled as he opened his eyes long enough to get a look at her before plopping his head back down on his arms and falling back to sleep.

The Chieftain smiled. "Let me guess…"

"I can't do this," Elysia blurted out. "What if Cathillian's right? What if Nika's right? I can't bear the thought of Arryn hating me any more than I can of Cathillian. I feel like I've betrayed one of my children and set her up for failure." There was a pause as the Chieftain's eyes stared into Elysia's. "What? Why aren't you speaking?"

"You didn't even let me guess!" he said, his amused expression spreading across his face.

Elysia rolled her eyes. "Father, I'm not playing games."

"Oh, I know. I didn't need to guess anyway. I knew the problem as soon as I saw your face. That being said, I'm going to relieve your guilt."

Elysia felt relief flooding through her. "You'll let me pick another warrior? Thank you!"

He shook his head. "No. I didn't say that. I simply said I was relieving your guilt. By that, I mean I'm taking the responsibility from you and putting it on myself. Arryn *will* compete in the Versuch, and she *will* do it with the warriors you've chosen. There. Now, it isn't your fault. It's mine."

"No! It doesn't have to be either of ours. We can fix this. Just allow me to pick another warrior," Elysia pleaded.

"Why? So you can insult her again?" the Chieftain asked. Elysia's eyes narrowed as she thought over his words. "You wanted to deny her the right to compete at all, but it was against our laws. Instead, you underestimated her again by choosing the strongest warriors we have to pit her against because you were *absolutely certain* of her weakness. So sure, in fact, that you knew without a doubt Arryn couldn't beat those warriors."

"That's not true!" Elysia interrupted. "I just thought if she can beat them, then she can beat anyone! Your words are untrue."

"Ah, but that *is* the truth, daughter. If she lost, she'd stay here—where it's safe. Now, you insult her again by coming to me and asking me to give her a weaker opponent. I won't. You're too scared of losing her to see how much she's grown. She's *exactly* the person you brought her here to be. She's spent more time with us here than she did with her parents in

Arcadia. That makes her one of us. She knows who her opponents are and knows who you've chosen. The damage is done. If you do this now, it'll tell her that you really do think she's weak."

Elysia was stunned to silence. Her intentions had been good. She'd never meant to hurt Arryn, but one bad decision led her to another.

She only wanted to keep her away from the dangers that Arcadia faced, especially after Ezekiel had come and told them of the horrible nature of his visit. Instead, she'd only managed to act like a child not getting her way and hurt a girl that she'd come to love.

"You're right," Elysia said.

He smiled. "Of course, I am! I'm pretty great, you know. That's why everyone calls me the greatest."

"No one calls you that," Elysia countered, trying to hide her smile. "But they should."

"That's all I ask," the Chieftain joked while shrugging his shoulders, his palms in the air. He stood then, walking over to Elysia. He placed his hands on her shoulders and kissed her forehead. "Now—the time has come. Are you ready to watch our little girl grow up?"

Elysia nodded. "I am. But first, I think I need to talk to her."

"I think that would be wise," the Chieftain said before heading west, in the direction of the Versuch grounds.

Arryn ducked, only narrowly missing a punch from Cathillian. "Good!" he said. "Remember to keep your eyes on your opponent at all times. Watch her body language. Same goes for Ryel when it comes time to battle with magic."

She nodded. "I think I can do this."

"You think?" he asked incredulously. "You're gonna need to do a hell of a lot better than *think.*"

She sighed. "Yeah. Very true. Damn it! I hate this. No one else needs to be an *expert* to leave. They just need to make sure that they don't die within five minutes of passing through the border. I'm trying hard not to focus on the fact this is stupid and uncalled for, but it's hard."

"I know," Cathillian said, nodding. "I did my best, but she's stubborn. She worries about you just like she does me."

Arryn laughed. "Is that so? Then why doesn't she give a shit that you're a warrior? You might have to go protect the tribe and you could die in battle. I bet if you requested the Versuch, she'd have no problem. She'd probably give you Jenna."

"It's not that," Elysia said, stepping out from behind the trees. "I would absolutely have a problem with it. And Jenna?" Elysia looked at her incredulously before rolling her eyes. "I'd *never* assign him Jenna. What's wrong with you, child? I'd need to make sure he's strong enough to leave. She's the weakest warrior we have."

Elysia stopped in front of Arryn, their eyes locked on one another.

"I just don't understand why you did this. I really don't think you would have put him through this. Either you're scared—and I've never seen you scared of anything—or you just have no faith in me."

Elysia sighed, giving Arryn a sad smile. "He's my only child, and Arryn, you're my responsibility. One that I came to care very much for. The problem is with me. I thought I was trying to protect you, but I wasn't. I refused to see how much you'd accomplished. When I look at Cathillian, I see a druid that's been trained since he was old enough to walk."

"And when you look at me, you see a poor, Arcadian orphan that doesn't belong in either place," Arryn said.

Elysia nodded. "I think part of me did. But today that changes. Today, you prove me wrong. I want you to go out there and beat their asses. Your physical magic is weak, but don't be afraid to use it. Use any means necessary. They're trained for that. They can handle it, and in any real fight, you'd use both, so it's fair."

Arryn smiled. "Thanks, Elysia. I planned to kick their asses anyway. I wanted a really good *rub it in* moment. I was working on my victory speech and everything. But now that you're on board, you've screwed it all up."

Elysia patted her on the back. "No problem. Maybe I'll let you give that speech anyway. But on the downside, if you lose, I'll kick your ass myself. Understand?"

Cathillian rolled his eyes. "I think that's her stubborn way of saying she loves you and good luck."

"Yeah," Elysia replied. "What he said."

Arryn looked to the sky. The sun was directly overhead. "It's time."

SIX

Talia had just finished eating the breakfast that she had unfortunately burned and walked out her front door when it started to rain. She groaned to herself, regretting having taken the time to even attempt to look nice. Her hair became a matted mess in only moments, and she didn't have an umbrella, though she did have something else.

She felt the energy swirling around her as she lifted her hand above her head, a magical barrier appearing just above her. It certainly wasn't practical like a non-energy-draining umbrella, but it protected her from getting any wetter.

As she walked into the school, she nearly slipped and fell because of a puddle of water that was just inside the entrance on the floor. She groaned again, silently cursing the matriarch, hoping she could hear her swears.

As she moved down the hallway toward the stairs that would lead to her office, she heard someone calling her name.

"Dean Talia!" the voice called out.

Already annoyed, just from hearing the tone of his miserable voice, she closed her eyes and sighed heavily, her shoulders momentarily slumping. She heard the footsteps rapidly approaching, so she gathered herself and pasted on what small smile she could manage.

Turning, she saw Alec, a new teacher at the Academy, approaching her with a student on each arm.

"That face doesn't look very happy," Talia said, knowing that her bad day was about to continue as she saw the teacher angrily look from one student to the other. "What seems to be the issue?"

"We have a little problem with these two. They were fighting." The man looked at her with a matter-of-fact expression, acting like he expected her to do something right that moment.

"*And*?" Talia asked. She could hardly keep the disdain from her voice. He was a grown ass man that couldn't take care of a couple of students. He could vaporize them for all she cared. Especially right then.

He looked at her incredulously. "Fighting is forbidden. This is supposed to be a safe area for students. Jackson here thinks that the Boulevard students have no right to be in the Academy. Amos here *is* from the Boulevard. Do you see now why we have a problem?"

Talia's eyes momentarily narrowed, her terrible morning affecting her ability to feign even the most basic of interest. More than anything, she hated his smartass tone. If he didn't watch it, he would be in her office before those students.

Talia smiled. "Actually, Alec, I do see the problem. The problem here is that these students were thrown into a situation that neither one of them asked for. They're both struggling to fit into this new structure. You came from the Boulevard as well, which baffles me, considering most Boulevard residents didn't know their ass from their elbow when it came to magic. Yet, here you are. A teacher. But you were hired before me, so that explains the desperation."

His eyes widened as her words cut him through like an icy knife.

Talia paused to enjoy his momentary fear of her before continuing. "Anyway—being from the Boulevard, you're just as sensitive as they are. I, however, am a neutral party. I'm very equipped to handle the situation, but only if I have all the information—which you did not give me upon demanding my assistance, then persisted to get angry with *me*. And that tone you just took with me? I don't appreciate. Especially in front of the students."

A look of momentary worry crossed the man's face before he looked down to the floor.

"Now, judging by the look on your face, I'd say you don't like me calling you out in front of students. Well, I don't like it when you do that to me either. We're all in this together. We'll speak to each other with respect. Is that understood?" She looked to each one, demanding responses.

All three of them nodded. Alec looked up and did his best to change his expression to something a bit more pleasant. "I'm sorry, Dean. You're right. All this does hit a little bit close. I got angry and impatient."

Talia sighed before allowing her face to show some form of sympathy. "And I understand that. This is why it's very important to have patience. Now, Alec, I believe that you have class to teach. I'll let you get to it, and I'll deal with these two."

Alec nodded. "Thank you, Dean. And again, I'm very sorry."

Talia turned her attention away from the newest history teacher and focused on the two students before her. She looked them over, wondering exactly how the situation could benefit her.

This is exactly what she'd been waiting for, an opportunity to find someone like her, that thought like her.

It wasn't necessarily that she believed in her father's mission; she couldn't care less about that. What she cared about was seeking revenge on the people that killed him, and those people were mostly from the Boulevard.

She turned to Jackson, a taller man with nicely cut, black hair, and dark, chocolatey brown eyes. He had darker skin and a fierce passion in his expression. He didn't plan to back down on the way he felt. He certainly didn't plan to back down to Amos.

"I know that you have a problem with the Boulevard students," she said. "But we all have to figure out how to coexist. I will need to talk to you more later. So, you and I are gonna meet in my office. Got it?"

Jackson nodded. She watched his eyes as they momentarily looked her over. At that moment, she knew exactly how to get to him. By using her charm. He was like any other eighteen-year-old boy.

"Good. Jackson, I'd like for you to go to class."

He nodded once, slowly turning to walk away, but not before looking back at her one last time. Once he was out of earshot, she turned her attention to Amos.

"And what about you? I think all you Boulevard students feel like you have something to prove. But that isn't necessarily a bad thing, but blending in isn't bad either. I don't have time right now to deal with this. But I *will* deal with this—"

Amos didn't wait for her to finish, interrupting her mid-sentence. "That bastard has no respect for anyone. He and his secret group of assholes are all the same. I don't expect him or any of the rest of them to like me, but I *do* expect them to respect me. I didn't know any magic before the Founder and Hannah returned."

Talia had to work hard to keep from punching the little bastard in the face. She wished he'd shut his mouth, but he only continued, forcing her to bite harder on her tongue.

"I fought for the right to be here, just like a lot of my friends did." He nodded down the hall in the direction Jackson had just walked. "That bitch didn't do shit. I'm tired of us getting bullied by them. It shouldn't be happening anymore."

Talia was stunned to silence. She was filled with a terrible mix of volatile emotion. Something between annoyance and anger at being interrupted, surprise that the little jerk had the balls to do it, and rage that the man standing before her was part of the reason why her father was dead.

It was one thing to walk around in the city realizing that everyone, or at least most everyone, had played some part. There was an anonymity to it because she had no idea who had done what. But it was another thing entirely to know details and put a face to her terrible imagination.

This little shit just fucked up and said the wrong thing on the wrong day to the wrong person.

"Hmm. This is definitely a conversation worth having," she said, doing her best to keep her voice level. "I believe I can help you find a solution to your problem. Why don't you stay after school today? Come to my office this evening, and we'll discuss things further. I want to see *exactly* what we can do about the situation in our great Academy."

Amos nodded. "Finally, someone that wants to do something. Everyone else just keeps preaching to ignore it, turn the other way."

Talia laughed. "Oh, I can assure you that I'm not one of those who just stand by and let things happen as they may. I *absolutely* plan to do something."

She dismissed him, sending him off to class. She quickly went upstairs and dropped things off in her office before leaving again, heading toward the secret place in the Academy that her father had described to her in detail, but no one else knew existed.

If things were to go her way, she would need to prepare.

Arryn took a deep breath as she approached the Versuch grounds. To the western side of the tribal houses was the pit. The ground was bare, completely void of any plant—not even a blade of grass. Above, the limbs of the trees seemed to avoid growing over the area, allowing the sun to shine down on the soil there.

The crowd had grown. Everyone from their small village as well as from the other two small, druid communities in the Dark Forest were there. She could feel the tremors in her hands growing stronger.

She hadn't even been able to take part in Laurel's Versuch, though it sounded like hers had been very private and quickly thrown together. She'd never seen one quite like this. It occurred to her that was more than likely because of who she was—more so, where she came from.

"How are you feeling?" Nika, her first opponent, asked.

Like all druids, Nika was tall and lean. She was only a couple inches shy of six feet, and unlike most of the other females in the tribe, her hair was shoulder length. She always wore it in a tight braid that started at her forehead and was tied off at the start of her neck.

All druids had green eyes, though they varied in color. Hers were dark and lightened to a frightful whitish-green when she cast. Her face was beautiful, but her expressions were always fearsome like she was ready for battle at any moment. She was a warrior by nature, possibly the best one in the entire tribe.

"That good, huh?" Nika said when Arryn took too long to answer.

"Nervous. Very nervous," Arryn replied. "Or scared shitless. Depends on how you want to word it."

"Come. I'll walk with you. We'll go in together," Nika said, throwing her arm around Arryn's shoulder and walking alongside her. The crowd parted, allowing them to step through, and Nika led Arryn to the center of the pit. "They don't exist. Got it?"

"Why are you helping me? Is this allowed?" she asked.

Nika smiled. "You're pitted against me for a reason. I'm the strongest fighter here, male or female. No one can beat me. If you're to stand a chance—which I only find fair given these unfair circumstances—you need to know what to look for."

Arryn nodded. "You can't pull punches. Elysia had second thoughts, so if she told you to—don't. It's disgraceful. I *can* do this. If I lose, I wanna lose honorably. If I win, I want the same."

Nika laughed. "You have no worries at all. I have a reputation to uphold. If you win, you'll do it honestly. Believe me—something of yours *will* be broken before you leave today."

Arryn's eyes widened. "Well, that sounds fantastic. Alright. What advice do you have for a novice and future, *proud* owner of a broken face?"

"You're not just a novice. I've trained you before, though not as often as Cathillian has. Look for weakness in me. Study me. I'm not gonna go easy. Not even a little, but that doesn't change the fact that *everyone* has a weakness. Everyone will give an opening at some point. You won't walk out of here winning by strength alone because I'm way stronger. So, use your damn head for something else other than taking punches from me. Got it?"

Arryn swallowed hard and nodded in response.

"I'm sorry to say, kid, but you're gonna lose. Just make sure you break something of mine—or I'll kick your ass later for fun."

Nika was a hardened warrior, but she was as good hearted as they come.

She was only being so harsh because of the situation at hand. Not only that, but Cathillian had let it slip that Nika was very against Elysia's request.

"I understand," Arryn said, her expression just as serious as Nika's. "Thanks for the tips."

Nika touched her right fist to her chest, just over her heart, before walking to the opposite side of the pit.

"Arryn!" Elysia called out. Arryn turned her attention to the head of the crowd where the Chieftain, Elysia, and Cathillian stood. "She's taller than you, but you're thicker. Use that to your advantage."

"Did you just call me a fatass?" Arryn joked. She was only a bit over five feet tall, but she weighed more than Nika—who was nearly eight inches taller—because of the difference in muscle and skeletal structure. Arryn's body packed a lot of power into a smaller package.

Elysia's hand involuntarily covered her face, exasperated at Arryn's ability to joke at such a time. "No—dear. You're heavier because you're built differently than native druids. Use your lower height and difference of weight against her."

"Is there going to be a fight any time today?" Nika asked.

Arryn turned back to her opponent who had a frightening smile on her face. It was obvious that friendly Nika was gone. This was warrior Nika she stared down.

Just… Don't piss your pants, Arryn thought to herself as she tried to focus.

Nika swung her arms back and forth and moved her neck side to side, stretching out. "I'm good to go. I think she is, too."

"Shit," Arryn said, suddenly worried just how badly she was about to get her ass kicked. But she sure as hell didn't plan to show Nika that. "Bring it on, hot stuff!"

The only thing that could have made the druid's evil smile more terrifying was a set of jagged teeth. Arryn imagined Nika had them as the warrior stared her down like prey.

"Begin!" the Chieftain shouted. Immediately, the crowd erupted in shouts, everyone cheering for their favorite fighter.

Arryn cleared her mind, feeling the nature surround her. Relying heavily on magic during this fight was forbidden, though simple magic could be used. Just as no fight she encountered in the outside world would have strict rules, neither would this one, save for two.

No *heavy* magic.

No weapons.

Those would come later as this round was all about skill.

Nika circled Arryn as she found her calm center, the druid's long, lean body like a deadly animal ready to strike. Arryn took the woman's advice, studying her from head to toe. Nika favored her right side, which Arryn assumed meant that she was right handed.

While Arryn hadn't actually planned to learn anything from studying this particular opponent, she was pleasantly surprised to figure out that helpful nugget of information.

Nika attacked first, rushing at Arryn from a few yards away. Knowing Nika's strong side, Arryn was able to duck and lunge to her left, under the quickly approaching fist, but not missing the woman's swift foot.

Arryn ungracefully fell to the ground on her back. She grumbled to herself, coughing from the hard landing before rolling over onto her stomach before getting back on her feet.

"Very nice, but you can't dodge me all day, sweetheart. I have more stamina than you," Nika said. "With honor! No matter if you win or lose. Don't forget."

Arryn grumbled under her breath. *I'll show you honor.*

"Nika wins this round!" the Chieftain called out.

Arryn turned, her brows furrowed. "What the shit? Are you serious? I dodged that punch!"

"You were grounded for more than three seconds," Cathillian said. "If your opponent makes any contact, and you go down for too long, you lose the round. How easy would it've been for her to round on you and deliver a death blow while you lay there coughing and catching your breath?"

"Gah! I call bullshit," Arryn said, not caring at all about her language in the heat of the moment. She turned back to her opponent. She didn't have time to argue anymore on the subject as the fight immediately commenced once again.

"Aw," Nika said, pushing out her bottom lip. "Does everyone's favorite little Arcadian girl have a problem with the rules? You can always forfeit." She smiled at Arryn, that dark, evil grin that had intimidated her earlier, but not anymore.

"*Never*," Arryn spat. "This is for my mother."

Nika nodded once, then moved, but this time Arryn didn't move to dodge. Widening her feet, she braced for the brunt of the impact.

Nika was so focused on the attack that she didn't see Arryn's eyes turn coal black.

Arryn flexed her upper body, her hands in tight fists as a small forcefield appeared before her. Nika didn't have time to react as her momentum propelled her forward, fist slamming hard into the shield. The power of her strike was enough to break through the weak, novice shield and connect with the side of Arryn's face, blood spurting from her nose.

She wasn't sure if the bone had broken, but it certainly felt like it. She was grateful the shield had taken most of the attack, or she'd have been knocked out completely.

As the impact forced Arryn's head down to the side, she recoiled quickly from the hit that was *far* less severe than she'd anticipated. She rebounded, bringing her fist upward in an uppercut, catching Nika under the chin.

As Nika stumbled backward, Arryn lifted her foot and kicked her opponent hard in the chest, sending her backward onto the ground.

"Arryn wins this round!" the Chieftain shouted after a few moments when Nika was slow to get up.

More cheers erupted among the druids watching. It seemed to her that many people were rooting for her.

"One more round!" Cathillian shouted. "If you win this—it's yours!"

Arryn nodded, taking a step toward Cathillian. "Define *if you go down* for me. What about going down to the ground for strategy?"

Cathillian shook his head. "No, that's fine. If she attacks, and you're grounded and unable to get up quickly enough while she's still upright, you lose. If the two of you take it to the ground and wrestle it out—

well, that's always *very* nice, and I wouldn't mind seeing that." Cathillian winked, giving a smile. "As long as the fight continues, of course."

"Good to know," Arryn said. "Minus the pervy bits. Dick."

Arryn sighed as she turned back to Nika who was dusting herself off.

"And this is for my father," she said. She stood tall, rolling her head from shoulder to shoulder, her neck popping in several places.

"Ready to end this, precious?" Nika asked.

"I'm going to kick your ass for that," Arryn said, her face deadly serious as she took the offensive, circling her opponent. Her confidence higher than ever.

Elysia watched as Arryn circled Nika, her prized fighter. She couldn't believe Arryn had ever made contact, let alone taken her down, but she couldn't deny the pride that she felt. Her nerves were on edge, her gut twisting as she watched, cheering for Arryn, but hoping for whichever outcome would be the best for her.

Arryn's face turned just as dark and terrifying as Nika's had been earlier, each woman trying their best to intimidate the other. Her eyes turned black again, but somehow even blacker than before. "I had no idea she could still use her physical magic so well," Elysia said out loud.

"She practices. I catch her sometimes," Cathillian said. He stepped closer to his mother. "She didn't want anyone here to be disappointed in her for still having a connection to it instead of abandoning it completely for nature magic."

"That's ridiculous. She's able to do both. She *should* use both. She's special. Look at her. Have you ever seen her like that?"

Cathillian smiled. "Only when she's pissed at me."

Elysia threw an elbow into her son's ribs, shaking her head at him before turning her focus back on the fight. Both women ran for each other. Nika dropped to her knees, leaning back as she slid, attempting to take Arryn to the ground again, but Arryn was ready.

She leapt forward, extending her hands as she dove over Nika, landing on the ground hands first before tumbling over once and bouncing back on her feet.

"Ha!" Cathillian shouted, throwing a fist in the air. "Taught her that just this morning!"

"Shh!" Elysia scolded before focusing her wide eyes back in on the fight.

"You're gonna lose!" Nika shouted. "And when you do—you can kiss Arcadia goodbye. You'll never be good enough to go back. Your father will rot there! That is—if he hasn't already."

The crowd went silent as the words flowed through the ears of everyone there, each person understanding the weight of their meaning. As important as family was to Arryn, it was *everything* to a druid.

Nothing was more sacred.

That was an insult worthy of swift consequences, and everyone there knew it, especially after what she'd gone through with them. Arryn stilled as her eyes closed and her nostrils flared. It was obvious that she was beyond pissed.

Elysia's eyes were wide as she nervously watched to see what would happen. Would she attack recklessly? Would that make her work harder? She had no real idea what Arryn was capable of, but that was the coldest thing possible to say to her.

Especially with everything she fought for right then.

To Elysia's side, she saw Cathillian looking around and even to the sky.

"Oh, shit," Cathillian said. "Do you feel that?"

"Uh, oh," Elysia replied, turning to the Chieftain. "Father, we need to stop this. Now."

He shook his head. "Nope. Nika was way out of line. Leave it be. Let our little Arcadian druid teach the warrior a lesson in honor in battle."

Elysia nodded, exhaling deeply. The last thing she wanted was another argument with her father. She'd underestimated Arryn too much. She needed to trust her for once—even if she was about to wield magic she had no control over. *Just focus, Arryn. Just focus.*

Thunder cracked overhead, wind whipping through the trees as thick clouds came in to darken the skies. Arryn's eyes snapped open, and Elysia gasped as she saw her irises glowing a vibrant green, bleeding into a color that was blacker than black where they were normally white.

Nika nervously shifted her weight from one foot to the other in the pit, looking from Arryn's terrifying eyes to the sky that was quickly darkening and over to the Chieftain. Her own eyes flashed whitish-green as she turned her attention to the sky.

It was obvious to Elysia that Nika was trying to will away what Arryn was pulling in, but it was impossible. Arryn's emotions were too high, and she was somehow overpowering the warrior.

"Grandfather," Cathillian said. "I can feel Nika trying to control it, but she can't. Let me in there. I can bring Arryn back."

The Chieftain shook his head, his eyes wide as he excitedly smiled like a kid that just got a brand-new toy. "The girl has a gift! If things get outta hand, I'll stop it. Stand back and watch the show! This is even better than I expected! Did we bring snacks?"

Elysia and Cathillian both shot him stupefied looks.

He shrugged. "I'll take that as a no. There's no need to be so hostile. Who taught you manners? Certainly wasn't me." He turned his attention back to Nika. "*Fight!*"

Arryn heard the Chieftain's command over the wind whipping around her, but it meant nothing. There was no meaning in anything. There was only the emotion she'd felt over the past few days, bubbling up in every dream, every thought.

All the fear, worry, and regret that she'd been repressing for ten years finally coming to the surface.

Do not fail. Do not fail. Do not fail, were the only words that occupied her mind. It was empty otherwise.

Nika rushed forward as Arryn's arms lifted to her sides, palms up as buckets of rain then fell from the sky in thick, heavy drops. The bare ground immediately became muddy with the beating that the rain gave, allowing Arryn to take the extra moment that she needed.

Just as before, she tightened her entire upper body, her fist clenching hard as a barrier sprang forth—only this time *much* more powerful. Nika hit it full force, stumbling back. She slipped and fell hard on the ground, landing on her hand.

Arryn heard the snap of a bone in Nika's wrist, causing the warrior to cry out as she rolled onto her back and tried to sit. Arryn wasn't sure if that was a loss for Nika, but she wanted to make certain.

As Nika tried to stand, Arryn took a step forward, quickly swinging her arm to the left. As she did, the water in the ground under Nika froze, causing the woman to slip back into the ice and mud. Before Nika could correct herself, Arryn was on top of her.

She landed a hard punch and then another to Nika's face before Nika pulled Arryn down and headbutted her in the nose, blood once again spurting out. The wind and rain died down as the women struggled on the ground.

Nika managed to get her feet under Arryn's stomach to kick her backward over her head. Arryn was tossed in an impressive arc behind Nika, landing hard in the mud flat on her back, their heads only inches from one another. Nika was lightning fast as she flipped backwards and straddled Arryn, punching her in the face again.

"Enough!" the Chieftain shouted. "The battle is over."

Arryn laid in the mud, dazed and weak. The magic had taken a hell of a toll on her physically and mentally. It had been her rage and emotion that allowed her to touch that much power, but it fed on those negativities and drained her dry, leaving her only half-conscious on the ground. Her entire body felt like it had been beaten the hell out of, not just her face.

"Sorry, about that," Arryn choked out, turning her head to spit out a mouthful of blood.

"For which part exactly? My broken face? Or the heart attack when I thought you'd actually kill me?" Nika asked, her brows furrowed.

Arryn smiled, even though it was incredibly painful. "No. Not that. You deserved it for being a bitch." Arryn's eyes were growing very heavy. She was very close to passing out. "I'm sorry that my head took so many punches. I really meant for it to be yours instead."

"What the hell? You're as bad as that shit, Cathillian," Nika said as Arryn's consciousness faded.

SEVEN

Cathillian jumped the barrier and rushed to Arryn's side, sliding a bit from the momentum as he dropped to his knees in the mud. He passed a dirty look to Nika who wisely backed away. He turned his attention back on Arryn. Her face was covered in blood and mud. Her hair was matted with it.

"Let me help—" Nika began.

"I think you've helped enough," Cathillian interrupted, placing a hand on the side of Arryn's face.

He immediately felt the swell of the magic in the elements and nature around him, allowing him to borrow enough energy to push it toward Arryn. Her eyes fluttered open, though it was obviously hard for her to keep them that way.

"Are you OK?" he asked.

Arryn nodded her head, but the movement was barely visible. "Oh, hell. I feel like I got punched in the face five hundred times by some super crazy bitch." Her face scrunched a bit as she moaned. "Oh, wait… I did."

"You're ridiculous," Cathillian said. He stood then, picking her up in his arms and carrying her off the field.

"The fight isn't over," Jenna, another warrior, said.

She stepped across the barrier and into the pit, her long, porcelain face and fighter's body displaying intense aggression. Her dark, blonde hair hung loose down her back, blowing in what was left of the now gentle wind.

Her arms were crossed defiantly over her chest. "The Chieftain has to call the winner."

"The fight is done, Jenna," Cathillian said, his expression angry.

He had no idea what her issue was, but she'd never much cared for Arryn. It didn't matter what she tried to do, Jenna was always there to kick her while she was down.

Cathillian continued, interrupting the argument the angry warrior was about to make. "With her half passed out, it *might* be a bit hard for her to swing a spear or throw an axe, wouldn't you say? Now, unless you wanna try to stop me from carrying her out of here, I'd have to say that you should step the fuck back."

"Cathillian is right," the Chieftain said. "The fight is over right now."

"Right now?" Jenna asked. "She cheated! She used heavy magic! Or am I the only one that noticed that shitstorm she just conjured? The rules are clear. Small amounts of magic can be used, but it *cannot* be used to overwhelm, disorient, or completely subdue the opponent."

Nika stepped forward then. "She was unfairly pitted against me in the first place. It should have been *you* in there. Someone she could stand a chance against. I don't know why you're coming to my defense, but I have a feeling it's not for my own benefit. Her heavy use of magic was completely my fault. I never should have mentioned her father."

"That doesn't excuse the outsider bitch for cheating. She lost. She can't carry on if she loses one of the battles. She has to pass all three," Jenna said, her fists clenched at her sides.

Cathillian turned to face Jenna, Arryn still unconscious in his arms. He was about to unleash hell on the girl, but Nika stepped in.

"You heard him. Back the fuck off," Nika said. "The Chieftain has made the call. Once Arryn's made a recovery, I'm sure we'll continue. Until then, you'd be wise not to completely disrespect the man that's responsible for your position. Everyone knows it sure as shit isn't your talent. Your brother had the skill to make it. You only got lucky the Chieftain was feeling sorry for you that day."

"Don't *ever* mention my brother again," Jenna said, her eyes glowing greener.

"Why? Because he had more talent? Or because he disgraced his family and his entire tribe? Don't dare flash those eyes at me, little girl. You'd do well to sit your ass down before you get yourself hurt. We *both* know, even with a busted wrist, I'd lay you out faster than you could cry for help. Or do I need to remind you of the last time I made you cry? When was that—just a week ago?"

Nika gave a shitty smile and turned away, leaving a young and silently raging druid in her wake.

"Thank you," Cathillian said as Nika helped him cross over the barrier to carry Arryn back home to be properly healed.

She waved a hand in the air. "It was the least that I could do. We may not like her much because she's a condescending bitch, but we're all still very kind to her. I wasn't allowing her to get away with that today. That girl has a serious attitude problem."

Nika sighed heavily as she shook her head, clearly still angry about the dispute.

She rubbed at her aching wrist before continuing. "Anyway, I know Arryn hates me for what I said. I'd hate me, too, but my intentions were good."

"I know," Cathillian said. "You were trying to piss her off so she'd kick your ass. I'm sorry I got so shitty with you back there. I was just worried about her."

Nika gave a small laugh. "It's fine. I deserved it. And I was definitely trying to make her angry. I thought if she was mad enough, she'd get stronger." She shook her head again, this time with a smile on her face. "I *never* expected that. If I'm to be honest, she scared the hell out of me. There is a *lot* of pent up emotion hidden away in that girl."

Cathillian walked in silence for a moment as he thought over what Nika had said, but also the things he'd seen Arryn do.

He'd never seen anyone wield two kinds of magic in person. In fact, he'd *barely* seen Arryn do it. He hadn't lied when telling Elysia he'd caught her practicing physical magic. Mostly fireballs, creating ice, and even trying to teleport—though she'd never even come close to that. It was far too advanced for a novice like her.

Still, it didn't stop her from trying.

Her fireballs were strong for their size, but he would never forget the day Elayne, Arryn's mother, had saved him. She was a *very* strong physical magic user. Her fireballs were powerful, and still to this day, he'd never seen a fire burn as bright or hot.

Arryn's were only slightly larger than her fist, but packed an impressive punch for how small they were. If she'd been formally taught, it was hard to say just how powerful she'd have been by then. She was great with ice because of her affinity for nature magic to add to it, but even her nature magic was weak in comparison to Cathillian's.

"I think Arryn's watched us and learned from us over the years. She has the knowledge—she's only been lacking the execution. The form. She's memorized all our movements, our lessons, and our ways—but she had no idea how to connect her own body with the things that her brain knew."

"Until today," Nika said.

Cathillian nodded. "Exactly. You may feel terrible for what you said, and she might be angry at you for a while—she did call you a crazy bitch after all—but I think it was the best thing for her. Especially if she plans to run off to Arcadia."

Nika laughed. "I heard it. I just didn't say anything. I can't blame her for saying it." They took a few more steps in silence. Nika reached over and wiped some wet mud away from Arryn's face. "Do you think she's ready now? I mean, she's learned a lot of our magic, but there is an enormous difference between learning a few things and thriving with it."

"After what I just saw?" Cathillian asked, briefly looking at Nika. "I think she's finally broken her mind open in a way that she can now channel that pain—if she'll allow it."

"Jenna said she cheated, but she didn't use the storm against me. All she did was use a bit of rain water to freeze the ground beneath me so she could physically pin me down and end the fight. The rest was all for show, a big threat, and the Chieftain should know she kicked my ass in two of the three categories."

"So, you want to request that she's the victor in both?" Cathillian asked.

Nika nodded. "Cathillian—I *tried* to control the magic she was using. I was terrified she'd release lightning and kill herself. I couldn't even influence the wind in another direction. I was *powerless* against her. That being said, admitting my embarrassing failure against a novice is not why I brought it up."

"Then, why did you tell me?" he asked.

"Because if she wins that, and then wins the weapons category, she'll be free to go to Arcadia. With this breakthrough, and with all she's proven herself capable of, she *needs* instruction. Power like that can't just be found and left. She *needs* a mentor."

Cathillian paused outside the door of Arryn's house as Nika walked ahead to open it for him. She helped him get Arryn through and on the floor next to her bed to avoid getting blood and mud all over the bedding.

"I've already thought of that," Cathillian said. "That's why I've asked my grandfather for permission to take the Versuch along with her. When

I saw how much power she was using, I just had a feeling she'd win. I can't let her go alone. I'll accompany her to Arcadia when she goes."

Arryn cried out and ground her teeth as she awoke to the sensation of her nose snapping in several places, quickly followed by her left brow bone as well as her left cheek. As soon as the pain came, it was gone. She still felt exhausted, but she no longer suffered from her injuries.

"Sorry," Cathillian said. "Can't cure the fatigue right away. That's from the magic use. You depleted yourself pretty heavily out there today, so it'll probably take a few healings or just some good sleep."

"I don't even understand how that happened. I kept drifting in and out while you carried me back here, or I'd have thought it was a dream," Arryn said.

"You don't remember doing it?" Cathillian asked.

"No, I remember all of it. It's just—nothing about it seemed real. I remember Nika saying…" Arryn shook her head. "Anyway, after that, there's nothing. It was like I felt so much all at once that I ended up feeling nothing at all. I guess I snapped. I didn't even have to work to push things out of my mind. It just happened. Well, until I got slammed in the face. That let everything pour back in *super* fast."

"Have you ever felt like that before?" Cathillian asked.

She shook her head. "Never. I'm so scatterbrained most of the time that I have a hard time clearing my mind. That was—strange, and I think that's an understatement."

Cathillian nodded. "Well, let's not worry about it right now. We have time for that later. How do you feel? Can you walk?"

Arryn tried to sit, but with her level of exhaustion, she could barely even accomplish that. "I can hardly even sit, so I doubt it."

"Do you think you could handle a ride on Chaos? Slow and steady?"

Arryn shook her head. "No. I can't ride alone. Why do I need to ride anywhere?"

"I'm gonna take you to the river. You're covered in mud and blood. Your hair's matted to your head."

"I'll live. Just let me sleep in my bed. I have to wash those nasty, wolf-slobber blankets anyway, remember?" she asked. "A little mud and blood won't hurt much."

Nika smiled. "Luna get you again?" Arryn nodded. "Don't fight so much. Let him help you. You're weak. I'll change your bedding for you while you're gone. It was my wolf that did it anyway. When you come back, everything will smell much better—so will you."

"I appreciate that," Arryn said, thinking it over. She desperately wanted to get cleaned up and sleep as long as possible in a clean bed, but she also wanted no part of needing to move. "I know you're probably offering because you feel bad, but don't. I only heard half of it, but it was enough to know you weren't being a crazy bitch. Just a regular bitch." She smiled, and Nika returned it.

"Yeah, well, I have a feeling you'll thank me for it later. Now, go get cleaned up. I'll take care of your room and bring you some clean clothes, too," Nika said.

Arryn didn't protest when Cathillian once again reached for her. She wrapped her arm around his shoulders as he picked her up. Once they were outside, he saw Elysia and the Chieftain walking toward Arryn's house.

"You looking for us?" Cathillian asked.

"Of course," Elysia said. "How are you, Arryn?"

She shrugged. "Tired enough to let this jackass carry me around like a baby, if that tells you anything."

"Well, you must really feel like shit then," the Chieftain joked.

"Dad!" Elysia grumbled. "I swear—you get worse the older you get. I try to teach these kids respect for you, and you go and act just like them."

"Oh, relax. It's a *word*. A word never killed anyone. Well..." He thoughtfully looked to the sky for a moment, placing a single finger on his chin. "Unless someone used a word to order someone else's death. Then I suppose, in that instance, words *do* kill."

Elysia closed her eyes as she shook her head. Arryn heard the words *fuck... me...* mumbled, but she wasn't certain. Elysia spoke a bit louder then. "I'm about to relinquish this old man of his responsibilities."

"Not to break up the good mood, but Arryn really does feel terrible. I just want to get her down to the river and help clean her up. Can we take Chaos? He'll be the gentlest out of the horses."

"Of course," Elysia said, closing her eyes for a moment. When she opened them, the dark green glow faded to the normal green of her eyes. "Is there anything that I can do to help?"

"I think we have it," Cathillian replied. "Nika's bringing some clothes.

I'm just gonna make sure she gets there without falling off the horse."

"Oh, like you wouldn't find that hilarious," Arryn said.

He smiled. "If you weren't as helpless as a little, baby bird, yeah. I'd probably find it hilarious."

"You're a dick," Arryn said as the sound of Chaos's hooves echoed around them.

The horse trotted up to the group before stopping completely. His head twisted side to side as he tossed his long, black mane back and forth.

"Chaos," Elysia said, placing her hand on his powerful jaw. He leaned into her touch as she spoke to him. "Please take Arryn and Cathillian to the river. No sudden movements."

Chaos snorted as he nodded his large head. He then extended his front legs, lowering himself enough that Cathillian could lift Arryn on the horse's very tall back.

She was able to throw her leg over, but immediately leaned forward to lie on Chaos's massive shoulders. Cathillian quickly hopped on before Chaos once again lifted himself.

"You should be safe lying like that," Cathillian said. "But if you start to slide off in one direction or another, I'm pulling you back against me—got it?"

Arryn gave him a thumbs up before her arm flopped back down to the horse's side. Chaos began walking west, toward the Kalt river, the sounds of his snorts and heavy breaths soothing Aaryn as she relaxed against him.

There was a loud screech as Echo flew by. She landed in a tree ahead, waiting for the trio to walk by before flying ahead of them again.

It didn't take long for Arryn to fall unconscious again, but Chaos's broad back and shoulders gave her a sufficient area to lay in. Cathillian had to center her a few times, but she didn't care. Right then, she didn't care about anything other than sleep.

EIGHT

It was quite a long hike for Samuel to get back to Arcadia, but that journey had finally come to an end. It never seemed possible to him—a rearick—that he would ever be excited to see the city, but that had certainly been the case after days of walking.

Food.

Drink.

The rearick was *very* excited to see the city.

The only thing he'd managed to catch and eat on his journey back were some rabbits and a few berries. He wasn't a big fan of rabbit meat, but it kept him strong. That was good enough for him in the Forest, but he wasn't about to pass up stopping for some real food now.

The hard ground had been no good for his old bones, and he needed rest.

Samuel could still fight with the best of them, but his sleep was important.

To keep up with the younger men, he'd need good rest. The idea of looking weaker by comparison annoyed him, as it would any other rearick, to no end.

When he finally arrived at Sully's, there was a cute little barmaid working that evening who brought his food and drink. Among all the ugly mugs in attendance, he was happy to see a pretty face. Something that didn't kill his appetite while eating.

He ate in silence as he imagined how wonderful it would be to get back to Craigston. It felt like forever since he'd been home. He didn't have a family there waiting on him, but it was still more home than this damn city.

"Can I get anything else for you?" the young woman asked.

Samuel pulled his mug way too fast, a stream of ale spilling down his beard as he coughed. He hadn't seen her coming, and he'd been lost in thought, allowing himself to be easily startled.

He cleared his throat one last time before speaking. "Well, since me clumsy arse just spilt half the beer, I think I'll need another. Have any of the mystics' brew back there?"

She smiled and pulled a cloth from her belt before handing it to him. He almost blushed at the kindness of the younger beauty, thanking his thick, bushy beard for hiding any color that had flooded to his face.

He wiped his mouth before giving her an embarrassed smile.

"We do, but it's pretty expensive."

"Expensive? Ye mean expensive inna way ol' Samuel here can't afford it even with him bein' one ta deliver it?" Samuel smiled, not wanting the woman to think he was giving *her* a hard time as much as having a problem with the situation.

She shrugged. "I'm sorry. We can't really afford to put in an order for more than a barrel at a time. Two at the most. None of the men around here have money. They're all outta work with the factory down and all. Noble money is all that keeps us up and runnin'."

Samuel groaned, the sound lost in the loud voices. After journeying alone and on foot for that long without any supplies or proper food, he was a bit more than annoyed to be unable to partake in the good shit. He'd earned it by constantly doing underpaid work for the city—and even helping to save it—or so he'd thought, but apparently not.

The rearick men were always in and out of the town. He realized his men were still working for the damned Arcadians, yet they couldn't even get a decent night's rest or entertainment because the city was too far gone.

Everything was too expensive for them, even though they were the reason it was possible. All work and no good ale made for very testy rearick—and they were already as rough and smartassed as they came.

"Sounds like the Chancellor needs ta put tagether a group fer rebuildin'."

The barmaid smiled. "She has. Otherwise there'd be a lot more guys here. All the others are outta town takin' jobs from nobles or out in the forests by the Madlands cuttin' wood for their new houses."

She paused, shifting her weight from one foot to the other before continuing. "I'm sorry for the expense, but I can get you another beer. I might even be able to sneak you one of them big corn muffins I saw back there."

When she placed her hand on his shoulder, Samuel felt another blush spread across his face.

"Thanks, lass," he said with a curt nod, turning away. "I'd like that."

She gave his shoulder a squeeze, that felt better than he'd liked to admit, and she winked at him before walking away.

"Damn it all," he said to himself. "I've completely lost me charm. Ugh. It's been too long."

Samuel shook his head, cursing himself for having been so awkward. He was a rearick, and rearick men didn't get nervous. With another nod, he avoided eye contact when the young woman brought back his beer and a large corn muffin—as promised. He quickly thanked her and went back to eating.

I can't wait to get back home, he thought, but then he thought of something else. What home would there be to return to if he couldn't find work? None of his people would be living very nice lives if there wasn't enough coin to go around. *I might be stuck here after all.*

Once Arryn and Cathillian reached the side of the river, Chaos lowered himself to the ground, allowing Cathillian to gracefully dismount without falling and potentially taking Arryn with him. Arryn awoke to Cathillian picking her up, and she curled into him.

"Shit," she said, yawning.

"What?"

"I can't stay awake. This is terrible."

He smiled. "Well, aside from getting your nasty ass cleaned up, I have something for you. A new lesson."

Arryn groaned. "Can't you see I feel craptacular? I don't feel like learning anything."

The sun was intense over the river, forcing Arryn to keep her eyes squinted. It was a beautiful day. The clouds had all retreated from her earlier assault. It looked as though they'd never even existed.

"If you can use words like craptacular, then you're energetic enough to learn this. Besides, you'll thank me. Not many druids can do it. I'm one of the few. Other than me, only my mother and the Chieftain are strong enough."

"Then why would you think I could?" Arryn asked.

Cathillian was silent, taking slow, careful steps as he walked into the river, Arryn still in his arms. Once the water was to his hips, he gently dropped to his knees, submerging Arryn up to the chest in the process.

"*Whoa*, that water is cold," she said. Her body was sore, even after being healed, and the cooler temperatures helped quickly numb away some of the pain.

"You'll get used to it soon enough," Cathillian said. "Lean your head back."

Arryn did as she was asked, her hair moving in the water as it rushed along with the current. Within moments, her hair was washed clean of the dirt and blood with no effort at all.

The water had cleaned away most of the mess. Her face was all that was left, and Cathillian wiped that away with a gentle, wet hand.

"You're clean now. Are you ready for your lesson?" he asked.

Arryn shook her head. "I really just want to go to sleep. Besides, if you, your mother, and your grandfather are the only ones able to do whatever this is, I'm not going to be able to even attempt it while I'm so weak."

"Way to give up before you even try, quitter. You'll never regret it if you learn it. Now, stop being a shit. You're too weak to fight me on this anyway."

Arryn rolled her eyes. "Delightful."

"You asked why I believe you can do this when no one else can. The reason is because I just saw something in you that we haven't seen in a long time. Raw, untapped power. You have a lot of potential—but not if you hold on to your Arcadian ways."

"What the hell is that supposed to mean?" Arryn asked. "I let go of my Arcadian ways forever ago. I'm more druid than Arcadian. I just don't have the fancy, pointy ears to go along with it."

Cathillian laughed. "Don't make fun of the ears. You're just jealous that yours are rounded and boring. Look, what I'm trying to say is it's fine to learn your physical magic. You're good at it—for a novice. But there are some things you need to learn about our magic, too. So, can you just trust me for maybe five seconds?"

Arryn nodded, fighting the urge to fall asleep in his arms while the cool water rushed around them.

Cathillian adjusted her in his arms when her eyes started to close again. "Using magic drains the hell out of your energy. Physical magic is the worst because it takes more energy than any other type and it doesn't give anything back at all. Mystical magic isn't much better, but they can heal themselves some with meditation. Nature magic is the opposite. It's pure. It's life."

Arryn fought heavy eyes again before shaking her head to wake herself more. "I suppose that makes sense, but I still don't see where you're going with this."

"That's because you have zero patience." He smiled, but Arryn couldn't see it for the bright sun blinding her. "Touch the energy from the water. Feel it and pull it into yourself. When you can learn to absorb the energy, you can learn how to recycle it and heal yourself."

"Yeah, I can feel it, but I can't move it right now, let alone do something I've never even seen done before. You can?" she asked with a yawn.

He nodded. "Yes. We walk around barefoot to have a constant connection with nature. But water's stronger. We just can't carry it with us. When any other druid heals, they only use their own magic—meaning their own energy—and push it toward whatever they are healing."

Arryn nodded, unable to manage much else.

Cathillian smiled. "That means they get weak quickly—just like if they'd used physical or mystical magic. If you learn to use the energy of nature around you instead of just yours, then it won't drain you so much. You're essentially healing yourself as you cast, but it has its limits, and I doubt it would work well with any other type of magic use—like physical."

"Heal yourself as you cast? But—that would mean that druids could have almost endless energy in battle if they just learned how to recycle the energy around them," Arryn said.

Cathillian shook his head. "No. Not even close. My grandfather doesn't even have that kind of power, but it *would* allow someone to fight a little longer. As for powerful healing, there is only one element that can deliver a lot of life energy at one time, and we're standing in it."

"This sounds like a lot of bullshit, and I don't believe you. Carry me back to the grass; I'm exhausted. I'd have noticed you, Elysia, or the Chieftain do that kind of magic. I can feel energy, and I'm not a native druid, so everyone has to be able to do it," she said.

Cathillian dropped Arryn's legs down while still holding onto her with the other arm. He pulled a knife from a small sheath on his belt and struggled for a moment to keep hold of her in the river while using the knife to make a deep cut down his free forearm.

Blood immediately poured through the wound and into the water. Without saying a word, he lowered his arm into the river.

Arryn's eyes widened as she watched the wound close almost instantly without him touching it as she'd seen other druids do while healing themselves or others. And she only felt a tiny amount of energy come from him as he healed himself.

"How?" she asked. "I—That's incredible!"

He smiled. "I told you. The point is, once you're comfortable enough with the power nature offers, and once you can control it, you'll use half the energy, but yield greater results. It's the only type of magic that gives as much as it takes. I think I can teach you how to use nature magic in a way that will help you *grow* your physical magic right along with druid abilities."

"Why can't other druids do that?" she asked.

"It's not for a lack of trying," Nika said from behind them. She rotated the wrist that had broken in the battle. Seemed like it was feeling much better. "If I could do what he can, I wouldn't have to have others heal me."

Cathillian turned with Arryn in hand. He sheathed his knife before picking Arryn up once again and carrying her to the grass. He gently sat her down.

"I wanted you to use the water to regain your energy, but I guess you'll just have to sleep it off. I'll let you off easy this time—but only because you got the shit kicked out of you. But next time, I'm not gonna be so gentle with you." He winked and stood.

"Do you really think I could do that?" Arryn asked, her voice sounding a bit more lively and excited.

Nika kneeled then, a towel and some fresh clothes in hand. "After what I saw today—I'll never doubt your abilities again. That doesn't mean I won't doubt your skill in controlling them, however. I really don't think you could call on that kind of power again without another trigger, but you definitely have something."

"We'll talk more about it later," Cathillian said. "I'm gonna walk back so you can get changed in private. Nika, can you get her on Chaos without a problem?"

"Your mom healed my wrist, so I'm good to go. I'm gonna heal Arryn a bit more. See if it helps give her a bit more strength. She's much more awake. Seems she syphoned a little from the water without realizing it. We should be just fine," Nika said.

"Wait, what?" Arryn asked. "I did?"

Cathillian laughed. "Never paying attention! It's no wonder why I always sneak up on you. You really do make it too easy."

Arryn and Cathillian had always spent their time arguing and insulting one another. It was their favorite pastime. But it had been a long few days, and he had been there for her without fail. He was a much better man and friend than she'd given him credit for.

It was obvious that he believed in her, and that meant more to her than she realized.

"Cathillian," Arryn said as he walked away.

"Yeah?" he said, turning back to face her.

"Thanks for everything. I don't know if you're right or not, but I'm more than willing to learn. If it turns out that I'll be allowed to leave for Arcadia, though, it'll have to wait."

"No. No, it won't," he said, a devious smile on his face. Her expression turned inquisitive before he answered. "I demanded to take the Versuch. Looks like you're stuck with my ass. We both *know* I won't lose."

"Oh, hell," she said out loud.

NINE

The sun was beginning to set, the daylight hours still short from winter. Amos made his way back to the Academy, having just finished helping a friend, John, home after class. John had been injured in the Battle for Arcadia, suffering a broken leg, and Amos liked to help make sure he made it home OK every day.

Amos hadn't told anyone about meeting the Dean later, not having wanted to make a bigger deal out of the earlier fight than what was necessary. He didn't like fighting and arguing, and he certainly didn't like making himself look like an ass.

Still, when people like Jackson got in his face, it was difficult for him to back down. All he wanted was to live alongside everyone in Arcadia in peace, no matter what their background was. But there were still people like Jackson that had a hard time adjusting.

As he crossed the front entrance of the school, he wondered what the Dean could possibly have to say. He didn't like the idea of needing to stay after class, but if it managed to get some problems solved, then he'd do what he needed to.

He regretted being so rude to Talia earlier, that having been the first time he'd really met her, though he'd seen her around campus. He hadn't wanted to upset her further; it was obvious she was annoyed with Alec, the new history teacher. Amos had only added to it, and he knew it.

He took a deep breath and knocked on the door of the Dean's office, the sound of her voice echoing through the wood almost immediately.

He pushed the door open and made his way inside before closing it behind him. Talia sat behind her desk, standing to meet him as he stepped away from the threshold.

"I'm so glad you could make it," she said. "I know staying over isn't ideal, but I appreciate you coming back."

Her words were kind, but there was something in her voice that chilled him to the bone. He couldn't place it, but something just didn't seem right.

She slowly walked toward him, her head was held high, her shoulders squared, and her pace was slow and deliberate.

Very confident.

His gut began to roll as a bad feeling crept cross him. He couldn't understand why, but he was suddenly very afraid of her.

Talia smiled, the very tone of it terrifying. "You look nervous, Amos," she said, her voice low.

Amos shook his head. "No, not at all. My mom's just expecting me soon, so I need to get home before it gets too dark outside. Still, I wanted to come here, since you asked."

Talia stopped only a couple of feet away from him, nodding her head as she looked him over. "So, you said you fought in the revolution?"

"Y-yes, ma'am," he said, silently kicking himself for allowing his voice to crack.

He'd stared death down and came out on the other side, having fought against an army of Arcadian Guards and alongside his friends. He'd never been alone with Adrien, though he'd heard stories of how terrifying he was.

From the stories he'd been told, the feeling coursing through him at that very moment was very similar.

He swallowed hard. "I did. I fought in the forest, and then we came to Arcadia to take everything back while Hannah destroyed Adrien."

"And even though you never spent any time with him, you weren't enamored with the Chancellor like some of your now-fellow students, is that right? Like Jackson?"

Amos' expression reflected just how repulsive and offensive he found that thought. "*Jackson* didn't even like Adrien, but he *did* believe most of the crap he said. Like Only the richest people deserved to learn magic. Adrien was a vile, disgusting human being, and I'm glad he's dead. We should all be glad. He *destroyed* so many lives. And anyone enamored with that is just as cold, black hearted, and soulless as he is. Or, I guess I should say, *was.*"

A dark smile spread across Talia's lips before she broke into laughter, the sound of which echoed against the walls of her office. It was a terrifying sound, one that pierced the ears and went straight down his body into his bones.

At that moment, his heart began to race, his body urging him to turn and run. But he had a feeling that if he did, he wouldn't get very far. There was something very disturbed about this woman. And no one seemed to notice except him.

Talia slowly shook her head as her laugh faded. "Not entirely. He didn't destroy *every*one's life. In fact, he happened to *create* one—just one."

Created one? he asked himself. Then, the reality of the situation that he was in settled around him.

Truth struck him as he looked into her eyes, fear bringing tiny goosebumps to his skin. Those eyes. It was hard—even impossible—to see without knowing what to look for, but there they were.

They were Adrien's eyes, eyes he'd only seen a few times, but would know anywhere. His strong features somehow set in her delicate, feminine beauty. There was no doubt that Talia was his daughter.

"You're..." he said, unable to finish his words, his voice trembling along with his body.

Talia closed her eyes and bowed her head before raising it again. When she opened them, they were jet black. "Yes, me. I am Adrien's daughter. Which makes you one *very* unlucky young man." Her dark voice oozed with a seductive tone, adding to the terror he felt.

Amos' breath caught in his throat as his predicament became more and more clear.

He knew there was no way in hell she would tell him who she really was without being absolutely certain that he wouldn't say anything to anyone. And because of how he'd so blatantly sided *against* her a few moments ago, she had to know there was no way he would keep that a secret.

Which told him only one thing…

"You plan to kill me," he said matter-of-factly, his voice barely a whisper.

Talia laughed again. "See! You little rebels are so wrapped up in right and wrong, good and bad you have absolutely no imagination. Kill you? What would be the fun in that?"

Amos swallowed hard, the imagination that she accused him of not having suddenly coming alive with a number of terrible scenarios. "And what do you plan to do with me?"

"You'll see," Talia said. "I have a secret place to show you. I think you'll like it. I have things that I need to know. About my father, his death, and anyone here that may still have loyalty to him, and it seems like you know quite a bit."

His head shook wildly, denying her words. "You should talk to Jackson, not me. I'm not giving you anything. I don't even have anything to give."

"Oh, I plan to talk to him. You—well, you're just for fun. See, I can't be completely honest with him and tell him who I am until I can trust him. And if I take him like I've done to you, he won't trust or help me at all, and I'll have to kill him instead of use him. In other words, you're completely dispensable."

"I'd die before helping you," he said, finding a bit more courage to put in his words. He figured that he was going to die anyway. May as well go out a hero instead of a puppet.

"You'll definitely die, but unfortunately for you, that day's not today."

At that moment, Talia lashed out, punching him square in the face. As he fell back and tripped, landing hard on the floor, she walked over and brought her foot down hard in a painful kick to the side of his head, rendering him completely unconscious.

Pain gripped Amos, his head feeling like it could split open at any time. His lips felt wet. As he extended his tongue, it was the taste of blood that greeted him. That seemed to bring him around to consciousness a bit faster.

His eyes snapped open, but he had to blink away the haziness in the room. Slowly, things began to come into focus.

The room around him was massive, easily able to hold a hundred people and comfortably so. The lights were dim, even for magitech, and the walls were red.

Had it been brighter, he thought the room might have been beautiful—elegant even—with all its rich colors, elaborate torches, paintings, and furniture.

But it wasn't.

Instead, it was dim. The color of the walls looked like blood and the faint glow of the lighting appeared more threatening than warm.

He took in his situation. There were no windows, so he imagined that he was in a basement. Underground where no one could hear his cries for help.

His wrists were bound above his head, chained to the ceiling and forced to stand on his toes. Deep, dull aches filled his shoulders, and his hands felt tingly from the way they were tied.

"Ah!" Talia's familiar voice flittered through the room. "My pet has awoken. How lovely that you've finally graced me with your consciousness."

Amos groaned, having hoped that it was all a dream. Unfortunately, the throbbing in his face from a potentially broken nose and the headache that went along with it screamed at him, telling him this was as real as it gets.

"Where am I?" he asked, his voice forced, yet still barely above a whisper.

"You're still in the Academy," she said, fidgeting with something noisy that he couldn't see.

"I've never seen this place, and I snuck all around this place when I first started here."

Talia came to stand in front of him, smiling as she did. "You haven't been everywhere, my pet. Well, *now* you have. My father had the basement sealed off shortly after the Founder left. I only know that because he told me about it in detail, including its location. The only entrance is through a hidden passage in Adrien's office in the tower, which I now have access to."

"You're a monster, just like your father," he said, coughing as he did. He could barely get the words out due to weakness and the ever-rising pain level with every added moment of being awake.

Talia laughed, the sound dark and sinister, wrapping around him and chilling him. He'd known just how awful Adrien could be because of the battle they'd just fought, but somehow, she seemed worse.

"Oh, Amos," she said. "That is a compliment of the highest order. He was a visionary. Growing up, he couldn't visit often, but when he did, he spent his time with me wisely. Teaching me everything that I needed to know, conditioning me. He knew his fall may come, whether it be naturally or by the hands of assholes like yourself, and he wanted to make sure that things were taken care of."

"So- what? You plan to continue on with a massive airship and destroying the world?" Amos asked.

Talia scoffed as she turned to walk across the room. She sat in a chair, crossing her legs as she looked around. "No. My father lost a bit of his senses toward the end. I didn't quite agree with his plan for world domination."

A confused—and therefore painful—expression crossed Amos' face. "Then what the hell do you want?"

"Revenge," she said matter-of-factly, like it was the most obvious thing in the world. "Not only did this city keep my father from me for my entire life, denying me of the one thing in this world that I wanted more than anything, it also turned its back on him. *Wasting* everything it had taken from us. It had all been for nothing. This city will burn for taking him away from me—not once, but twice."

"Holy shit," Amos said. "You're a fucking psycho."

She smiled again. "You have no idea. So, how about we talk about something else? Like your fellow students for instance."

Her eyes bore into his from across the room. Amos hated the way that she looked at him. Those eyes were cold, calculating.

A psychotic mind in a beautiful package.

There was no denying the fear he felt. All he could hope for was a miracle. That someone might find him—though, given what she'd told him about the secrecy of this place, he highly doubted it.

"I ain't tellin' you *shit*, lady." Suddenly, his voice had found itself, sounding strong and confident.

Talia stood and sauntered across the room, one foot directly in front of the other as her hips confidently swayed from side to side with every step.

She placed her fingers under his chin, gently grazing his lip with her thumb. Amos' eyes narrowed as she leaned forward, her tongue grazing his swollen, bloodied lip.

"Do you know what this tastes like?" she asked, her voice soft.

Unable to find words, Amos shook his head.

"It tastes like failure, like the key to getting anything that I want." He watched as she moved back a few inches and looked down at his chest, his shirt having been stripped away. "Because if I don't—I'll have to take more."

As those last few words left her mouth, she gently traced a finger down his chest, intense heat burning into his skin with every painful inch. Clenching his jaws hard enough that he thought his teeth might break, he somehow managed to keep from crying out.

Talia smiled. "Impressive. It's a shame that flawless skin of yours will be scarred now, though." Her bottom lip pushed out as she looked over her work. "Let's not put too many more of those on you, huh? Just do as I ask."

"You're lower than scum," Amos spat.

Talia's mouth opened in feigned insult. "Now, that's not very nice to say to your gracious hostess. To be honest, I don't actually *want* to hurt you. You're just a necessity. Tell me what I need to know, and I'll kill you quickly."

"And what do you want to know that I would be able to tell you? Part of the city is destroyed, and the other parts are broke. That's not news."

Talia shrugged, turning to head back to her chair. She sat down and once again crossed her legs, swinging the one on top. "I'll be the judge of what's interesting and what isn't. So, *pet*, let's start with your best friend, Jackson. Then—I want to know in explicit detail the steps that led to my father's undoing."

TEN

"**H**e said what?" *Arryn asked,* a hesitant smile spreading across her face.

Her hands fell to her sides, no longer caring about their training session. They'd been sparring for a while before Cathillian had decided to let her in on the big news. She was so excited about his words that she nearly dropped her spear.

"He said he'll grant you a pass on the Versuch. You might not be the best in hand-to-hand combat, but you sure as hell showed you knew how to take *and* deliver a hard punch to the face, and you're also capable of dodging attacks. You *did* take her down, both with and without the use of magic—so his decision wasn't him feeling sorry for you."

Arryn's eyes were wide, still unable to believe it.

Cathillian continued when she said nothing. "You won fair and square. Granted, I've taught you a lot over the years, and you've had various other warriors teaching you things, but you never had much interest in walking the path of a real warrior. So, for someone with only general training, you did amazing."

"Well, it wasn't that I didn't *want* to learn," Arryn said. She shrugged. "It's just that I knew I'd go back to Arcadia one day so I could find my dad. If I became a warrior, my alliance and dedication would be to the druid people. *Only* the druid people."

Cathillian stepped back, raising his spear. He motioned with his free hand for Arryn to do the same. "You didn't want to make promises that you couldn't keep. I understand. We all do. Still, you did great. My grandfather isn't blind, and he's not cruel. He saw how much potential you had. He's just worried—we all are."

Cathillian stepped forward, thrusting his spear at Arryn.

She jumped back. Then holding her spear in both hands, she quickly raised her hands, her spear hitting his higher into the air and out of her way. She dropped to the ground and thrust hers forward, the tip coming to rest just under his rib cage where his light armor didn't cover.

"Good! I should have been paying better attention," he said.

Arryn lowered her spear and stood. "Ugh. You were paying plenty of attention. You just don't want to admit you screwed up."

He laughed. "And admit losing to a stinky old girl? Ha! I don't think so."

She rolled her eyes. "You'd do good to remember just which of the two of us have actually had a hot shower, sir," Arryn said, pointing a finger at her opponent.

"Another point to the stinky old girl!" he said.

"Call me that… one more time. I'll bitch slap you with this spear," she said, pointing her spear at him as she backed away. "Now, back to the topic at hand. Why's he granting me a pass on the Versuch? That's a druid law. Why's he breaking it?"

Cathillian shook his head as he circled Arryn. "He's not breaking the law. More like a gentle bending. Believe me, there are a lot of requirements."

"Requirements? Like what?"

"First. I told you I requested the Versuch. He doesn't plan to make a huge deal of it. It'll be just like Laurel's was. We'll take to the pit in front of him and my mother, and a few other warriors. If I pass, I'll be allowed to leave with you, but you're only allowed to leave *with* me."

Her jaw dropped a little. "Seriously? Can't I just retake the Versuch?" Arryn asked.

She was only partly joking. Going back to Arcadia wasn't a journey that she wanted to make with a partner. It would be very intense for her.

She'd grown very strong in her time with the druids, but like the trial she'd just taken, she knew there would be times where her weakness might shine through. It wasn't something she enjoyed, nor would she want a witness.

"Cute, but no. Sorry, sweetheart, you're stuck with me."

Cathillian lunged, and Arryn leaned her body to the right to dodge, but he'd anticipated her movement. His spear was a blur as it circled around and smacked her hard on the calf, using her uneven balance to easily take her to the ground. He then stepped forward and put his spear at her throat.

"Point," Arryn said.

Cathillian stepped back, extending a hand to help her up. "My grandfather's worried about you; Mom is, too. Actually, if I'm honest, so are the warriors and even me."

"But why? I know everyone thinks I'm weak, but—"

Cathillian gave a hearty sarcastic laugh. "Are you kidding? No. That's the furthest thing from our minds. Before, we worried about you going without *protection*. We weren't sure if you'd be able to take care of yourself if something bad happened. Now?" He smiled as he took a step closer. "Well, now we're terrified of you going off without training and wasting the gifts you have."

Arryn's mind swam with the possibilities. They believed in her enough to bypass a total redo of the Versuch with only the stipulation that Cathillian go to accompany her. They wanted her trained. That didn't seem so bad. More than that, it meant a lot for them to have so much faith in her.

Arryn fidgeted with a small knot in the wood of her spear. "So, you'd be my trainer?"

He nodded. "The warriors, my grandfather, my mother, and me—we all saw something break open in you when you battled. To ignore it and not train it… To just let it go would be way worse than you missing out on a traditional Versuch. You fought. You won. The only thing you aren't battling in is the weapons portion."

"I'd love the chance to learn how to control my powers. And if I can

126

learn that trick that you showed me?" Arryn shook her head. "I could do a hell of a lot if the time ever came. Do you think you could put me through warrior training?"

He smiled. "You mean *actual* warrior training? The whole bit where I *actively* try to stab and beat you with things? The same kind of training I went through? Because I train you all the time, and I think you're doing just fine with the general type. I didn't feel comfortable trying to hurt you."

She looked at him with confusion. "Why do you feel uncomfortable? It's the way it's done with druids. It's what's normal. You aren't trying to *hurt* me. You're trying to *teach* me, and if I get hit or stabbed, then it's because I'm too slow, and I guess I'll learn to move really fast, now won't I? Elysia still trains that way. So does Nika. Both of them are total badasses!"

Cathillian laughed. "We'll, how can I deny a request like that? It's painful, but effective if you *really* wanna learn—and fast. Just keep in mind that you can tell me to stop at any point. You don't have to train that way."

Arryn stepped forward and slapped him in the thigh with the broad side of her spear. "And tap out like a bitch? Hell no. If I'm going to cry like a baby then what's the point of training at all? Nika broke my face... it's not so bad. Besides, it's not like you weren't going to train me anyway. This is just better, and I think it would be good for me. You, too. It would keep you fresh with it."

He paused for a moment, examining the tip of his spear before turning his focus back to her, smiling. "You're a very special girl," Cathillian said. "You're also a jackass. And quite the sarcastic asshole."

He paused for a moment, a look of confusion crossing his face.

"Where was I going with that? All I can remember is that you're a jackass and a sarcastic asshole. That's all I got."

"Special girl. You used the words special girl—dick," she replied, her expression as flat as her voice.

"Oh, yeah! That," he said exaggerating his excitement to annoy her. "If you want real warrior training, I'm good with it."

"Fantastic. And battle magic?" she asked.

Cathillian nodded. "Of course. Now, something to remember... Our magic is only as strong as our will is. Basically, there's a magical door that we all open when we begin doing magic. Most of the time, it's only a crack. Enough to learn to heal or grow basic plants. In other cases, like the Chieftain and the Founder, it opens more and more all the time with practice and dedication."

Arryn nodded. "That's basically all I can do—unless I'm pissed, apparently. And animals seem to like me quite a bit, even if I can't bond with one."

"You're pretty talented whether you want to admit it or not. You have the potential that my family has. Personally, I think that's pretty cool since we were raised together. It would be an honor to train you and teach you to harness it."

"Do you think that's limited to nature magic?" she asked.

Cathillian looked at her inquisitively. "You mean, do I think it would transfer over into your physical magic, too?"

Arryn nodded. "Yeah! I mean, if I'm going back to Arcadia, maybe I can attend the school. They wanted to see me attend the Academy with all kinds of students, regardless of their background. Maybe I could go and learn a few things."

"I'd say you'd be crazy to let that go. I highly doubt your connection to magic is limited to nature alone."

She smiled. "Fine. I accept these conditions. You can come with me, and you can be my teacher."

"That sounds like a positive thing, but I just don't know if I trust you. You're going to make my life hell, aren't you?"

"Did you think for a second that I wouldn't? That's kind of my job at this point," she said. "Now—game on! Next point wins this round."

Talia made her way down the hall, a small stack of applications in her hand. She had other things on her mind—like her pet in the basement—and she had no interest in parting with those to do interviews, but when Amelia approached her, she smiled and agreed.

It was too important to stay in Amelia's good graces.

Being too impatient had been the mistake that Adrien had made. He came in and dominated everyone, putting himself above all and letting everyone know it. Talia was smarter than her dearly departed father.

She refused to recreate his mistakes.

The true secret to dominance was to allow everyone else believe they were in control. Then, she would never be challenged.

Amos had given in a little, telling her there were other students and teachers she needed to check out, though he didn't have names. She'd tortured him long enough he'd have given them if he did. That would require her talking to Jackson, but she hadn't had a chance to do so.

She hadn't even been able to go to the bar yet, which she planned to do *very* soon. That was no longer a question. Smiling so much gave her a headache, and she was ready to go unwind. People-watching wouldn't be a bad thing either. Learning about the city's people could come in very handy.

"Are you fucking stupid? Do you have a clue what you're talking about? Why should they be punished for where they were born?"

Talia heard a young woman screaming at someone from down the hall.

"Their parents could have bettered themselves, but they didn't. Bad genes, Mikhaila. That means the kids are just as stupid and lazy as their parents. Do you *really* trust them to learn how to use magic? People like that will only use it for their own greed."

Damn it. I know that voice. They're fighting about the Boulevard students joining the Academy—again, Talia thought as she picked up her pace.

"Jackson, just stop it. You sound ignorant as hell. They weren't lazy. Those people worked harder in a single day than you have in your whole life. Do you even know how to wash a dish? Do you know how to clean your clothes? No. You have someone do that *for* you."

"You have servants, too! What the hell point are you trying to make? Besides, I don't think you really get what I'm saying. They've lied, cheated, and thieved their entire lives. What the hell do you think they'll do if they get magic?" Jackson yelled back.

Talia came to the corner of an intersecting hallway, standing just out of sight to listen for a moment. She did promise to take care of it, though she hadn't planned for that to be today.

"I saw how non-nobles and servants were treated—so I learned how to do that shit myself. And do you hear how stupid you sound? The Boulevard families did those things because they were *forced* to just to survive. *Not* because they're bad people, you asshole. Don't look down on people you don't understand. They deserve to be here just as much as we do."

Talia stepped out from behind the corner, faking a stern expression as she approached. "Whoa! Hey—what's going on? Why are you guys fighting about nobles and Boulevard students? Especially *you*, Jackson. Really?"

Jackson wasted no time arguing for his innocence. "She started it by giving me grief about the fight with Amos. No one cares to see the obvious. Those Unlawful bastards are going to get us all killed. I'm telling you—they have a vendetta against us nobles. You just wait."

Talia shook her head. "They aren't Unlawful anymore, Jackson. Those laws have been rewritten."

He shook his head, clearly exasperated with the argument. "Mark my words. Bad shit's coming. I'm telling you."

Talia fought a smile from forming. "Jackson, I told you before that I didn't have time for this. We *are* going to continue this talk in private at some point, but right now I have to go interview more teachers. I expect this argument to be over for now. Those from the Boulevard *will* be a part of the school, and we'll do all we can to make them welcome. Understand?"

Jackson was annoyed, but he wasn't defiant. He nodded. "Yes, ma'am. I understand."

Talia turned to Mikhaila. "That goes for you, too. No antagonizing. He can't help how he feels. Perhaps over time he'll see the other students are friendly. His mind might change. There's no need for such arguments. The recent revolution settled all this for us."

Mikhaila nodded. "Yes, ma'am. I should get to class," she said before turning and walking away.

Talia silently watched the girl walk away as she turned her attention back on Jackson. "I meant what I said. Drop it. I'm sure you don't want your other fellow students or teachers to make you feel like an outsider, do you?" she asked. He shook his head, looking down to the floor. "You need to vent in private. You can come to me, but stop causing problems. That's not how anything gets solved."

He sighed. "I didn't even want to get into that argument. I just exploded when she came at me like that. I don't know what happened."

Talia nodded. "Don't beat yourself up over it. Just stop and think next time. We could begin a counseling program to help others with adapting. One-on-ones, of course. But I could start with you."

He nodded. "I do have friends that think the same. I know some teachers, too. I just don't think it should be *me* that changes. No one asked *me* what I wanted when all these changes took place. Or anyone else. They just happened. Why should I have to give up my sense of security for scum..." He closed his eyes and clenched his fists as he tried to calm himself.

Talia gave one of her first genuine smiles. "Relax. It'll all get better. I promise. We'll start with you and see how this goes. Just keep your head down and no more fighting." Her smile grew as she placed a hand on his shoulder. "It's important that everyone here feels safe. Even those who may not share whatever the popular opinion is."

The tension melted away from his expression. He was putty in her hands. Her soft tone, beautiful face, and position of authority gave him a strong respect of her, maybe even a bit of healthy fear.

He trusted her, and that was all that mattered to her. As long as she had that trust, she had him. All the molding would take time anyway, and she was a *very* patient woman.

"Thank you, ma'am," he said. "I'm sorry again."

"Not a problem. Things are still very sensitive around here. Maybe even apologize to Mikhaila." She held up her hand as Jackson began to protest.

It occurred to her that with this latest fight, he could end up blamed for what would happen to Amos, and Jackson wouldn't be any good to her in a cell.

She needed to protect him for now, so she added, "It'll only cause you more problems than being stubborn will solve if you don't. Just keep that in mind. Now, as I mentioned when I first arrived, I have a few interviews to attend! Get to class and try to salvage the day."

She flashed one more beautiful smile in his direction, and he smiled back. As she walked away, her smile faded into something a bit more devious.

This may be easier than I thought.

Amelia waited in Talia's office for her return. The interviews had gone better than expected. With lack of funds for ample salaries, she expected the men and women applying to be far less inclined to accept, but that hadn't been the case at all.

Only a few declined the position afterward—though Amelia couldn't exactly understand why.

Where else would they work?

The factory was destroyed, and it would take volunteers to rebuild it because there was no funding for materials, let alone for the workers to start.

But even with all the issues surrounding the city as well as getting the school back on track, there were bigger things pressing on her mind.

There had been some leads on finding Doyle, but they'd turned out to be a loss. The Hunters visited a farmhouse and discovered he'd spent a few nights there, having pretended to be a kind man from Arcadia, one who fled because he'd lost his wife and children—neither of which he actually had—and the city was a painful reminder.

They had no idea who he was and had sent him on his way. They were currently searching the area, but she knew the weaselly bastard had slipped away. Still, even with Doyle's location a mystery, other terrible news had reached her...

A student had gone missing. One that she'd worked with personally.

She sighed, trying to push it out of her mind for the time being. She needed to keep herself together. She flipped through the papers in her hand, thinking back to the many things floating around in her mind.

Doyle.

New jobs.

Homes.

Poor, missing Amos.

She was pulled from her thoughts when Talia walked into the office. She didn't seem to even notice Amelia sitting across the room by the window.

"Talia," Amelia said.

Talia looked over to see her guest. Amelia had expected her to jump from the surprise, but she didn't. "Hello," Talia said, her voice level and calm. "What can I do for you, Chancellor?"

Talia hung her jacket on a hook before turning to take a seat behind her desk. Amelia stood and crossed the room to sit across from her. She placed five applications on the desk and slid them toward the Dean.

"I had a few things that I needed to go over with you," she said, pointing to the applications. "First is this. These men and women showed a lot of promise. They understand the situation that we have with rebuilding. They also welcomed the challenge of teaching the Boulevard students. We both know that'll take a lot of time and patience on their behalf due to past laws."

"Adrien," Talia said. There was a flash of something that crossed her face, but Amelia couldn't read it before Talia continued speaking again. "Right. He definitely created quite an educational gap for these people. Hmm. Yes, I'll look these over. If you feel they're promising, I'm sure I'll feel the same." She smiled, and Amelia followed suit.

"I'm so happy to hear that, but really—don't hire someone for my own benefit. Please make sure these are people you would want to work with as well. You met them as well as I did, so you can judge on their personalities for yourself. I don't want to tell you how to do your job. I only wanted to give you the options that I felt was best. You can take or leave them."

"Thank you, Chancellor," Talia said.

Amelia waved her hand in the air. "I just can't get used to that. Please, feel free to call me Amelia."

Talia smiled again. "As you wish. Thank you for the suggestions. I'll look them over and let you know what I think tomorrow morning at the latest."

"Wonderful! The sooner we can get the classes back to normal, the better. That being said, I'm afraid I gave the good news first."

"Oh?" Talia asked, concern in her expression.

Amelia nodded, hoping the new Dean didn't take the news terribly. "Unfortunately, one of the students, Amos, a young man that I grew very close to during the rebellion, was reported missing to the Guard. They filled me in immediately, of course, and it appears his mother said he never came home last night."

Talia's expression fell further as she leaned forward, placing her arms on the edge of her desk. "Missing like maybe he went hunting or fishing and didn't say anything? Or…" she didn't finish, allowing the silence to finish the question for her.

Amelia shook her head. "I'm afraid not. We'd hoped so, but no one saw him leave. If he did, he would have had to sneak out somewhere other than the gates, and there's no reason to do such a thing. No guard saw anyone leave or come in. He must be somewhere in the city. There was talk about an earlier argument with Jackson—"

Talia's eyes briefly widened before her previous cool, yet worried demeanor returned. "Jackson? Yes, there was. But I talked to him myself, and he mentioned apologizing. I know he's upset, but do you really think he's capable of actually *harming* another student?"

Amelia wasn't sure. She certainly hoped not, but there was no real way to tell. "I don't know. I would think not, but we need to check all angles. We have to find him."

Talia nodded. "I'll ask around and see if anyone saw him, but Jackson is a good man. Misguided, but I'm working with him. Leave him to me. If he knows anything, I'll get it out of him. I would say we shouldn't alert everyone. I fear they may worry for their safety after so much has been done to grant it in the first place."

Amelia shifted in her chair. "I thought the same thing, but if we don't warn them and something else happens, then it would be on us. Better safe than sorry."

"I suppose that's true. Thank you for stopping by to tell me. I just spoke to him yesterday, and we were supposed to meet once I had more free time to discuss how to make the school a better place. This is truly devastating. I'll keep my eyes open."

"Thanks again, Talia. I'll let you get back to it. Have a wonderful day."

Amelia left the room, leaving Talia to look over the stack of applications in front of her.

ELEVEN

R_ain had started to fall,_ making the chill in the air a thousand times worse, but that didn't stop Marie from keeping her promise to Amelia.

In the few weeks that she'd worked for the new Chancellor, things had changed in ways she never imagined. Marie was untrusting of those that were mean to her—for obvious reason—but through working for Amelia, she discovered that she was even more nervous around people that treated her nicely.

The new Chancellor seemed to understand her, though, which had gone a long way to ease her worries, and she no longer feared knocking on that door.

She admired Amelia and her strength. It was obvious why she held the positions that she did. Her entire life, she imagined what it would be like to be stronger. What it would be like to be the kind of person who stood up for people—including herself—but she couldn't ever really believe that could be her.

Until now.

It was amazing how much a person could change in such a short time when she was allowed to believe in herself. Every day was a new challenge, and she met it with excitement. She *would* help Amelia get the Queen's Boulevard rebuilt and restore the quality of life for the people that lived there.

Marie pulled the hood of her thick, red cloak over her head and made her way to the street. She wasn't exactly sure what she would find when she went to the Boulevard, but she was excited to see what the progression looked like.

It had been days since she'd found some help to rebuild the destroyed area. Only a few men and women had volunteered, but it was a start.

It was still so new to see the people of Arcadia freely mixing in the streets. Students, potential teachers, and out-of-work laborers walked around the city together.

At the moment, it was difficult to balance the need of men for the new and improved Arcadian Guard and needing strong hands for the rebuild.

Hundreds of Adrien's followers were lost in the Battle for Arcadia. Hundreds more survivors that still somehow worshipped him fled. And hundreds more begrudgingly thought they could adjust, but soon decided they couldn't—then fled.

Most of the sympathizers went of their own accord, going to the country to build their own homes, or they went north to Cella to build new lives in another city, but some were forcibly removed. There was no place in the new Arcadia for hatred and violence.

So far, most everyone seemed to be adjusting well, and it warmed Marie to see it in action as she walked through town.

As she came to the old intersection that once held the toll to the entrance to the Boulevard, she was stopped in her tracks, unable to believe what she saw.

Just outside of the Boulevard were huge piles of debris. The largest piles consisted of burned, busted, or otherwise unusable wood and materials. The other smaller piles had salvageable wood varying in size from large beams to what could be used to make new furniture.

Stones that weren't blown to pieces by the cannons on Adrien's warship were also put in with those items.

Looking around, she saw loads of furniture in with the good things, and she wondered just how much of what she saw looked just as terrible *before* the devastation.

Her brows furrowed as she thought about how they must have been forced to live. The sound of a small stack of wood dropping startled Marie, bringing her attention to a couple of men coming out of the Boulevard to sort them.

"Hey, Andrew!" she said, a large smile spreading across her face. "I don't believe it. You guys have been hard at work! This is incredible. I never imagined you'd get so much done in so little time. How are you guys doing?"

Andrew stepped forward, using the back of his forearm to wipe sweat away from his face. "We've been working morning to night, ma'am. This was our home. We want to see it restored. If you can make that happen, we'll do whatever we need to to help."

"That's wonderful to hear!" Marie said, her excited smile still intact.

Andrew paused for a moment, looking down at the ground before looking back at her. "I don't trust nobles. Never have. I imagine you can understand why."

Her smile faded a bit. She wasn't offended by his words, but she understood them. She may not have lived in torn down conditions like he did, but she certainly lived under Adrien's thumb. She knew his wrath just as much as anyone.

"I do. Very much. I can't fault you for that." She took a step forward, her expression reflecting the compassion she felt for him. "But I hope you'll extend just enough trust my way to let me help you."

"What do you get out of it?" he asked.

She shook her head. "Nothing. And I don't *want* anything. I know what it was like to be under his thumb. Adrien's, I mean. I worked directly under him for years, if you can imagine that. You don't have to trust me—or *any* of us for that matter—but I hope you'll at least give us a cautious chance."

He looked behind him at the few guys that had come to stand several yards back. They said nothing, but seemed to share a silent conversation.

Andrew looked back to Marie and extended his hand. She paused for a moment as she looked from his eyes down to his hand and then back. She smiled and accepted it, hope filling her.

"I guess we can give you a shot. You seem harmless enough,"

Andrew relented.

"Thank you. You won't regret it," Marie replied. "I saw the remnants of some broken furniture, but have you been able to salvage any of the sinks or bathtubs? And what about the magitech lighting? Even just the cores would be helpful."

All of the men stopped and turned to face her, confusion on their faces.

"You're joking—right?" Andrew asked. Her brows furrowed as she shook her head a bit. "Oh, wow, lady. You really ain't joking. OK... So, poor folk don't get magitech crystals. We have no reason to have tubs or sinks. We don't have a lot of access to water. Just a pump in the street that everyone shares. When you're that limited with water, a bath of any kind is a luxury. We don't get to bathe often. So, to answer your question, no. We haven't recovered anything like that."

Tears welled in Marie's eyes. She knew they had it bad, but the thought of not even having something as simple as a hot bath or shower really hit her hard.

She cleared her throat. "It's raining. You guys are done for the day."

"We ain't even close to done," Andrew protested. "We have too much work to do."

Normally, she would back down to anyone that pushed back, especially a large man, but not today. "No, you guys are far ahead of the schedule that I had in mind. Have you even eaten?"

Andrew once again looked back to his men before turning his attention back to her. "We'll be fine, ma'am. We just need to get this done. If you plan to keep your word, you'll need us to keep ours, or this'll never get done."

She nodded. "I agree, but you can take a break. It's raining, and it's freezing. You'll all get sick, and then where will you be? Behind schedule. Now—why don't you all follow me to the city building? You must be hungry. We have a kitchen there, among other things, like a private bathroom with a shower in it. Adrien had it put in."

"That sounds uncharacteristically kind of him," one of the other men said, a sarcastic laugh following it.

She shrugged. "Not really. As with most things, there were ulterior motives. Most of the time, he was in the Academy tower. But the city building is where the rest of us worked for him. He liked to overwork people, but he didn't like having to smell them if they went too long without bathing. It was his way of keeping people living there to do whatever shit work he created until the factory was operational. Now, it'll be used for a good cause."

"I hate to agree with the noble," one of the other men said, taking a few steps forward. "But we could really use a hot meal. I can't say I'd be all that upset to have a hot shower after this cold rain either."

"Great!" she cheered. "Then it's settled! You guys will come back with me. You can use the shower, and I'll get something hot to eat for you. It's the least that I can do."

The corner of Andrew's lips curled in a grin. "If you're not careful, we might just start to like you after all."

Unsure of how to respond, Marie nodded once and turned to lead them back to the city building to treat them with the decency they'd clearly never been shown by the nobles, and maybe even to build a bridge between the new government and the people of the Boulevard.

And after, I need to find extra hands. These men can't do it alone, she thought.

TWELVE

Things had calmed down a bit after Talia handed in the applications and accepted three of the five candidates.

Amelia seemed happy with Talia's choices, and she was relieved that the Chancellor didn't ask any questions about turning down the other two from out of town. She didn't want to take the chances on them knowing her or having plans of their own.

Calm as things may be, it was only because the shitstorm had yet to hit.

Those teachers would start in the morning, and Talia would be expected to give them the tour, introduce them to the students, and go over all the boring bullshit that came with being a new teacher—though, she assumed they would have at least a basic knowledge of how things worked, having been students at the Academy once themselves.

It had been over a week, and she had yet to get even the slightest bit of good rest. She couldn't figure out what she wanted to do with her little stowaway, but she had a feeling his time was coming.

Things had been progressing, and Jackson had come to her office twice. It was possible that she wouldn't need Amos any longer. He'd given her all that he would—possibly even all he *could*. He was becoming even more stubborn somehow, not weaker over time as she'd assumed.

Now with Jackson in her grasp, things would move much smoother. She'd had to feign interest as he whined about the Boulevard students— trying to gain his trust and feel out just how serious he was.

The only interest she'd had was looking for places where she might be able to plant seeds of her own. She was looking forward to his next few visits now that the groundwork had been laid, and she was ready to begin her real work.

Still, she'd run herself exhausted. She'd managed to be the little bitch for none other than the woman she knew firsthand had betrayed her father and was moonlighting as something far more sinister. Playing both parts was difficult at best, and she was drained. She was in need of some *Talia* time.

Tonight was the night. Screw everything else. Getting drunk was number one on the list, and she debated the possibility of even more than that. It just depended on what kind of men the city had to offer.

Though, she doubted there would be very many that could keep up with her—or her interests.

She pulled the hood of her cloak over her head and made her way to

Sully's Tavern. While she needed a night out, she didn't want to be seen heading there. Appearances and all. She'd need to be careful.

There was a bit of aged mystics' brew in her office that she brought from home, but she'd need a lot more than what she had.

With shit money currently flowing around Arcadia, it was almost impossible to get more than a little of the drink into the city, though it had been rumored that Julianne, the master mystic that had helped with the rebellion, donated a bit at a time to Amelia to do with as she pleased. As some kind of morale booster.

Talia didn't care if that were true or not.

She didn't want any part of accepting anything from her or any other bitch or bastard that was tied to her father's death. She'd have her relaxation the good old-fashioned way.

As she crossed the cobblestone road to the bar, she saw that the building had been damaged right along with the rest of that side of the city.

Most things in the noble quarter hadn't been bothered too badly, but Sully's wasn't quite *noble*, not by a long shot. It sat on the edge of the Boulevard, and had always been theirs and theirs alone. But once the revolution was over, more and more nobles—at least those in the middle class—seemed comfortable going in there.

With the mixing classes, some had even become friends, and that seemed to have benefitted the establishment, as they were able to quickly repair it due to increased demand. The repairs had obviously been hurried and unappealing at best, but it had still been salvaged.

The Dragon's Lair—the town brothel—had also been through a

rushed rebuild, though that came as a surprise to no one. There were needs to be met, after all.

She opened the door to the bar and found the place brimming with life. Nobles and the lower class littered the bar at the back and tables all over.

Knowing how the city had been before, it surprised her to see just how many smiles there were and how much fun was being had. She groaned to herself, the sound lost in loudness of the shouts and laughs.

Fuck their happiness, she thought, her brows furrowing.

The stress of her long days and lack of sleep bubbled to the surface. She saw every one of them as a target. Each one an enemy of Adrien that now celebrated his death. They stayed after his defeat. There was no other reason for them to be there, disgracing the boundaries he'd put in place for good reason.

"Hey, beautiful," a large man said, stepping in front of her. He was at least three times her size—all brawn. "You should come with me. Let me wipe that scowl off your face. Looks like no one's done that in a while. I'm sure you could use it."

Talia smiled, but it was dark and sinister. Then—it was gone. Her hand was a blur as it shot out from under her cloak and grabbed hold of his endowments.

His eyes immediately widened as he slumped forward, the lump in his throat bobbing up and down with every nervous swallow. His nose almost rested right against hers as she spoke.

"And exactly what do you plan to do once I tear this off and shove it down your throat?" She laughed as she applied pressure. "Funny. A man your size, I thought it would be more of a handful."

His face scrunched in a pain-filled grimace. "H-holy shit," he said, swallowing nervously again. "Not what I expected. I'm sorry."

"Oh, sweetheart. Don't be sorry for flirting," Talia said, her voice soft, yet sadistic as she squeezed a bit more. "Be sorry for how you approached me. I'm a *fucking* lady. Learn how to approach a woman. The wrong approach to the wrong woman could end in you never needing to worry about such things ever again. Understand?"

"Yes! Yes, ma'am," he choked out, his eyes briefly squinting at the pain before opening them and nodding wildly.

Talia smiled. "Good. Now, buy me a drink, and I'll forgive you," she said, releasing him.

He stumbled backward a few feet, taking several deep breaths as he regained his composure. After a few moments, he stood upright again, nearly a foot taller than Talia. Her brow rose as she placed her hands on her hips, impatiently waiting for his answer.

"Yes, ma'am," he said. "Please, accompany me to the bar. You can have whatever you like."

She smiled. "See? Now, how hard was that? You should know that I still plan to go nowhere with you, but I'm not a very happy woman, and you just made it worse. I feel like you should fix that with something *other* than your dick."

"Honest and powerful. You must have a line of men after you at all times," he said, his voice still a bit shaky from catching his breath.

A grin crossed her full lips. "When I choose for there to be, yes."

She stepped forward then, signaling for him to move out of her way. Without a word spoken, he understood her demand and stepped to the side, allowing her to move toward the bar. He followed her, but didn't sit, instead choosing to stand next to her.

There was stirring to her other side. "Wow," a very drunk man next to her said.

"Uh-uh, buddy," Talia's new behemoth acquaintance said, looking over her head to the man on the other side that had her in his sights. "If you wanna keep your dick, don't even think about it."

"I didn't realize you were taken, sweetheart," he said.

Talia sighed, her eyes briefly closing as she forced her irritation to calm. She could feel the itch of her power licking at her palms, and she desperately wanted to use it, but knew better.

She had to remain—for the most part—virtuous in the public eye.

Her stunt earlier with the giant of a man was nothing she felt the Chancellor herself wouldn't have wanted to do in the same situation, though she doubted Amelia would have had the balls to do it. She seemed too goody goody.

Her eyes twisted to the right, her head slowly following. He was a filthy, lower class man. Small. Thin. He looked weak. It only took a single handful of big boy on her left to completely control him.

This guy, she could break in half, and it made her sick that he found the confidence to approach her at all. The look on her face must have exuded every ounce of irritation and anger that she felt because his eyes widened.

Her voice was level and calm as she spoke, but her intention easily bled through. "I would like to sit here. Alone. And enjoy a beer... or twelve. I assume that will be quite alright with you. Because—I assure you that if it isn't—I *will* see that it is."

She couldn't see the mountain of a man behind her, but she saw her target's eyes look over her to the other man before nodding, picking up his beer, and walking away. She turned back to her new acquaintance.

She sighed. "What's your name?"

"Erik, ma'am," he said.

She nodded. "Good. Sit there. Don't speak a word. Keep the other ass fucks away from me. Understood?"

He smiled. "And what exactly do I get out of this?"

She didn't even bother looking at him, staring at the alcohol along the back wall. "You get to buy my first round, sit there, not speak a word, and keep the other ass fucks away from me. Is there a problem? Did I stutter?"

His smile grew as he shook his head. "I get the feeling if I say anything other than *no,* I'll walk out of here more woman than man. So, no ma'am. No problem at all. Order your drink—whatever you want."

"Good boy," she said, waving the bartender over.

"What's your name?" Erik asked. The bartender came to stand in front of them, and Erik briefly turned his attention. "Whatever she wants."

"Do you have stock of the mystics' brew?" she asked.

The man behind the counter nodded. "I do. We only have but a couple barrels left, so the price ain't cheap, but we've got it."

She looked to Erik before turning back to the bartender. "He's good for it. I'd like a pitcher."

There was a hearty laugh from her left. "First round, huh?"

"I said you'd buy my first drink. You never stated what size drink I should order. I'm sure if I got a normal sized mug, but asked for shot glasses to pour it into, you'd have still considered it one drink. Well, think of it as a very large mug, and consider yourself thoroughly educated on how to approach a woman and not piss her off," she said, turning back to the bartender who was retreating to the back to fetch the brew.

"Duly noted. Not a mistake I'll make twice. It's rather loud in here, so I'm sure you didn't hear me. What's your name?" Erik shouted over the din.

"Oh, I heard you. I chose not to answer, which I'm choosing to do again. You know, for a large, *silent* bodyguard, you sure talk a lot. Maybe you should work on that. Right now would be fantastic," she said. The bartender returned then, setting down a full pitcher and a glass. "Oh! Thank you."

"Very welcome, ma'am. Thank you for coming in," the bartender said, smiling as he turned to Erik.

Erik shook his head and reached into his pockets to fetch the coins before handing them to the bartender. "You're not cheap to make up to, you know that? Also, calling me a bodyguard implies work. Work means getting paid. I'm the only one paying around here."

"Careful, big boy. You'll talk yourself into a second pitcher and out of a second date. Besides, you didn't approach me because I looked cheap; we both know that. *Also,* my presence is payment enough. It makes you look good. Now, if I could only get that silence I asked for..."

He sighed. "Yeah, yeah. I hear ya. I'll be at that table over there if you need me to rough anyone up for ya, princess."

She flashed him a sarcastic smile before turning back to her drink. A heavy sigh of contentment escaped her as she drank from her glass.

It was loud, but it still relaxed her. It wouldn't take long for the brew to kick in. As thoughts about work and even her father threatened to invade her mind, she pushed them right back out.

Being a magician had its benefits past the obvious. It also trained her to clear her head at a moment's notice.

"Can I have everyone's attention please?" a familiar feminine voice shouted above the crowd.

Talia groaned as she turned to see Marie standing just inside the door with a couple of large, strong looking men. She quickly faced forward again, lifting her hood back over her head. It wasn't like she was doing anything wrong, but she didn't want to risk it.

Marie was a mousy sort of woman. Almost a pointless creature except she was very loyal. Especially to the new Chancellor.

The bar still roared after a few more weak shouts from the small, submissive woman. In the end, it had to be one of the men that walked in with her that quieted down the rest.

"Hi, everyone!" Marie said. Talia could actually hear the smile in the woman's voice as she spoke. "I'm sorry to interrupt your evening, but I have wonderful news regarding the Boulevard."

"What Boulevard?" one patron shouted. "It was blown to hell by that bastard!"

There were some shouts, but Marie recovered—much to Talia's

dismay. "Yes, I know, but things are changing! I have with me a couple of the men that are responsible for clearing it out. Right now, we're working to restore the homes. I'll let Andrew here explain a bit more."

Talia turned only enough that she could see what was happening, but was careful to keep her cloak in place. A rather handsome man came from behind Mousy Marie to stand beside her.

He stood tall, his broad shoulders squared as he looked to his people with confidence. He was the kind of man she could get used to looking at.

"We've spent days gutting the houses. We're salvaging all we can and scrapping the rest, but we need help. We need hands to get in there and help us finish gutting everything, and we even need magicians that can help us with the rebuild."

"What the hell are we gonna rebuild with?" a man shouted from the corner. "The city's broke!"

"That's not wrong," Andrew said. "The whole city is hurting. Now more than ever, we're all equal. I didn't believe it until I went to the Capitol building and saw exactly how much they're struggling to find solutions to problems that don't only affect them, but *all* of us. They wanna rebuild the factory—"

There was a loud laugh from the man that had shouted from the corner. Talia looked over to see him stand from a table and step forward.

He pulled off his shirt, her eyes fixated on what she found to be beautiful flaws, ones she wished she'd witnessed—or caused—herself. Deep scars and burns up and down his arms, chest, and she figured his back was covered as well.

"You see this? And you want us to go back to that damn factory?" the angry patron asked. "Most of the men here spent a *long* time there. Weeks. Months. To anyone else, that doesn't seem like a long time, but when every moment of every day is filled with fear and torture…" He paused for a moment as he looked down to the floor before casting his gaze back on Andrew. "That's a damn long time."

Andrew stepped forward and pulled his own shirt off, revealing scars that were similar to the patron's though there weren't as many. "I understand, friend. When I initially thought of going back… I couldn't even imagine it. I know it's hard to consider, but things are changing. That factory will be used to build materials that Boulevard people have never had before."

The other man shook his head. "And what do you figure we rebuild it with? Our good looks? 'Cuz in case ya didn't notice, I ain't got so much of that left now."

The other patrons laughed. A few slapped him on his bare, scarred back.

Andrew seemed confident to Talia as he continued. "I know many of you in here are only able to buy drinks because you're working outside the city. Cutting wood and doing runs to the nobles outside the walls building homes. Why not cut a bit extra and bring it back here? Why not grab a few extra stones? It'll go a long way. The city plans to give us things we've never had before. A real chance at a normal, good life. Basic necessities."

"Like what? Running water?" the patron said, shouts erupting around him.

Talia wasn't exactly sure what was transpiring, but it occurred to her then exactly how she could get into the good graces of the city and make her job *so* much easier in the process.

Once her name was synonymous with hero, it would be very hard to discredit her. Then she could find the allies she needed and begin planning to overthrow Amelia.

"Yes!" Andrew said, a smile on his face. "We *will* have running water! We need volunteers to help us rebuild the factory. With the help of magicians, it'll fly by. Once we get the factory up and running, we can have an export again. The city will begin to make money again. The rebuild will come, and we will have everything that we need."

Talia continued to listen to them talk about the total overhaul of the city, the patrons slowly coming around to the idea of helping the government as the government tried to help the people.

"So much for a clear mind," she mumbled out loud to herself before draining the rest of her glass and pouring another. *Time for a distraction... I think I should work on my next move.*

THIRTEEN

Arryn looked down the shaft of each of her newly-crafted, river cane arrow shafts to ensure they would be straight enough for a good shot. She'd already stripped them, dried them—which was a much faster process, thanks to nature magic—straightened them, and had just finished cutting them the way that she liked.

All that was left to do was assemble them. She wanted to fill her quiver before they set off. There was still plenty of time given Cathillian still needed to take the Versuch, but she wanted to be prepared.

"How do they look?" Elysia asked.

Arryn looked up, giving her a smile. "Looking great so far. This is my last bit for the day. The first couple dozen turned out great. So far, so good on these. There have only been a couple of duds."

"I'm proud of you," Elysia said. "You grew up right in front of my eyes, and I never noticed. You're a woman now."

"Depends on who you ask." Arryn smirked. "Cathillian seems to think of me as a little brat. But that's OK. Because he drives me batshit crazy, too."

"That's because Cathillian cares more for you than he might admit," Elysia said. "But you didn't hear that from me."

Arryn put her hands in the air for a moment before dropping them. "Trust me—I didn't hear a word. He's an overgrown man-child. He inherited it from your father, I think."

Elysia sighed. "Don't even get me started. I'm not sure if it skipped a generation, or if it's just the men in this family that are just naturally born missing something in their brain, but there is definitely a correlation there. I agree." She sat down next to Arryn and picked up an arrow, looking down the shaft. "How soon are you planning to take off?"

Arryn finished tying off one of her arrowheads before once again looking down the shaft to ensure proper placement. "I think I should leave soon. There's a lot that I need to do. Housing won't be much of an issue. I can sleep outside for all I care. It's obviously not a problem, but I really want to look around the city. I worry about how I'll feel going back, but I have to."

"For your father?" Elysia asked.

Arryn put the nearly complete arrow down before picking up another one to begin securing the next arrowhead to the river cane. "My brain tells me he's dead. Thinking like that is the only thing that kept me from running for Arcadia the moment I heard it had been liberated. Hope, however, is another matter. I can't accept that he's dead. I hold enough hope to pull me back there to find out—one way or another—what happened."

She smiled then as she finished tying off her arrow and pulled it to eye level. "And if I get to spit on Adrien's grave, then I can assure you that it will *not* be a wasted trip. I just have to know for sure."

"From what Samuel said, it seems like things are going much better. I understand why you need to do this." She paused for a moment again as she twirled a bare shaft in her hand. "Please don't forget about us. About me. If you decide that Arcadia is more home to you than here, please know you're always welcome home here. Don't make yourself a stranger to the Forest."

Arryn smiled as she looked at Elysia. "I could never forget you or what you've done for me. Everyone here—aside from Jenna anyway. She just hates me, and I have no clue why."

"It's a long story," Elysia said with an exaggerated sigh. "Her older brother, Aeris…"

"What?" Arryn finally asked after Elysia paused.

"He left when you came." Elysia's eyes cut away toward the woods. "She blames you for it."

"Me? Why would she blame me for it? And why hasn't anyone told me about this before now?"

"Because we didn't want you to worry about it. The truth is her parents are very against outsiders. They resisted us bringing you in, but a vow was a vow. I wasn't about to cast a child to the Arcadian Guard or to the lycanthropes and let her die. I told them they'd have to accept and respect my decision as an Elder if they couldn't respect me as a fellow druid, or they could leave."

Arryn sighed. "And the brother chose to leave, I take it."

Elysia nodded as she inspected another of the shafts. "This one's slightly off. You might wanna heat and adjust it." She put it in a separate pile. "Honestly, I'm shocked all of them didn't leave. Their dedication to our people was the only thing that saved them from being removed—I do know that."

Elysia's body had gone a bit rigid as her annoyance for Aeris grew.

She took a breath before continuing. "Still, their behavior and Aeris' departure did nothing to reassure us. I've always kept an eye on them— especially when it came to you. Aeris left with little warning. He didn't even take the Versuch. He said that druid laws were shit if we could break them at will whenever we wanted to fit our selfish needs. I believe the words, 'harbingers of chaos' left his mouth."

Arryn laughed. "Harbingers of chaos? You guys? Now, *that* is hilarious. It's also insanely dramatic. Well... then again... You did choose to name your familiar *Chaos*."

Elysia laughed. "Oh, my. I didn't even think about that. He *must* be right. As for his theatrics, that's not the worst of it. He wound up going to the dark druids."

Arryn looked at her inquisitively. "The dark druids actually exist?" She sighed, her eyes closing for a moment as her hands fell to her lap. "You know, I'm starting to get the idea that someone might have kept a thing or two away from me."

"I've learned we made several mistakes with you, but we're fixing them now. That's what matters. Right?" Elysia asked, nudging Arryn with her shoulder.

Arryn was amused by Elysia's behavior. It really seemed like Elysia opened her eyes and saw Aaryn was all grown up. Like she'd been blinded to it the entire time.

Arryn playfully pushed back against Elysia and smiled. "Better late than never, I suppose. So—tell me more about these dark druids that I never heard of before today."

They each picked up another arrow shaft and continued talking as they worked.

"Well, there are good and bad in all classes and types of people. In all forms of magic. So, naturally, they would exist. They split long ago, their *Chieftain* was a very dear friend of my father's. Shortly after we came here, there was infighting and squabbles. Eventually, he and my father had a falling out, and they left. They're rotten to the core. Even their magic is dark and corrupt. When they harness nature, their magic poisons it. The crops they grow are consumed by bacteria and insects, but they eat it anyway."

"Fucking gross! I can't even understand how it's possible to grow things like that, let alone eat it. How the hell aren't they all dead?" Arryn shivered and picked up another stalk of river cane to occupy her mind from thinking too far in detail.

"Our bodies have adapted over the years, which is why we look like we do. They're no different. Their bodies have grown used to eating that way and can filter out the harsher poisons by healing, but it doesn't get rid of everything."

Elysia and Arryn both shared a disgusted shiver at thinking of living that way.

"Their terrible diet and twisting of nature turns their skin an ashen grey that varies from light to dark, and their green eyes have gone mostly grey, too—though a hint of green still exists around the edges. It's even brighter when they cast. If you ever meet one, you'll never mistake them for anything else. Their magic destroys them, yet somehow they still manage to live long lives."

"They sound far more terrifying than any lycanthrope." Arryn said. "Why would her brother join them? That takes being a little whiny bitch to a whole new level."

"Because they're lawless and have no responsibilities to anyone or anything except each other. Even that's negotiable." Elysia sighed as she fumbled with another arrow. "Like I mentioned earlier, he said we were all chaotic. Our laws were pointless, and he refused the stay under the *rule* of Elders that couldn't even follow their own laws."

"We were better off without that bastard. Don't let it bother you." Arryn shrugged before setting down another arrow with a freshly tied arrowhead. "I'm sure as hell not bothered by it. Little Suzy Sunshine needs to watch her ass, though. I understand problems with family better than anyone, but I didn't *cause* shit by coming here. You didn't *cause* anything by accepting me. Her brother made those choices. I won't be nice if she comes at me or anyone else like that again."

Elysia smiled. "If you do come back, I think you should train to be a warrior. You'd make one hell of a fighter. Cathillian told me that you asked him to train you. He's wonderful, but if you come back, a structured experience with many instructors will do you good."

She scooted closer and put her arm around Arryn's shoulders, pulling her close. "Please listen to Cathillian. He might be just as goofy and ridiculous as his grandfather, but he would give his life to protect yours. He'll teach you the right way. In ways that I never could. I tried, but he's always had a better connection to the way you learn. Just pay close attention. He'll keep you safe."

Arryn nodded. "This whole thing just started a few days ago, but I've already figured out exactly how much I have to learn. So, don't worry. I'll listen to him, I promise"

FOURTEEN

*C*athillian stood in the middle of the pit, taking in the sights around him. The birds chirping, the sun shining, and the cool air that surrounded him. He pulled the sword from its sheath on his side and began swinging back and forth as he fought an imaginary opponent.

It wouldn't be long before he had to take the trials. He wanted a few moments to himself to gather his thoughts and practice. Like Laurel's before him, only his mother, his grandfather, and a few of his closest comrades would be there to witness.

Even over the swishing of his sword cutting through the air, he could hear Arryn's soft footsteps as she approached. "How are you feeling?"

His concentration was unbroken, even by the sound of her voice. Cathillian continued to swing and block with his sword as though he were fighting a real opponent. "I'm actually more nervous than I expected."

He lunged, and the sword thrusted forward. He pulled back, coming to stand still for a moment as he looked Arryn over.

"They paired me against Nika. I was surprised, given that she's already participated in a trial with you just a few days ago. But she's our strongest warrior, so it was the only one that was fair. Ryel's good, but not nearly as good as she is."

Arryn smiled. "Not scared, are ya? I can see why you would be, being a loser and all. Comes natural, I'd say."

Cathillian laughed before returning back to his preparation. "I don't think you understand just how much I let you get away with sometimes. You're the loser, not me." He turned back and winked at her. "Never forget."

Arryn shrugged. "Well, all I'm saying is I actually kicked Nika's ass. You're the one sitting here all worried about it, and you're the trained warrior. I think you might be more worried about it than I was."

She loved to give him a hard time, and he knew it. They both enjoyed their mutual torture of one another.

Right then, however, he wasn't sure if she was trying to distract him from his worry or annoy him to fire him up enough to win. Either way, he knew that her ribbing was for more of a purpose than obvious good humor.

"Do you give everyone a hard time, or am I just special?" he asked.

She smiled. "I guess you're pretty special. I like to give everyone a hard time, but don't be jealous, sweetheart... I could *never* treat *anyone* as shitty as I treat you. You're the best girl for me." She fluttered her lashes, her hands clasped in front of her to exaggerate her sarcastic innocence.

He turned only his head to meet her amused gaze. "To quote a moderately attractive, extremely abusive girl I know—who needs enemies when I have you?"

Arryn's left brow rose as her hands went to her hips. "Moderately attractive?"

Cathillian shook his head. "That's the negative you took away from that? Not the extremely abusive part?" He said as he went back to swinging his sword.

"My vanity knows no bounds, good sir," Arryn replied, twirling her long, black braid around her finger.

"Good to know." Cathillian looked to the sky, checking the placement of the sun through the trees. "It won't be long now. They should be on their way."

Arryn nodded, going silent for a moment before speaking again. "And here I thought I was distracting you with my great sense of humor and *moderate* attractiveness."

"You were doing a great job. I'm just focused. I don't want to screw this up. I know how much it means to you, and you go *nowhere* without me. I know that's shitty. Eventually, you could take the Versuch again and go alone, of course, but I know you want to go now."

Arryn waved a hand in the air. "I hate you lots, you know that. But..." she sighed, stepping forward and placing her hands on one of the posts surrounding the pit. "If I'm to be completely honest, there are only two people in this world in whose hands I'd place my fate."

"My mother and grandfather?" he asked, turning his head just enough to give her a wide smile.

"Yep! Exactly!"

At that moment, Echo's screech cut through the sky as she announced herself, coming to rest on a post just to the left of Arryn. With just shy of a twelve-foot wingspan and just over four feet tall, the golden eagle was the largest bird that Cathillian or Arryn had ever seen. Not quite twice the size of others like her, but she'd gotten close.

The bond between she and Cathillian had made her larger, one of the few bonds in the tribe that had changed the size of their familiar. Echo was a terrifying bird to encounter for anyone that didn't know her.

Arryn smiled at Echo as she reached out to give her broad chest a scratch. "I guess she came to see the show. So, are you ready yet?"

Cathillian sighed as he swung his sword back-and-forth again, reminding himself then of a small, nervous child. "I'm nervous. But... I've been around long enough to know that nervousness keeps you on your toes. To give you a straight answer—yeah, I think I'm gonna kick her ass."

Arryn smiled and nodded. "Good luck, loser. Knock her dead—literally. Wait. No, not literally. She's pretty cool. But break a leg. Not yours, hers. We'll fix it later."

Arryn walked away, leaving Cathillian to his thoughts. His trials meant a lot more to him than just his freedom. That was something he'd always wanted, but was afraid to seek. But this was for the future of someone else, someone that he'd come to care quite a lot for.

Arryn stood outside the barrier of the pit, Elysia and the Chieftain approaching. Nika had only just arrived, and she had her weapons sitting to the side just to the edge of the barrier.

As promised, there were only three other warriors to witness, and Ryel was among them. Arryn could tell that Elysia was nervous. It was her expression, her smile, and her body language. Still, Elysia acted as though she weren't bothered by anything.

"Are you ready for this?" Elysia asked.

Arryn nodded, her eyes never leaving the pit or Cathillian. "I know I am, but I don't know if he is."

The Chieftain laughed. "Cathillian's been ready for this his entire life. That kid has always wanted adventure. I'm sure he's more excited than nervous right now. He might be worried, but he's more worried about failing you than failing himself. Whether he wants to admit it or not, he wants to leave; he always has. He wants to see the world beyond our borders."

"Yeah," Elysia said. "That doesn't mean that *I'm* ready for him to. That's my baby out there. My only one."

"Have no fear, daughter," the Chieftain said. "Cathillian is much stronger than you or I know. He holds greatness in him, just like our young, Arcadian druid. They'll make a fine team. This is the best-case scenario you or I could have ever hoped for because they'll be able to protect each other. Now, relax and enjoy the show."

Elysia took a deep breath and exhaled, obviously steeling herself. Arryn smiled and reached over for Elysia's hand, squeezing it. "We're gonna be fine. I promise. I know you're worried, but you don't have to be. We aren't leaving forever. You'll see us again soon."

The Chieftain smiled and clapped his daughter on the back. "See? Nothing to worry about. The kids are all grown up, and they're gonna be just fine. Can we watch the fight please? *Please?* I've been expecting this one for quite some time, and I'm ready to see what he's got."

Elysia rolled her eyes at her father's begging. "Just like you to be so excited for your grandson to leave."

The Chieftain laughed. "I'm not excited to see him go, I'm excited to see him grow up into the man that I always knew that he would be. Plus, this kid's been driving me nuts for years, wanting to get beyond the Forest's edge. It'll be nice to shove him out of the nest for once."

"I'm kind of excited to see what he has, too," Arryn said. "He's constantly going on about how much of a badass he is. Now, we actually get to see if he is one."

Elysia laughed. "I guess that's a good point. It's his make or break moment. If he fails, we get bragging rights for the rest of his life. He lost to a girl."

They all laughed, catching Cathillian's attention as he briefly looked back to narrow his eyes at the trio. "You bastards better not be laughing at me over there."

"Us?" Elysia asked with a wink. "Never."

The Chieftain quieted then, his face growing a bit more serious as he raised his hand, and the few in the crowd quieted. "Cathillian it's time. Nika, please initiate battle."

Nika nodded, stepping further into the ring. Just as she had with Arryn, she circled Cathillian, measuring his every movement. Arryn watched the two as they studied one another, preying on one another.

Nika was the first to make the move, just as she had with Arryn. She realized then that Nika was quite the aggressor. The warrior ran forward, thrusting her fist through the air, but Cathillian was easily able to dodge it with little effort.

He twirled out of the way, dropping down to his knee and sweep-kicking Nika from behind as she passed. She was very agile and adjusted her bodyweight to throw herself backward in a well-executed backflip before landing on her feet.

A smile crossed Cathillian's face as he measured his opponent once again, more than a few feet standing between them. This time, it was Cathillian that attacked first.

Arryn watched as Cathillian ran for Nika, but she didn't move. She broadened her stance, preparing for him.

Cathillian dove for her, and she was able to dodge his initial blow, but as she twisted to the side, he stopped hard, jerking his arm back to land a hard elbow to the side of her face instead.

Nika dropped to her knee, but she returned his attack with a hard punch to the gut causing Cathillian to double over.

Nika used his moment of weakness as an opportunity to scramble to her feet and knee him in the face, throwing him back off balance. She copied his move, dropping again to one knee, spinning, and sweep-kicking his legs out from underneath him.

It wasn't difficult to take him down at that point.

As soon as he was on the ground, she put her foot on his throat, signaling the end of the round. Nika had won that round.

"Point to Nika!" the Chieftain called out. "Cathillian take a moment, right yourself, then get on with it."

Nika smiled as she reached out for Cathillian's hand, and he gladly took it. She helped him stand before they both went to their respective sides.

Cathillian jumped up and down for a moment, rolling his head around in circles as he did. Arryn had seen him doing it before the trial had started. He was boosting himself back up for the next round.

Arryn watched as Cathillian's hands flattened parallel to the ground from his tall height. She saw his fingers moving, and even from where she stood, she could hear the bones in his face snapping.

He was healing himself, just as he'd said he could do—by recycling the energy through his body instead of expending it all on his own.

She could feel the energy that he called on, but it was so small that it was barely noticeable at all. And just like before, he didn't touch the wound—he only channeled the power. She smiled as she realized that he could do that anywhere and not only in water.

Once again, Cathillian charged first. He ran for Nika, but he didn't attack. As he approached, she kicked him in the stomach. He fell to his knees, but only long enough to punch her hard in the side of the knee that held all of her weight.

She cried out and fell to the ground right alongside him. He then grabbed her by the throat, throwing her back onto the ground and pinning her down. Arryn was surprised to see Cathillian be quite so rough, but she'd seen how Nika sparred with him.

If he'd taken it easy on her, she'd do far worse to him.

"Point to Cathillian!" the Chieftain called out. "The next round determines the winner. Let's try not to kill each other with wicked storms or anything." He looked over to Arryn and winked.

Arryn couldn't help but smile as she saw the humored expression on his face. She would miss her druid family when they went to the city—more than they could possibly realize.

Both opponents climbed to their feet and once again moved to their respective sides. There was no waste of time when starting this round. Nika charged at Cathillian, jumping in the air as she did. She tumbled over once, her legs wrapping around his neck.

Arryn's eyes widened as Nika then planted her hands on the ground and used her strength and body weight to pull back, slinging him over her and onto the hard earth behind her. The warrior quickly repositioned herself so she straddled his chest, ready to pin his shoulders down.

But Cathillian wasn't so easy to subdue.

His long legs kicked up, striking her in the back of the head and loosening her grip on him enough that he could throw her off. She rolled twice and got back onto her knees before lunging for him.

All her speed and strength was lost because of her hastiness.

It only served to ensure her undoing as Cathillian paired his own strength with her momentum and landed a hard punch to her face. Once again, Arryn could hear the sound of bone crunching, the terrible noise echoing through the air.

It made her want to puke, remembering how her own nose had broken when Nika had punched her so many times.

Nika fell back and Cathillian jumped on her back as she rolled over to her stomach to climb to her feet. He used his heavy weight against her, pinning the woman down for a few seconds before her round was considered ended.

"The winning point goes to Cathillian!" the Chieftain cheered. "Cathillian is the winner of the first trial! Next, are weapons. Swords. As always, the best two out of three wins."

Cathillian briefly laid his hand on Nika's face, healing her before he stepped away. Ryel stepped across the boundary, bringing Nika her favorite sword before retreating back across. Cathillian already had his on his hip.

Both opponents bowed to one another, their hands briefly crossing their chests as they did. They righted themselves and lifted their swords outward, briefly clinging steel against steel as if they were toasting at a dinner.

Arryn saw a brief smile creep across Nika's face as she made the first move. Arryn couldn't believe how fast the warrior moved. She was like a whirlwind with her weapon.

Nika was smaller than Cathillian, long and thin, though her body was very lean. In addition to training with her strength, it was obvious that she spent the most time training on her speed. Cathillian could hardly keep up with her as fast as she was moving.

Cathillian was all defense as she attacked, unable to take an offensive strike. But, there are other means for him to get what he needed in a sword fight.

As she sliced through the air on the upswing, Cathillian went low, dropping down and spinning around behind her. He kicked her legs out from under her, sending her falling hard to the ground.

As she landed hard on her back, he brought the blade down on her throat signaling that he had won that first round.

With this round, there wouldn't be a pause, the fight would have to go on. Cathillian tumbled out of the way, and Nika righted herself, coming at him full force.

Once again, she was a fury of speed and determination, confusing her opponent and forcing him to go on full defense. With every thrust of Nika's sword, Cathillian countered harder and harder.

Arryn knew what he was doing. He'd done it when sparring with Arryn several times. As they trained, Arryn would swing, and he would use his brute strength to deflect with his own sword. The effects soon would make Arryn's hands ache with the amount of strength it took to hold on through the vibrations and heavy hits.

Eventually, she would drop the sword and Cathillian would win every time. With Nika being so much faster, it was his only option.

Soon, Nika did just that.

She dropped her sword, and Cathillian placed the tip of his blade against her chest, signaling the total end of that round.

"Cathillian wins the weapons category!" Chieftain said. "Onto the final round. Magic."

Nika smiled, shaking her head a bit. "It seems that congrats are in order, Cathillian. I think we both know who's gonna win this round. Your bloodline, is as strong as they get. Honestly, I don't even know why they're having us do this round."

Cathillian laughed. "Oh, come on now, it's not that bad. You kicked my ass pretty good," he said as he once again flattened his palms parallel to the ground, a small amount of energy pulling as it healed his body.

Nika nodded. "Just end this quickly. This is already humiliating enough. I had my ass kicked twice in one week. Once by a promising warrior, once by total loser."

"Hey," Cathillian said, smiling. "Don't talk about Arryn that way. It's not nice to call her a loser. Only I get to do that."

Nika laughed loudly and nodded toward Arryn. "I didn't. She's the promising warrior."

"Oh, that's just cold," Cathillian said. "Damn. I get no respect around here."

The Chieftain, Elysia, and Arryn all laughed, the few others in attendance also taking part in the joke. The Chieftain then stepped forward, raising his hand. "This is the final round. We all know who will win, no offense, Nika."

"None taken, Chieftain," Nika said.

"But as is law, the final round must be fought. A single round for the magical category. Winner takes all. Cathillian, show us what ya got," the Chieftain said with excitement.

Nika's eyes glowed whitish-green; Arryn could see them from where she stood. Cathillian's back was to her, so she was unable to see his, but she could feel his power. Nika's magic was strong, but it was nothing in comparison to what Cathillian had.

The ground trembled under their feet, everyone looking around to see what would happen. Cathillian managed to jump high in the air, narrowly missing a root that shot out of the ground straight for his feet. He tumbled over backward and landed, but Nika's attack was not over. Her hands shot forward as another root reached from the ground.

Cathillian jumped over them, tumbling across the ground. Arryn could feel the swell of energy in the area as his hands came to rest flat on the ground. It then looked like he grabbed hold of the dirt and pulled up.

The ground under Nika lifted, knocking her down flat on her back. Cathillian stood and gripped his fist at his sides, the ground wrapping around Nika's wrists as he did. She tried to fight, but it was pointless. The round was over in only seconds.

Arryn stood slack-jawed, as she looked at Cathillian, realizing what had just happened.

He'd won.

That was it.

He'd won the trials, and now she would be able to return to Arcadia.

Her life began anew ten years ago when the druids took her in, and her life was about to begin again now with her new journey back to the city that had forgotten her. Back to the place her parents died helping her escape from.

"*So, what did you say* your name was again?" Marie asked.

"The name's Samuel," the rearick, said.

"And you want to help rebuild the city?" Marie asked, a smile on her face, but a level of disbelief in her tone.

"Aye," Samuel said. "The way I see it, there ain't no work around here. My people ain't been making any coin, except fer the few brew runs we get from the bars. But even that's not enough ta sustain us. And the long trip we have ta make to go all the way up to Cella, well, that ain't no fun either. I'd rather rebuild the factory here in town for free, get the damned Arcadians workin' again, and get my people back up and running, than to make shit runs from the Heights all the way to Cella fer very little coin."

"That sounds like a pretty reasonable cause," Marie said. "We'd be needing gems for magitech, too, once we can start manufacturing them again."

Samuel nodded. "That's very true, lass. So, tell me what ye need, and I'll do my best ta get it fer ya. I might even find a couple of guys willin' ta help out. Especially if ye agree to let 'em take a few items once that factory's up and runnin' so they can sell 'em. Consider it back pay. I bet ye we could run business from that factory to Cella and make some coin coming in the city that way, too."

Marie's eyes widened. She hadn't thought of that, she wasn't even sure if Amelia had thought about that yet. It wasn't like Amelia was able to focus so much here lately with everything else going on. She still had so much to do.

But if Samuel was right, if the factory got up and running, they'd be able to fund the things that they needed for Arcadia by selling things to the people in Cella and even more so to the Arcadian people that fled to the hills and other bare land in hopes of building their own homes. They would need supplies for the build.

Cella didn't have a factory, not a good one anyway. That was at least one answer to the problems they'd been having.

"How many men do you think you could get to help?" Marie asked.

"Oh, I don't know. A few dozen or so. I wouldn't expect too many to get on board. Unfortunately, a lot of my people have become greedy sons of bitches. Adrien's reign spoiled some of 'em." Samuel laughed then. "But it ain't like they're gonna get any money like that again anytime soon without a factory and without men who can afford to pay for brew shipments. With the Academy here, people will want to see the city heal. Some of those rich bastards in Cella might even be so inclined to invest in businesses."

Marie nodded. "Yes, but I doubt that many people around here, poor or not, would want to give up a fraction of their business to some greedy soul in Cella. Perhaps if there was a timeline on it."

She shook her head. "I don't know. This is all so confusing to me. I've never had to deal with any of this before, but I'm up for the challenge. Let me think about this, and I'll talk to Amelia, and we'll see what we can get done. You go back to Craigston and see what you can dredge up in the form of help."

Samuel smiled. "Ya got yerself a deal, lass."

He shook her hand and turned to leave the office. As he opened the door, she could see a small line of men standing outside the room, waiting to have a similar interview. Men from the bar that she'd gone to who were anxious to get the rebuild started.

She was glad that Samuel had been her first interview of the day. Now, she had ideas to work with, things that she could talk about with the other men. Perhaps by the end of the day, she would have one hell of a plan to take back to Amelia. They might even be on their way to getting their city back.

"I'm ready for the next one," Marie said.

The door opened, and a man walked in. "Hello sir, I'm Marie. I'll be the one talking to you about the future of the city." The man sat down and Marie smiled at him, excited to see where this conversation and all those following would take her.

FIFTEEN

Talia *impatiently waited at the* base of the stairs for the three people she would have to show around the Academy. There were three new hires for physical magic teachers, and as the Dean, it was her job to show them around.

Their appointment was set for 9:00 a.m. that morning, and she was happy to see that every one of them showed up no less than ten minutes early. Punctuality worked for her; the earlier the better.

The last thing she wanted to happen was to be pulled away from her own work and her own plans to be a substitute for the day for any of their classes. After all, things were about to be set in motion.

While her dungeon friend hadn't been as forthcoming as she'd hoped, he'd certainly been able to tell her a few good things about Jackson—

which she'd used to her advantage.

Still, she'd had to gather the good stuff the hard way, gaining Jackson's trust and trying to pry information out little by little. Slowly—dreadfully so for her liking—it was coming together.

Today, she'd find out just how successful she'd been.

Talia smiled as she walked towards the door as the last new hire walked through. The first was a tall man named Jakob, relatively handsome with light hair. He seemed like the do-gooder type.

Next up was Shelly, a tall brunette with overly rosy cheeks, bright, hazel eyes, and an almost too-excited attitude towards teaching children.

Children of all ages were assholes. Talia couldn't imagine anyone willingly teaching them, let alone being *excited* about it. Even at eighteen or nineteen years old, there were hormones, attitudes, and most of those students seemed to think they were better than everyone.

She hated them.

All of them.

Shelly seemed nice enough, but Talia assumed that there was undoubtedly something loose with that one.

Finally, there was a tall blonde, inquisitive, yet quiet. She studied everything as she looked around, but said nothing. Scarlett was her name. She was stunningly beautiful. If Talia hadn't been the all-too-confident woman that she was, she would have been quite worried about the new employee.

The neckline on the teacher's dress was cut lower than most, yet it looked very tasteful on her. Her seemingly long hair was pulled up high with messy tendrils hanging down. It gave her an overall sexy look.

Even Talia had to admit that she was a little taken aback. During her interview process, Talia remembered the woman being very cool, calm. Her answers were calculated, smart. She seemed to be the only one out of all the applicants that might not drive her insane.

In fact, Talia was a bit surprised to think that she might actually like the woman had circumstances been much different.

But that was fine with her. She didn't have to like her to get what she wanted.

"Thank you all for joining me," Talia said with a broad smile as her hands gestured around her. "I just want to take the time to welcome you to your first day at the Academy. Most of today is just going to be touring, sitting in on a couple classes, and just getting to know the layout here at the school. Many of those I'm still learning myself! As I'm sure you understand, we're in a transition period. The school is still recovering from all the changes that have been made. But don't let that fool you, everyone here is strong, and things will get better. Especially with all of you here now."

Jakob stepped forward, a large smile on his face. With the way he'd eyeballed Talia in the interview and even now, she knew he'd be one hell of an ass-kisser. But that was fine by her. The more people she had willing to bow at her feet, the better.

"I'm just excited to be here," he said. "Thank you for this opportunity. I went here as a child, but things were a lot different back then. Everything was very—how should I say this—for the *elite*."

Talia almost scoffed and rolled her eyes.

Jakob continued, much to Talia's displeasure. "I'm excited to see what bringing in the new blood from the Boulevard will do. I really think those kids have a lot to offer; I always have. I always thought those rules were a crock, and now things seem to be a lot fairer."

Talia struggled to keep her fake smile as she inwardly rolled her eyes. He was a liar if she'd ever seen one. She could tell by the way he'd said elite. He believed he was better than those Boulevard bastards, and she could tell that he'd only said otherwise because of wanting to impress the new boss.

Talia hated him, but she'd chosen him for his weakness in the first place. At his level, it was easy to spot.

"That's very true!" she said, trying to power through the introduction. "Over the next few months, the integration of the Boulevard students is very important. Most of them have absolutely no experience with magic whatsoever because of the laws that were once in place. I know most of you are familiar with the things that happened in the city before, but I wanted to make sure you knew for empathetic purposes."

Talia saw movement out of the corner of her eye. Looking over, she saw Jackson approaching. He had something in his hand as he came closer, more than likely the item she'd asked for.

She felt very triumphant at that moment.

It had been a couple of days since they'd spoken, and before he left her office, Talia had then asked him to come back to her office today at nine.

This morning, she'd told her assistant that she'd be giving a tour, and if anyone came looking for her, send them to the front entrance, ensuring that the new teachers would see her new pet.

"Dean Talia," Jackson said. "I'm sorry, I didn't realize that you were doing a tour. We set an appointment to meet this morning."

"I'm sorry, Jackson," Talia said, reaching out and placing a hand on his shoulder, the other over her heart. "That was all my fault. I completely forgot that I'd be doing a tour for the new teachers this morning. I hope you can forgive me."

She looked down to his hand at the envelope that he carried. "Is that what I think it is?"

The Dean knew exactly what it was.

It was a little writing assignment that she'd asked him to partake in. She'd challenged him to write down his true feelings toward the Boulevard students and what he wished he could do about it—no matter how bad.

She'd asked him to write down the names of those who might feel the same. After only a couple of meetings, he'd agreed without a single protest. This had been her test to see just how in control she was. It appeared he'd given her exactly as she asked with little effort. And now, it was time for the show for the new people.

He looked down before smiling shyly and giving a nervous nod. "Yes, ma'am. It is. I wanted to take my time on it. It seemed important to you, and it kind of made me feel like it should be important to me, too. Anyway, here it is. I don't wanna take up any more of your time. I see you're busy."

He extended his hand, and Talia took the envelope from it.

She smiled again. "Thank you, Jackson. This will go a long way with helping you. You'll see. I'll be free later this afternoon to look it over, and I'll get back with you tomorrow. In a couple days at the latest. Is that OK?"

Talia asked.

An almost excited expression crossed his face as he nodded. "Yes! Yes, that's just fine. Thanks again. Have a great day, and it was nice to meet all of you. I'm sure I'll see you around school."

Talia watched Jackson as he made a hasty retreat down the hall, disappearing around the corner.

"What was that about, if you don't mind my asking?" Scarlett asked, her voice smooth and even-toned.

Talia turned back to the group, who all wore smiles as she replied, "Oh, that was Jackson. I promised that I wouldn't share the details of our conversations, but I will say that I've initiated something a little new around here."

She couldn't help the swell of pride while seeing the genuine look of interest on all their faces. *Puppets*, Talia thought to herself as she considered how well it had gone. Small plan or not, it was the little successes that led to true victory. Not the smash and dominate method many others, including her father, had chosen to use.

"You see, we have a lot of students that seem to be having a hard time adjusting to the changes in the city. It's all so new still. We're the only solid footing they have right now. Anything outside these walls is chaos."

"That's very kind of you," Scarlett said. "It seems he's taken quite a liking to you."

"Kids, even older ones, are *excellent* judges of character!" Shelly chirped. "It only goes to show just how good of a person she is for him to trust her so much so quickly. Good for you! So, it's like a counseling program?"

Talia hated the shrill sound of the woman's voice when she was excited. It annoyed her to no end, and her peppiness was about to crush her. Talia forced happiness to her face, though the disgust wanted to show most of all.

"Yes! Though, I'm leery to call it that. I don't want these students to feel like there's something *wrong* with them if they feel one way or another."

"Brilliant!" Jakob said, taking a step forward.

He reached out for Talia's shoulder, but he then pulled away. She hoped her expression didn't say anything, though she felt the bile rising in her throat as she thought of him having any physical contact with her. Especially in the form that he *really* wanted.

Jakob cleared his throat, clearly feeling tension where he hadn't before. "It really is a show of true character. You have an entire school to run and a list of things to do every day, yet you still put these students ahead of all that. Again, I just have to say thank you. This is an honor."

Talia swallowed, giving a nervous laugh as she feigned excitement for his words while simultaneously forcing her trembling hands to calm.

Lately, her anxiety had been getting to her, and her magic threatened to burst forth. Luckily, she was excellent at control, though apparently not as excellent as she'd once thought she was.

"I haven't yet discussed it with the Chancellor because she's quite busy. She has enough to worry about! I'll take care of this and know she'd be very excited that we're doing all we can to help the students in any way possible."

Shelly smiled like an idiot, placing her hand over her heart as her face scrunched up like she was looking at a newborn baby. It was obvious that she was truly touched by Talia's words.

It was exactly what she'd hoped for when she'd set it up. Now, it was almost a guarantee that when Amelia made her visit later that day to check on the new teachers, the word of Talia's generosity and dedication without seeking recognition would reach the Chancellor.

Talia turned, and took a few steps away, before using her happiest voice once again. "Let's get this started!"

Samuel and Andrew had set out east, heading toward the forest where a group of loggers were cutting down trees. They'd been commissioned by the nobles that had fled Arcadia and decided to live in the open country under their own rule.

The loggers were no doubt being paid handsomely for their efforts, but not nearly what they'd make working for the city again.

Rearick and Arcadian's alike took the outside jobs to earn what little money they could for their families. It wasn't wise to work that close to the Madlands, but the small forests that separated the Arcadian Valley from the Madlands were closer than the Dark Forest, and the Arcadian's were too terrified to touch the druids' territory anyway.

Too many stories had been told of the druids, and no one wanted to feel their wrath. Somehow, it was less terrifying to face down the remnant. They were more beast than human, but the rearick had fought them in battle often.

As Samuel and Andrew approached, Samuel spotted a familiar rearick carrying logs back to a cart that would be drawn by horse once it had been filled.

"Ren!" Samuel called out, a smile on his face. "I'd know that wrinkled, old, shit stain anywhere."

The other, older rearick looked up and smiled, dropping the logs into the back of the cart before running up to meet them. "Ye old bastard, what are you doing here?" He asked, clapping Samuel on the back. "Look at ye! That face of yers looks like weathered skin on a bull's undercarriage. It's good ta see ye, old friend."

Andrew shook his head. "I'll never understand you people. That was one of the worst insults I've ever heard in my entire life, and ya act like nothing happened."

Samuel looked at Andrew incredulously. "What are ye talking about? It would've been an insult if he'd told me I looked like some smooth, baby-arsed, pampered prick."

Ren laughed. "Yeah, kinda like yer friend here."

Samuel barked out a laugh and waved a hand in the air. "Na, this one might look soft as a newborn's arse, but he seems ta be all right."

"Well, I'll take yer word fer it. So, what brings ye out here? Lookin' fer work?" Ren asked.

"In a roundabout way. The Arcadian's are hurtin' fer help. They need resources. They need wood ta rebuild. I was comin' ta see if we might be able ta strike an arrangement," Samuel explained.

"Oh, no. How did they manage ta get their grip on ye? Workin' *with* the

Arcadian's is much different than workin' *for* the Arcadian's. It's worse, lad."

Samuel shook his head. "It ain't like that, old man. Do ye enjoy takin' shite work from those rat bastard nobles?"

Ren shook his head. "It was better working fer the city. We didn't really have a boss, just orders comin' in. We came and went as we pleased. Workin' fer the nobles, those entitled pricks think they own us. They'll send someone out after us if we don't get our work done in time."

"That's what I'm tryin' ta say," Samuel said. "If we can get that damn factory rebuilt, they can start sellin' goods to Cella. They start sellin' goods, they start pullin' in money," Samuel began.

Andrew took over. "If the city starts making money, they can start paying us. Once they start paying us, the city can employ the rearick again. The bars and private citizens will have enough money to order bigger shipments of the mystics' brew. We can start buying wood to start rebuilding the Boulevard. And we're gonna need stones for magitech. So, you see, while we're asking for a little free help, it'll do you a lot of good in the long run to give it."

Ren stroked his beard as he thought Andrew's words over. "Workin' fer ourselves again, eh? Can't say I don't like that. I call most of the shots around here, but this one doesn't just affect me. Lemme talk to the guys, and I'll see what we—"

A loud scream followed by gurgling breaths filled the area. Samuel looked around and saw a rusty battle ax cleaved into a man's rib cage. Those gurgled breaths he'd heard had certainly been the poor man's last. Screams erupted, the sound of loud footfall getting closer.

"*Scheisse!*" Ren called out. "It's the remnant."

Andrew drew a sword from the sheathe on his hip. Samuel looked up at him. "Do ye know how to use that, boy? Have ye ever seen battle?"

Andrew gave a wicked smile. "I'm just as handy with this sword as you are with the hammer at your belt."

Samuel smiled and nodded. "Let's see if ye have the stones to back up those words, lad."

A dozen remnant ran directly into the group, slashing, biting, and clawing their way through the loggers. Samuel, Andrew, and Ren all dashed forward, weapons at the ready.

A remnant knocked one of the fellow loggers to the ground, a large war-hammer—one that looked like it had been taken from a rearick—lifted over his head. He gave a wicked smile, laughing a guttural laugh before saying in an almost unintelligible deep voice, "Looks like I'm eatin' tonight!"

"Hey, ugly!" Samuel yelled at the remnant.

The remnant locked eyes with Samuel, his dark grin growing. He charged as Samuel ran up, swinging his hammer hard and hitting the beast right in the side of the knee, shattering it. He fell to the ground on his good knee, his weapon falling behind him.

Samuel swung around, lifting his weapon as he did just before bringing it down hard on the remnants head. He kicked the body over.

"Eat that, ye foul bastard," Samuel said, spitting on the corpse. He turned to the man sitting and almost shaking on the ground, extending a helping hand. "Can ye fight?"

The man took his hand before standing and nodding. "Y-yes, I can."

His eyes spread wide. "I've never actually seen them before."

"They're big and stupid. They fight with brute force and nothin' else, no common sense. They'll run right at ye, so stay low, and ye'll do fine." Samuel pointed at the remnant's weapon on the ground. "Grab that and get ta work."

Samuel didn't stick around to see if the man was strong enough to lift a hammer that big. Rearick were small, but they packed a lot of muscle into their stout bodies.

Samuel searched the area, hoping to find his companion and his old friend. Another remnant gave a loud battle cry. Just as he told the young man he'd saved, the remnant was running straight at him, planning to take Samuel to the ground with brute force.

Samuel ran forward, dropping down to his hip and sliding between the remnant's legs before rolling over and jumping to his feet.

He swung his hammer hard, hitting him right in the spine. As he fell, Samuel once again took the final swing at his head, forever ending the remnant's miserable life.

"Samuel!" someone called out.

He turned to see his friend, Ren, taking on two of the bastards. He took off in his friend's direction only to see Andrew running from the opposite side toward Ren as well.

"Take this!" Andrew threw his sword at Samuel, the blade slicing through the air and sticking into the ground only a few feet in front of his path.

Without stopping, Samuel shifted his hammer to his left hand while pulling the sword out of the dirt with his right.

Without hesitation, Samuel ran one of the remnant through the back, shoving the blade all the way through his gut, and with fluid motion, immediately turned to slam his hammer down on the foot of the other, smashing the remnant in the jaw on the upswing as it leaned over in pain.

Samuel heard a grunt and looked over to see Andrew pull the sword from the back of the other remnant and bring it down on his neck, cutting his head off before spinning around and swinging it again, taking the head off the other as it recovered from Samuel's attack.

"Fuckin' nice!" Samuel shouted. "I retract my previous statement."

"Save it. I expect you to buy me a drink later to celebrate me saving your ass," Andrew said.

"If the two of ye can keep fightin' like that and get me men outta here alive, I'll get both yer asses piss drunk," Ren said. "And ye can have yer resources, too."

"Ye got yerself a deal," Samuel said with a grin. "Now, let's go finish skinning these ugly bastards."

Samuel decided to stay close to Andrew after having seen his level of expertise with the sword. Ren was a tough rearick, and he could take care of himself, but Samuel and Andrew only had each other.

Several more remnant ran into the area, but Samuel and Andrew weaved through the crowd, using the distraction of the other loggers to take them out one by one. Soon, the final remnant fell, the group breaking out in cheers of celebration.

Ren walked up to the duo, a smile on his face. His teeth and his eyes were the only things that could be seen through all that blood. "We did it, lads."

"We did," Samuel said. "Now, how about those drinks?"

His friend laughed and clapped him on the back. "That's what these Arcadian boys don't realize. Battles're only challenges. They deserve ta be celebrated when won. Glad ta have one of me own ta drink with tonight. There's an empty cart over there. Any of the wood that's lying around that ye can fill it with, ye can keep."

Ren spat a mouthful of blood on the ground before smiling, one of his teeth missing. "Anything after today, ye have to come cut down yerself. I'll happily give it to ye. Let's pack up these carts and head back ta Arcadia. We have several injured, and I think it's time we had ourselves some drinks."

Samuel and Andrew finished chatting with Ren before heading off and gathering up an overstuffed cart full of wood while the others packed up the injured. They'd been lucky that everyone survived. That was all thanks to quick reaction, Samuel's and Andrew's expertise, and the low numbers of remnant. Twelve or so.

"This ain't exactly how I planned on this going," Samuel said. "But I guess it worked out fer the best anyway. Not only that, ye earned my respect today. Believe me when I say that's not easy ta do. 'Specially fer an Arcadian."

"I don't trust people at all, but here lately I've been learning that not everybody is quite so bad. Including ugly old bastards like you."

Samuel smiled. "Now yer gettin' it! And hey, tomorrow, ye might even wake up with some calluses on those baby hands of yers."

"You're still within sword's length, old man. I'd say that I'd cut you in half, but I'm not exactly sure if that's possible," Andrew said with a smile.

"Yer all right, Arcadian. Now, shut yer trap an' help me get this thing hitched to a horse. It's time ta go get drunk."

After having taken a few days to prepare before leaving, Arryn's nerves had certainly picked up. She was incredibly anxious, her stomach rolling at the thought of leaving. She couldn't decide if it was fear or excitement. Elysia assured her it was both.

"You're gonna do just fine," Elysia said. "I know you're worried. Believe me when I say I'm worried, too. I have no idea what you're gonna be doing, who you're gonna run into, if they'll be good or if they'll be terrible people. All I have to console me is my faith in both of you. I could *not* be happier that things worked out the way they did. If either one of you went out alone, I'd be a mess. But you can't let my worries affect you."

"I think what she's trying to say," the Chieftain said, placing a hand on Elysia's shoulder, "is that she's crazy. She is a borderline psychotic, overprotective mother, and deep down, she knows that you're a hell of a lot stronger than what she gives you credit for. Both of you."

Elysia scoffed, turning and hitting her father in the arm. "You can be a real dick." She shook her head. "You're lucky that, even in your old age, you're still stronger than me."

The Chieftain laughed. "Oh, daughter. You and your threats." He turned to Arryn then. "See? I told you. *Psychotic*," he said, whispering the last bit.

Arryn was happy for all the smiles in those moments, the silliness that surrounded them. They were good people. They'd raised her well and taught her everything that she needed to know about family.

Everything *everyone* needed to know about family. Things she wasn't even certain her own parents could've taught her.

Her parents had both been kind, loving people, but Arcadia didn't have the sense of family the druids do. In the forest, where there's nothing else, the people around are all they have. And even though Arryn was more like a family friend than true family, she knew they could never be replaced.

She looked up to the sky and saw that the sun was directly overhead. It was midday. "Time to go," Arryn said. "We need to get on our way. We've already wasted too much daylight saying goodbye to everyone."

Elysia and the Chieftain stepped closer to Arryn and Cathillian. The Chieftain extended his hand to Cathillian, two solid, carved, wooden bracers in his grip.

Cathillian took them and looked them over before slipping them over his forearms. While wooden bracers might have seemed impractical, to a druid, they were an honor.

"That wood was cut from the Heilig tree," the Chieftain said. "They'll give you strength, and will always tie you to nature."

Elysia took a step toward Arryn, a smile on her face. "I know you prefer the bow," she said. "So, I made this for you."

She lifted a stunning, expertly crafted bow and handed it to Arryn. Her jaw dropped, and her eyes widened as she inspected the beautiful piece.

There were small designs etched out and engraved in the length of the wood. The grip was perfect, and she knew by the color of the cord that it was made from none other than Chaos' mane.

"I hope you like it," Elysia said. "But that's not all. Somewhere down the road—while training with Cathillian, I imagine—something happened to make you decide you liked hand-to-hand combat. Even though it isn't customary, I wanted to give you something else."

Nika appeared then, carrying a long staff. It, too, had been carved of the same wood. Nika handed it to Elysia before giving Arryn a wink and stepping back.

"Eventually," Elysia began, "Cathillian will train you how to fight in close quarter combat like a true warrior. When that time comes, you'll rely more heavily on a different style of weapon, and you'll find that you use your bow less and less. Because of that, I made you a second gift. Actually, Cathillian helped me."

Arryn looked at Cathillian for a moment, a large smile on his face as he peered down at her. There was a look of pride in his expression. Arryn looked back to Elysia before replacing the bow that was on her back with the new one and taking the staff from her, inspecting it as well.

It was her full height, and light in color. The long staff twisted from the bottom all the way up. At the very top, the wood split into several vine-like pieces as they wrapped around a beautiful stone. It was green in color and reminded her of the green of the druids' eyes when they cast magic. It was breathtaking.

"This wood is nearly unbreakable," the Chieftain said. "It would take the strength of a man three times Cathillian's size to sever it, or the magic of a very powerful druid. In our tribe, when someone begins the death process, they're taken to the Heilig tree. In their final moments, they channel what is left of their life force and their power into that tree until they take their final breath, growing it and fortifying it. The tree itself does not have power, but what it does have is strength. It's stronger than any other tree in this forest and grows more and more so with the passing of any druid in our tribe."

Elysia took over. "Only an Elder druid has the power to cut even a single twig from one of its mighty limbs. This tree is used for protection. This tree is what is used to craft the shields that our warriors carry and the armor that they wear. While it may not be as sharp, it's certainly stronger than any steel. It's because of this, and because of your devotion to our people, that you both receive these gifts."

Arryn could hardly believe their words. She'd heard stories of the tree, but only in passing. She'd spent a lot of time there.

At nearly seventy feet in girth, and over two hundred feet tall, the giant sequoia had been a place of solitude for her. There had been many times when she'd found herself sitting on one of its massive roots while she watched the squirrels play in its branches.

All that time and she'd never known the true meaning behind it. She only thought the tree meant a lot to them because of its age and size, not that it was a physical symbol of what the druid people stood for and those they'd lost.

Arryn wiped a single tear from her cheek as she looked first into Elysia's eyes and then to the Chieftain's.

"I love you both, thank you for everything you've done for me, including this. It means more to me than you could possibly ever know." She stepped forward, giving each of them a hug before stepping away and allowing Cathillian to do the same.

Elysia began to cry, something that was quite uncommon for her. Arryn knew if she didn't leave soon, she would end up crying more than the tear she'd allowed to escape.

"I love you both," Elysia forced out. She sniffled. "Be safe, find ways to send word back to me." She gasped, a smile breaking across her face. "Take Chaos! One of you can ride him while the other rides another horse. That way, Chaos can come back to me and let me know that you're safe. Ha! I'm a genius."

Cathillian shook his head, exasperated. "I suppose there's no getting out of this one is there? I could always send Echo back, ya know."

Elysia shook her head. "No. No, there really isn't. I don't want Echo to have to fly all the way there, back here, and then back to you. It's only a single round trip for Chaos. You *will* do this for me because I'm your mother, and you don't want me to come to Arcadia to search for you."

Cathillian's eyes widened. "I think Granddad's right. Psychotic," he said.

Elysia's eyes narrowed as her hands came to rest on her hips.

Cathillian quickly changed his tone. "Well, that's settled! Because no, we absolutely do *not* want that. We don't need you coming in there raging like a crazy person. Nor do we need whatever death you're plotting with the look on your face right now. Stop it." As he said that last bit, he playfully tapped her on the forehead. "Stop it."

Elysia laughed, swatting his hand away. "I love you. Go, child, before I beat you."

At that moment, Chaos trotted his way up, another horse right behind him. They quickly packed their things on the backs of the horses, and climbed up.

After yet another round of goodbyes, Arryn and Cathillian set out on their way. Arryn heading back to her childhood home, and Cathillian finally getting the adventure he'd always wanted.

SIXTEEN

Samuel and Marie headed over to the site of what used to be the Arcadian factory. Marie knew Samuel had gone through a lot to get them the first small load of wood, and she was grateful.

Though he was a tough guy and didn't like to show his weaknesses, she could tell the fight had taken a lot out of him. He still rubbed at his shoulders and neck whenever he stood too long in one place. But it hadn't tempered his determination.

As they arrived at the site, Marie got a nervous look on her face as she looked to Samuel's worried expression. "What's that look," she asked. "I don't like that look."

She studied Samuel as he stared out into the large mounds of rubble. Shattered rock, wood, glass, and various other materials littered the area in a mess. She knew what he saw. It was the same thing she did while wondering where the hell to start, but they had to try.

"Well, lass. What I'm looking at appears ta be a massive pile of shite. Not exactly sure what ye expect me ta do with this, but if it's rebuild it…" He trailed off, shaking his head. "Well, I'm not quite sure yer gonna get what ye ask for."

"Darn it," Marie said, sighing a bit.

Samuel looked up at his new acquaintance, brows furrowed. "Did ye just say darn it?" he asked. An amused expression crossed his face as though he couldn't believe the word had exited her mouth.

She nodded. "Yes, why?"

Samuel shook his head. "Lass, we need ta teach ye some new words. If ye wanna be the backbone of the city, ye need ta *have* a backbone. While I hate ta say it, because I like working with me own two hands, we need some of those fancy magic users."

"How many do you think we'll need?" Marie asked, looking at the shorter man beside her.

He shrugged. "I don't know. Not too familiar with magic users, still ain't quite sure about 'em. But—I know what I'm up against. Anyone climbin' through that pile of shite, is gonna get cut up. We need some of that tele-whatever you people use ta help sort without touchin' much. If ye can get the glass sifted down ta the bottom, then all the normal folk can heave out the big shite and sort it proper. I'd say no less than ten. But even that's cuttin' it close. I guess it just depends on how quick ye want this done."

"I suppose that's fair," she said. "And telekinesis was the word you were looking for." She winked, and he waved her off. "We can shake the debris enough to get at least the small pieces down to the bottom and shatter the rest so they can fall through. As long as everyone has good footwear, that should be safe enough for the time being. Lucky for us, we have an entire Academy full of magic users."

The rearick laughed. "The way I understand it, ye have quite a few dummies in there, too. Those Boulevard kids can scrap with the best of 'em, but they're none too magically inclined, lass. You'll need strength, precision. You're gonna need teachers and advanced students."

Marie sighed. "I was afraid of that. The last time we specially chose people from the Academy, Adrien was literally sucking the life out of them. I'm not exactly sure how excited those students will be to volunteer for anything requiring *advanced* students."

She shrugged, looking around the demolished site. Everything was charred or in thousands upon thousands of tiny little pieces. As bad as the Boulevard had been, the factory was possibly worse. It had burned up and exploded from the inside.

"Well, it's a start," Samuel said.

Marie nodded, contemplating exactly how she was about to go ask the new Dean and also Amelia if she could have students and faculty for a few days, possibly a week. While it was a necessity, it certainly made her nervous.

Cathillian and Arryn made their way through the Dark Forest. The leaves, vines, and other plants getting thicker and thicker as they neared the edge.

Once they could travel no farther, they each dismounted and made their way to the deep wall standing in their path. Arryn looked up, and then to her left, and then her right, inspecting the massive barrier. The thorns and brush were so thick, she couldn't even see through to the other side.

Cathillian looked over to Arryn before motioning to the wall. "Kneel with me."

Arryn watched Cathillian as he knelt to the ground, placing both his hands flat against the earth. She followed his lead and did the same.

"This magic is a little different than healing. It's a little different than most things that you've done. Most of the time, we focus on the energy within nature and use our own to grow it into something more."

His eyes cut over to the thick hedge. "This time, we're making the connection to the life directly in front of us and asking it to move. Focus on what you want to happen, which in case you hadn't figured it out, is for the plants to part."

Arryn nodded, closing her eyes and focusing on the path directly before them. She could feel the energy of everything surrounding her, and she pushed her own toward it as she imagined everything moving out of her way.

After a few unsuccessful minutes, she sighed and pulled away. "It doesn't seem to be working," she said.

Cathillian smiled. "That's because you can't bully everything into doing what you want. Just watch. Study my movements and feel what I do."

Cathillian had been outside of the Dark Forest more than a few times.

He used to escape all the time as a child before the lycanthrope attack, and, as a warrior, he'd gone to check the perimeter both inside and out of the barrier. So, Cathillian was no stranger to opening the wall before them.

Arryn had seen it done, but she'd never had the opportunity to really pay attention or try herself.

Cathillian's eyes glowed brighter green as he summoned his power. She could feel the type of energy that he was calling on, and it felt different than what she had been using.

She realized then that she hadn't paid a bit of attention to anything he'd told her.

He told her it was nothing like healing, or even growing plant life. It was something almost similar to the power that was used when one of the druids communicated with their familiar. Not quite like telepathy, but a bond with nature.

She watched as the vines began to wrap themselves around the thorns, and the thorns began to move. While she had no way of knowing what it was like to communicate with a familiar, she did have a connection to animals.

She placed her hands on the ground again, focusing all of her energy toward the path before them.

Like Cathillian, she bonded with the life around her, willing it to do as she asked. She began to hear snapping and loud creaking.

She opened her eyes to see that the path was very rapidly opening now with her magic thrown into the mix. Soon, the passageway was several feet wide, just enough for them to comfortably walk through with their horses.

"Very good!" Cathillian said. "You're a damned fast learner."

"Thanks! Sometimes when my teacher actually takes situations seriously, I learn a thing or two."

His brows furrowed. "Well, now, I wouldn't say *that* exactly. No need to be rude and throw insults. We both know I take nothing seriously."

Arryn laughed as she stood, turning back to Chaos. She grabbed the reins, and waited for Cathillian's instructions. "What now?"

"We have about twenty feet of trail to walk through, but we also have to close it as we walk. That's why I'm not wearing my boots, so I can stay connected to nature. So, you're going to ride ahead of me, and I'm going to walk through on foot last, behind you and the horses, so I can close the passageway."

Arryn didn't respond as she got back on Chaos. Cathillian handed her the reins to Maia, the horse that he was riding. Arryn went first, making sure to hold Maia's reins behind her so the mare could follow directly behind.

Arryn could hear the popping and cracking again, and she looked back to see Cathillian, his eyes glowing green as he slowly paced behind them. His arms were extended out to his sides, his fingertips barely touching the brush on either side. The wall filled in just behind him with every step.

When they reached the other side, Arryn couldn't help but admire his handiwork. He was definitely strong and magically inclined. Having him as a teacher might not be so bad after all.

They had traveled for a couple of hours when Cathillian decided to probe Arryn about her intentions. "So, what is it that you plan to do first?" he asked. "Are ya gonna find shelter? Or are ya just gonna dive right in?"

"There's going to have to be an adjustment period," she replied. "I don't know what condition the city is in, so I don't know if there'll be any place to stay. Worst-case scenario, I figure we might end up staying just outside the walls. But I'm gonna need some time. I just wanna get there and get settled and get used to the idea of being back in the city again."

He sighed and Arryn thought it sounded almost relieved. "I think that's a pretty smart idea. There's no reason to rush since we're not going anywhere. Besides, I think the first thing we should do is figure out where we're sleeping. I honestly thought you were gonna run in there like all excited and wild and grab people while screaming questions about your father. Glad to see you have a little common sense to you."

"Has anyone ever told you that you're a dick?" she asked. "Besides me, of course."

He laughed. "Actually, I *have* been told that before."

"Well, good. Now you know it's popular opinion. Sometimes I think—" she started.

Arryn was interrupted by Chaos stopping almost immediately. His front hooves began prancing around the area as his head wildly nodded up and down. He made very aggressive noises, alerting Cathillian.

"Arryn," Cathillian said, his voice low and very serious. "Get off Chaos. Now."

Arryn had only nodded before Chaos knelt down, rolling halfway onto his side and gently dumping her off before standing again.

Chaos ran, moving in a circle around them as he huffed and nodded his head. He looked very agitated and angry. Arryn was about to ask Cathillian what was happening, but she was interrupted by a very loud growl.

"Echo!" Cathillian called out. The bird screeched before diving down and landing on the ground before Cathillian who was now dismounting his horse as well. "Go find it. Call to us when you do."

Echo's massive wings unfurled as she took off to the sky in the direction of the growl. With as fast as she could fly, it didn't take long before they heard a loud screech followed by another.

Cathillian's eyes glowed green just before he closed them. When he opened them again, only a moment later, he looked to Arryn, a serious look on his face.

"It's a lycanthrope. A big one," Cathillian grunted. "And it's heading straight for us."

Chaos still shifted between running circles around them and running back and forth. Arryn expected the horse to head for the hills, but he was no ordinary horse.

He was a familiar.

One that was ordered to make sure they arrived safely at their destination. If need be, Chaos would protect them with his life.

Just then, a large, brown lycanthrope revealed itself in the distance, charging them at full speed. It was far taller than a normal man, even taller than Cathillian.

Its body—half-man and half wolf—was lean and built for power, for hunting. Its growl echoed through the woods just before it came to a stop and howled. Its large muzzle pulled back in a hideous snarl, it's slobber dripping from its long, jagged teeth onto the ground.

"That looks just like the bitch that attacked me when I was a kid," Cathillian said.

Arryn held her staff tight, positioning her body so she was ready for any attack that may come. "Maybe it's a… *son of the bitch*," she said.

Cathillian laughed. "I see what you did there!"

The sound of Chaos running away caught their attention. Arryn turned her head just enough to see him heading west, toward the river.

"Well—looks like he's out," Arryn said. "So… You distract the lycanthrope while I take him with my bow?"

The lycanthrope lowered himself, his entire body poised for attack. He howled once again before his cry faded into a deep growl.

"No, trust me. He senses something. He'd never abandon us otherwise. And yes, I think that sounds reasonable enough," Cathillian said.

Cathillian drew his sword, rushing forward and to the left, giving Arryn a window to use her bow. She dropped her staff to the ground, and pulled her new bow from her back. She nocked an arrow before drawing back, her entire body steady, familiar with the movement.

She was impressed with how sturdy the wood felt in her hands, far better than any other bow she'd ever used. She let loose the first arrow, missing the beast as its increased senses heard it whistling through the air. It dodged the arrow, somehow catching it in the air before throwing it to the ground.

Arryn then decided to use a different technique. If he was that strong and that fast, there was no way Cathillian could take him. She immediately nocked another arrow, letting it loose directly in his path, just far enough out of reach so he couldn't grab it again.

As anticipated, the shot caused it to change direction. She drew another arrow and, one after another, she controlled its path with her shots, slowing it down.

Cathillian must have known what she was doing, because he planted his sword in the ground and came to a stop, his hands stretching out as though he were reaching for the large tree behind the beast.

Arryn heard loud cracks as the mighty tree followed his command, a giant root breaking free of the ground, knocking the lycanthrope back on the damp earth. Cathillian's hands swiped down in a quick motion, the root coming down to impale the monster through the chest.

"Nice work!" Cathillian called out as he returned the root to the ground.

He gently kneeled down, touching another root that belonged to that very tree. Arryn knew that he was thanking it for coming to his aid.

"Any idea where Chaos went?" Arryn asked.

Another screech ripped through the sky, and Arryn knew Echo wasn't just announcing herself. She was warning them.

There was another monstrous growl coming from the east as another came from the west, closing in on them. Arryn watched in horror as two more lycanthropes, each one bigger than the first, ran toward them.

Arryn looked to the sky as she heard Echo once again make herself known. She dove from the sky at an impossibly high speed, aiming herself directly at the beast coming from the west.

Arryn's eyes widened as she watched Echo dodge the large, clawed hands of the lycanthrope, her long, sharp talons ripping the monster's eyes from their sockets.

In Arryn's amazement, she had completely lost track of what was happening around her. A large branch snapped under the heavy foot of another one as it approached from the east, capturing her attention. She turned just in time to see it jump for her.

She dropped her bow to the ground, her eyes turning black just before arcing her hands over her chest and thrusting them forward. Two fireballs appeared, flying forward to hit the beast in the chest, sending it tumbling back a few feet. Adrenaline pumped through her veins, her heart racing in her chest as she thought about what to do.

She heard scuffling and growling to her left, and knew Cathillian was battling with another one. She wasn't sure if it was the same one Echo had attacked, but she assumed it wasn't because it had been blinded. She was too terrified to pull her eyes away to find out.

"Cathillian!" Arryn cried out.

"I'm fine! Focus on yourself," he grunted in reply. "Stay calm!"

That was certainly easier said than done. All she could think about right then was watching her mother skillfully take down one of these damnable creatures. She'd never known them to travel in packs. But clearly, they did.

Arryn quickly kicked off her boots, her bare feet touching the earth below. She immediately felt the connection to nature around her and focused as hard as she could.

Her eyes once again turned black, the irises a dark green as she wielded both types of magic. She once again arced her arms over her chest pulling them away, another fireball in each hand.

Through her feet, she willed the vines growing along the ground to move. The magic was still new to her, and her fireballs were weakening her faster than she'd like to admit.

At that moment, she wished that she had listened to Cathillian that day in the river. That she would have fought her fatigue from the Versuch and learned how to recycle nature's energy to increase the amount of power she could use.

That would've been a really good lesson to have had—even if it didn't grant a lot more power, it would have given her a few minutes longer.

The creature ran forward, and Arryn once again threw fireballs at him, each one hitting him in the chest. The beast howled in anger, his snarl growing, and his growls getting louder. She took a step forward, lifting her hands, praying to the Matriarch and Patriarch that nature would do her bidding.

The beast ran at her again, not staying down for long. Her head began to swim, dizziness taking her from the amount of strength it was taking to create the magic that she had used.

The vines wouldn't respond to her like she'd hoped, and she had no idea if she would be able to take the lycanthrope down. Arryn could still hear Cathillian battling and knew he wouldn't be able to save her.

Thundering hooves echoed through the forest, and Arryn looked over the head of the beast to see Chaos stopping, rising up on his hind legs as he let loose a loud cry of his own. The lycanthrope stopped and turned his attention to the oversized threat behind him.

Chaos turned and kicked the beast hard in the chest with his hind legs, sending him several feet back and smashing into a tree. Arryn's jaw dropped as she watched Chaos trot over to him, lift up on his hind legs, and drop hard onto its body.

The creature howled in pain as it fell over to its side, Chaos then trotted over and lifted one of his massive hooves before bringing it down hard on its head, smashing it into the ground. Chaos ran past Arryn, and she followed him with her eyes as he went for the one whose eyes Echo had taken.

Kicking with his front hooves, Chaos knocked him down to the ground before repeating what he done to the other one.

Arryn heard grunting and looked over to find Cathillian with his sword doing his best to battle off the beast. She wasn't sure how long he'd been fighting with it, but it was obvious that he was tiring.

She looked down to the ground, seeing her bow next to her legs. She grabbed it, nocking another arrow. She was one of the best bowmen in the entire tribe. It didn't ever take long for her to aim, and she rarely missed.

She didn't this time either.

Arryn let loose the arrow, the beast distracted by Cathillian and his sword. The arrow pierced through the throat of the lycanthrope before she nocked another one and let loose again. This time, hitting it in the leg closest to her. It dropped down to its knees, and Cathillian swung his sword, taking his head clean off.

Arryn fell to the ground, her jaw slack and her eyes wide as she caught her breath. She looked up to Cathillian and saw that he had also collapsed to the ground. "Are you OK?" she asked. "I'm sorry it took me so long. I wasn't able to take him by myself."

"I wasn't doing much better," he responded breathlessly. "You did great. *We* did great. All four of us. Not Maia, though. Bad horsey."

Arryn nodded. "I don't know what we would've done without them. When we come back from Arcadia, I'm bringing Chaos back the biggest damn bag of apples he's ever seen."

"And I'm going to buy Echo the biggest, smelliest fish she's ever seen," Cathillian said between breaths.

Arryn turned her eyes to Cathillian; it was all she had energy for. "Buy it with what? You have no money."

"With my good looks, of course," he replied. "They've gotta count for something. And if not, there's always *your* good looks."

"Did you just say you're gonna pimp me out?"

There was a laugh as Cathillian tried to sit up, but he fell back again and just accepted his place on the ground. "Well, we're gonna have to make money *somehow*."

"I'm too snarky to be a whore. I won't make any money when I tell 'em I've seen bigger dicks on chipmunks. You're full of shit, and you're high maintenance. All the best prostitutes are. Not to mention you'll be exotic with those big, dopey ears of yours. You have to be the whore."

"I'm totally OK with this," he laughed. "Now, we just need to find some women willing to pay. I'm sure that won't be too hard once they see me."

Arryn laughed. "Women? Oh, you're *so* funny sometimes. Women don't buy prostitutes in Arcadia, princess."

"Well, then who the hell were you planning to sell me to?"

Arryn pointedly turned her head to fully look in his direction as she gave a devious smile. He lifted his head enough to make eye contact with her.

"You—are a monster. You're gonna get it as soon as I have the energy to stand," Cathillian said.

Arryn sighed. "No, princess. Remember? We just established that *you* are the one that's gonna be getting it. Now, get up off your ass. We need to get out of here before anything else attacks."

Cathillian groaned. "Good point. I need to find Maia anyway. I think she ran off."

"Look at us," Arryn said. "Not even a few hours into our journey, and we've already been through one battle *and* came up with a business plan. A rather solid business plan at that. You do have that luscious blonde hair. I really think this is a sign of good things to come. What'll you call yourself? I bet I can help name you."

"I think this is a sign that only one of us is gonna make it to Arcadia. And it's not gonna be you."

Arryn laughed as she stumbled over to Chaos who was already kneeling for her to climb on.

She was glad, because she didn't have nearly the strength that it required to climb. She'd hoped they wouldn't need to stop so soon for rest, but it was obvious that they were going to have to stop far sooner than anticipated. All of them needed a lot of rest after that.

SEVENTEEN

melia climbed the steps that led to the Dean's office where she hoped to find Talia. Marie and Samuel had just left her office, having told her about an incredible plan to clean up the site of the old factory.

From there, they could rebuild once they had enough materials. With the help of enough magicians, anything could be possible.

They discussed the possibility of clearing out the area and building something small for the time being. Later, they could add on, expanding the factory as funds came in and materials were more readily available.

While Amelia wasn't the biggest fan of pulling students out of class, especially after all that had happened before, she was a fan of progression. Of people not starving. And of bringing money back into the city.

Finally reaching the Dean's door, she knocked. It only took a moment for Talia's voice to call for Amelia to come in.

"Ah, Chancellor," Talia said. "It's so lovely to see you. What can I do for you?"

Amelia was all smiles as she spoke. "Actually, I come with great news, though, there is a bit of bad. I know, I'm getting terrible about this. As before, the good news first. It seems that Marie has found some help with cleaning up the factory site. There was one rearick in particular with some pretty good ideas. If we put those in action, we could see some real results in no time."

Talia smiled, her eyes wide. "Really? That's fantastic! As good as it is, I'm assuming you didn't come here just to tell me the good and bad news, though. So, what is it that I can do to help?"

"Well," Amelia started, "some help from magicians would be fantastic. I was hesitant at first, because of Adrien's *special* program, but I know it's the right thing to do. I'd like to take a few of the best students and teachers to the factory site to help sort through the debris and repurpose some of it. With help, we could separate the glass, sift through it, melt it down, and make new windows while other laborers sorted through the wood and metal. We're thinking about a week will help a lot. What do you say?"

Talia looked thoughtful for a moment before getting excited again. "Actually, I think that's a brilliant idea. In fact, if you allow it, I might leave for that week. I think I can be of some significant help."

"Leaving? Where would you want to go?" Amelia asked.

"I have a lot of friends and acquaintances near Cella," Talia replied. "I bet I could get us all kinds of volunteers or resources. Maybe both. They need us. If they want to continue their rich lives, it would be in their best interest to assist us. And I know a group of people that might just do it. But it'll take a few days to talk to them and come back. Would that be possible?"

Amelia was overjoyed at her suggestion. The thought of others using their own pull to recruit from other places was wonderful. With the right team, anything was possible. "Yes! I think that's a great idea. If there's anything you need from me, please don't hesitate to ask. I'll do whatever I can to help."

"Thank you. What's the bad news?" Talia asked while fidgeting with some papers on her desk.

"First of all, there's still been no word on Amos. It's looking more and more like he was taken." There was a sigh as she shook her head. "I have no idea what's happening there, or more importantly—*why*—but we have to find him. That sadness aside, there was an attack at the eastern border of the valley. By the Madlands."

"The remnant?" Talia asked.

Amelia nodded. "Yes. A dozen or so, they said. A lot of our men have been logging there to build homes for the nobles that fled the city. Luckily, everyone survived. Though, more than a few were on death's door. They managed to get them back here in time to be properly cared for."

"How terrible. Are they doing better now?"

"They are. I'm sure I'll have more later. People are worried. They keep saying they hope those remnant don't come this way. I understand the concern. Evil like that..." Amelia shook her head. "They're terrible creatures. Mindless beasts that only want to destroy everything around them. Still, they know we have a large army. They wouldn't be stupid enough to come here. Mindless or not."

"Are they? Mindless?" Talia asked, sliding the papers to the edge of the desk.

"From what I heard, they're capable of communicating—talking and even coordinating plans. Only they're short-sighted. Impatient. They only want death and chaos. So, I suppose they aren't *truly* mindless. Still… our people don't need to worry about the possibility of them coming this way."

"Indeed. Please update me if you find out anything else."

Amelia stood and turned toward the door to leave, but stopped. She turned back to Talia, a large smile on her face. "With all this excitement, good and bad, I completely forgot the other good reason I came," she said.

"Oh?"

"I heard you've implemented a counseling project with students. I just wanted you to know I think it's a brilliant idea. The initiative you've taken since being here is nothing shy of phenomenal. I can't tell you how excited I am to have you on board. You've been a great asset. We're lucky to have you."

"Thank you, Chancellor," Talia said. "I do appreciate that. These students are the future of the city. We have to give them the best shot we can. I'm hoping to get more kids and even adults involved soon."

Amelia nodded. "That's great. I really appreciate the extra steps you're taking. It really is a huge help to me. In a couple months, it'll be like a brand-new city. Everything will be flourishing. At the very least, it'll be well on its way."

Talia smiled. "Oh, yes. The city will certainly see some *big* changes in the next couple months. Some of the biggest changes they've ever seen."

Arryn and Cathillian had been traveling for two days, and they'd only stopped long enough for sleep and food, mostly for Chaos. As the second day came to a close, they neared the edge of the woods just west of the city. It wouldn't be long before they would arrive at the Arcadian gate.

Cathillian was a bit worried about what Arryn's expectations might be. It seemed she was overly anxious, and he didn't want her to be discouraged if things weren't what she'd been hoping for. More than that, he was worried about what she would find out about her father.

Other than Elysia and the Chieftain, Arryn was the strongest person he'd ever met. She could handle just about anything, but he prayed that if she discovered the worst, she'd use it as a way to better herself.

"Not much longer," Arryn said. "I can't believe I'm going back home."

"Just keep an open mind and remember that everything's going to be totally different. Try to remind yourself it's something different. The people will be different, the friends that you had will have all grown up, some of them may have even lost their lives in battle or left the city afterward. A lot might have happened in your absence. Just keep an open mind, and you'll do fine."

"I know you're worried," Arryn said, "but I'll be fine. I know everything's gonna be different, but I'm ready. For the first time in my life, I'm ready. Just try and relax. This'll be fun for you. Just think of all the trouble you can get into in the city."

Cathillian hadn't even had a chance to make a smartass retort before he heard the light gasp from Arryn as the large city came into view. It was hard to make out details, but they could see the outlines of the buildings and the tall walls from that distance.

Cathillian knew if he looked over, Arryn would have a look of excitement and wonder on her face.

"There it is." Arryn's voice was barely above a whisper, and Cathillian could hear what sounded like tears in her voice.

"Well, what are we waiting for?" Cathillian asked. "Let's get you home. See what home looks like."

Arryn nodded and squeezed Chaos' side with her feet, sending him into a full run. The massive horse moved faster than any other she had ever ridden.

The occasional screech filled the air right along with the sound of powerful wings slicing through the wind as Echo played in flight. She flew in circles, diving down and recovering at the last moment before gliding back into the sky.

As they reached the main road, she pulled back on Chaos' reins, slowing him down to a brisk walk. They approached the front gate to the city, and four guards stepped away from the gates to meet them. Arryn slowed Chaos down to a stop several yards away from the men. A tall man with dark hair and a beard approached.

"Hello there," he said. "What can we do for ya?"

"Hey," Arryn said. "My name is Arryn. I lived here as a child. This is the first time I've been back in ten years. I heard things have changed; is this true?"

The guard smiled and stepped forward. "My name is Ken," he said, pride resonating from his voice. "I grew up in the Boulevard, and that's where I stayed until the ol' bastard was killed. He didn't deserve the title. The new Chancellor, Amelia, is a badass. She helped free the city and pulled a lot of us from the Boulevard and gave us jobs. So, to answer your question, yes. Things've changed."

Arryn couldn't help but smile. Ken's pride was intoxicating. She was happy for him, happy for all the people whose lives had been positively affected.

"You have no idea how happy that makes me. I can't wait to see it for myself," she said.

Ken smiled. "I'd be happy to let ya through so ya can. But first, I need some kind of proof you're an Arcadian. You don't look like an Arcadian to me, even one that's been gone ten years." He nodded toward Cathillian. "He sure as hell don't look like no Arcadian I ever seen."

"I don't have documentation of any kind," she said. "I look like this because I've spent the last decade living in the Dark Forest. Ever heard of a druid? This pointy-eared bastard to my right happens to be one."

Ken's eyes widened a bit as he looked back over to Cathillian. He took a step back, his grip tightening on his magitech weapon.

His gaze lingered for a few before he looked back to Arryn and nodded. "I understand and respect that, but I hope you understand we have a job to do. You seem kind enough, so I'll accompany you in. We'll go to the guards' quarters and look into the story you gave. That sound acceptable to you?"

Arryn thought it over. A battle had recently been fought there. She shouldn't have expected them to be any less than cautious. They probably would be for some time.

"Of course," Arryn said. "I don't trust you any more than you trust me, no offense."

He smiled. "None taken, ma'am."

"I honestly have no idea how much luck you'll have looking into my story, but hopefully we can find something. There must be someone around here that would remember me or my parents. Christopher and Elayne."

He nodded and gave a reassuring smile. "Follow me, and we'll get ya taken care of."

The gates opened, and Arryn saw inside. Her eyes fell to the familiar, cobblestone road, and all the buildings inside. She saw businesses and houses, and farther off in the distance, she saw the outline of the Academy. It stood tall and beautiful above everything else. She couldn't wait to get started.

EIGHTEEN

As *Amelia exited Talia's office,* she was startled by a guard standing in the hall. "Yes? What's wrong?"

"We have two people in the guard's quarters, and we ain't really sure what we should do. The guy clearly ain't from around here. Says he's a druid. If I didn't know any better, I'd say he was. Pointy ears and everything."

"A druid? Seriously? And what about the girl?" Amelia asked. A smile spread on her face as she thought of Laurel, the druid that had joined the fight against Adrien.

"Said her name's Arryn, and she lived here ten years ago. Her father worked for Adrien at some point, and the old Chancellor had him taken and her mother killed. You should definitely come hear this. She seems OK, nice enough, I guess. But we just wanted to be safe, never seen her around before. Especially the pointy-eared fella."

Amelia quickly followed the guard, wondering what on earth could be happening and who could have just shown up to Arcadia. She'd only known one druid—Laurel.

The druids had refused to help Arcadia, so she couldn't imagine why they'd want to show up now, but she intended to find out.

When Amelia arrived at the guard's quarters, she had no idea what to expect. When Ezekiel had returned and told them the people of the Dark Forest would offer no help, she wasn't quite sure how to feel about them. But Laurel had done quite a bit to salve any negative feelings she'd had towards the druids.

What could a druid possibly want, and what on earth would one be doing with an Arcadian girl?

She was intrigued to meet whoever waited for her and get to the bottom of it. If they were friendly visitors, then it couldn't have come at a better time.

Who better to have around than a druid when the city was in such need for food and resources? But they would be welcomed into the city no matter what as long as their intentions were pure.

As she opened the door to the guard's quarters, she was taken aback by the beautiful, porcelain skinned girl sitting before her. Raven black hair, medium height, and her body was built in such a way that Amelia knew the girl had trained every day for many years.

Next to her stood a tall man that stunned her to silence just as his traveling companion had. Long blonde hair, green eyes, and a body that was built for battle. As she looked him over, she saw his ears extending slightly out through his hair, coming to subtle points.

He was a warrior. There was no doubt in her mind. She imagined he would be able to easily take out any guard that stood in his way if he chose to.

But he hadn't.

He didn't even look annoyed. He just stood there, silently towering over everyone in the room in height and in confidence, taking a protective role over his young, Arcadian druid friend.

"Hello, I'm Amelia," she said, giving what she hoped was a sincere smile. While she was worried about their intentions, she also wanted to be diplomatic. "I apologize for the formalities, but I'm sure the guards were kind enough to explain it—I hope."

"Yes, they did," Cathillian said with a nod. "They've been surprisingly kind. Much nicer than I expected. I'm Cathillian."

Arryn gave a quick wave. "I'm Arryn."

Amelia sighed with relief. Unable to help herself, Amelia cleared her mind and slipped into the young woman's mind. It was wide open for her, even with Amelia being new to the world of mystical magic.

The young woman was nervous about being back in the city. From what Amelia could see, her intentions were pure. Due to her nervousness, her thoughts kept wildly switching from images of who Amelia imagined was her parents to Adrien to the Academy.

There would be no way to make sense of it except to speak to her directly.

"I'm glad. So, what can I do for you?" She turned to Arryn. "I understand you're originally from here. Is that right?"

"Yep. I lived here until I was nine," Arryn replied flatly. She'd already been over everything with the guards. "I made a promise to my mom that I'd come back to Arcadia when I was ready. The battle's over, and Adrien is dead, otherwise I never would've spoken a word to them about my past."

Amelia took a deep breath, exhaling in relief as she stepped forward. "I see. Well, I assure you the city isn't the one you left. I don't know if you came seeking vengeance for your family, but like you said, Adrien is long gone, and I'm nothing like him. You'll never have anything to fear from me—unless I'm given reason."

Arryn nodded. "I can tell just by looking in your eyes that you're nothing like Adrien. You actually have a soul. Plus, sitting here talking to the guards, I've learned you're the one that is partly responsible for the city being freed. So, no. I can promise you as long as you stay a good person, you'll never be *given reason* from me."

Amelia smiled. The girl had fire in her, not unlike another young woman that she knew. With everything going on in the search for Doyle, Amos, and all things regarding the economy and wellbeing of the city, it made Amelia happy to see someone with hope.

"Then it seems you and I have absolutely nothing to fear from one another." Amelia's smile grew. "And if I'm completely honest, I can't tell you how excited I am to have druids in the city."

"We saw some of the destruction when we came in," Cathillian said. "It looks like most of the city on the other side is destroyed."

Amelia nodded. "Unfortunately, that's true. That was once the Boulevard, where Adrien more or less forced the less fortunate to live, secluded from everyone else. Those people are struggling now, but once we get those houses rebuilt, they'll all have their own water and the ability to bathe their children. As for healing the city, I'd like to talk with you a bit about your magic and what it can do."

"That's a very noble cause," Cathillian said. "As for the magic, my family is pretty strong with nature magic."

Arryn rolled her eyes. "For once in his miserable life, he's being modest. I'm sure you can't see it, but this is my shocked face right now. Once you get to know him, you'll be quite shocked, too. Anyway, by *his family*, he means that he's the grandson of the Chieftain."

Amelia couldn't believe what she'd just been told. Someone like him could come in very handy. "Really? You must be *really* good with magic."

He smiled. "I know my way around the beauty in nature, beauty not unlike your own."

Arryn sighed heavily. "Oh, hell. *And...* he's back, everyone," Arryn chimed in. She elbowed him in the side. "Get to the point before she lights you on fire for good measure."

Amelia laughed at the two. She could tell they were great friends, even if they argued quite a bit.

Cathillian winked at Arryn before turning back to Amelia, his face a bit more serious. "If you don't mind, I'd like to look around the city. I can't guarantee that I'd be able to help, but Arryn's very passionate about the city. And if its lovely Chancellor is, too, then I see no reason why I wouldn't be able to at least try."

Amelia had no idea what to say. Apparently, neither did his companion, who looked to him with wide eyes.

"Really?" Arryn asked. "You would do that?"

"Aw, do you feel bad now? After that hard time you just gave me?" Arryn's eyes narrowed, and he laughed. "Like I said, I'm not gonna promise anything. I know at least one Arcadian that isn't half bad, so if there's life in the city that's honorable, and they're suffering, then it's our duty to help 'em."

Amelia was moved by his words. Coming from a druid, it meant even more. Outside of the city, Arcadians were greatly disliked. She'd learned that from random travelers who had no other choice but to come through the city for shelter or food.

The Arcadians had spent a lifetime treating everyone else that was lower than them like trash. To some of the wealthiest nobles, that was literally everyone.

Physical magic was also more destructive than the rest. So, the Arcadian's looked like slothy, rude, arrogant, harbingers of chaotic magic. Magic that was only taught to people rich enough to afford to learn in the Academy, and anyone less than that was killed for using it.

"Arryn," Amelia said. "What did you have planned for yourself here in the city?"

Arryn stood and stretched, her body more than likely still sore from riding on the back of a large horse for two days. Amelia had seen the horse she'd rode in on. He was a beautiful creature, but the biggest horse she'd ever seen.

"My goal was to come back and look for my father. I don't know if he's alive or dead, but I know he suffered. It's hard to say what I'll find. He might've died the night we escaped. Maybe he was taken into custody and tortured until he took his last breath. He might even be alive somewhere. I don't have a clue, but I intend to find him, even if it's only his memory. I need to know what happened."

Amelia nodded, coming to understand more of the images she saw when peering into Arryn's thoughts. "I think I can help you with that. I have one person in custody that might be able to shed light on it, and I'm currently hunting another one down. Adrien's right-hand man. Doyle. He escaped, and we need to find him before he causes any trouble. If we catch him, we might be able to get some answers out of him for you."

Amelia struggled to talk and look more into Arryn's head, but it became painfully obvious that Arryn could feel it. The young woman's brows furrowed as her eyes closed. She rubbed at her temples and forehead where Amelia knew the buzzing would be the worst for someone that was sensitive to the sensation.

Satisfied that she hadn't found anything other than what she'd been told, Amelia pulled back and continued. "I can't guarantee answers that'll lead anywhere, but I'm sure we can find someone around here that knew your father, or might know what could've happened. What do you plan to do in the meantime? You can't possibly plan to spend every moment of everyday searching—or do you?"

"Actually," Arryn replied. "I want to join the Academy. It was my parents dream that I would attend there when I was old enough—well, once I got strong enough to recruit an army and take back the city, of course. But since that's already done, I can just enjoy it the way they'd always wanted."

"Wonderful!" Amelia said. "I was the Dean of Students before the revolution. It was a position I took great pride in. We can definitely make that happen. Out of curiosity, do you remember any of your physical magic?"

Arryn's eyes suddenly turned black, as she arced her hands over her chest and then pulled away, a small fireball in each one.

They weren't much bigger than a grown man's fist, but they were there, and they were strong for their size. Amelia could tell.

The blackness faded from Arryn's eyes as she clenched her fists, extinguishing the fire in each one.

"My mother was one of the most powerful magic users in the city, at least that's what my father told me. That's why they wanted so badly to be a part of the rebellion. My mother and father taught me magic up until I was nine years old. But I've never learned how to grow past what I'd learned from them without a teacher. So, the things that I *did* know got stronger, though they never got any bigger."

"So, what you're saying," Cathillian said, pointing a finger at Arryn, "is that you have super small balls, but they're very mighty."

Without hesitation, Arryn smiled and looked over at her companion. "They're still bigger than yours. At least I *have* some."

Cathillian gasped, placing his hand over his heart to feign offense. "Well, I *never*…"

Amelia laughed at the two, enjoying the back and forth between them. Listening to them reminded her of Parker and Hannah—her old compatriots who had left after the revolution. "OK, Arryn. I want you to do a quick training exercise. Can you do that?"

Arryn was hesitant at first, but after Cathillian gave a nod of encouragement, she acquiesced. "Sure. Why not?"

Amelia stepped forward, taking Arryn's hands in her own. She turned Arryn's hands over so her palms faced up. "I know you've felt it, but I've been using mystical magic on you. Looking through your mind for signs of lying. I apologize, but I felt it was necessary."

There was a flash of confusion on the girl's face, but then it disappeared. "So, *that's* what that was. I should be pissed, but if I had that ability, I'd do the same before letting you in the Dark Forest. So, I understand."

Amelia smiled. "Great! Again, I'm sorry. It's impressive you could feel it, though. That's good. No one good *or* bad can ever get in your head without you knowing about it. OK, now that I've come clean, I'm going to use the same magic to guide you. Make sure you don't make any dangerous mistakes. Now, close your eyes," Amelia said.

Arryn did as she was asked, closing her eyes and exhaling. Amelia focused on Arryn's mind to feel for her emotions.

"I want you to empty your mind. Your father. Your mother. Adrien. All those years in the city. *None* of it exists. *You* are all that exists. The air that you breathe. The heat in this room. Feel the warm air around your hands. Even feel the warmth in my skin as it touches you. Focus on that heat."

Amelia knew from personal experience with the students from the Boulevard that what she was about to do was risky. Using such volatile emotion to fuel power was dangerous, but the girl had heart.

It was worth it to try, and she knew that she'd be able to control any downfall if anything bad happened. Amelia further cleared her own mind as she stared at the girl, hoping that she wouldn't need to take any action, but preparing in case.

"I want you to feel your physical magic and push it to your hands. When you feel it, shape it. And let it go. Conjure another fireball."

Arryn pulled her hands away, crossing them over her chest before she pushed them out to her sides, a fireball appearing in each one.

Again, they were small, but they were more powerful than the ones from before, as evident by the core color, an almost brilliant blue. The core heat was intense, but very small.

She'd never seen a spark so hot before. Most of the fireballs she'd ever seen were red and orange, though there were a few with the hint of blue at its core. Amelia took a deep breath, steadying herself.

"Now, magic is passion. When you feel the most intense, be it fear, rage, or desire to thrive, your magic will grow stronger. So, with your clear mind, I want you to gradually think about the night your mother died."

"Uh," Cathillian said. "This probably isn't the wisest idea. I've seen what happens when someone brings up her parents. It's very scary."

Amelia nodded. "Trust me, I've known someone just like that. That's why I'm choosing my words carefully." She turned her attention back to Arryn. "Were you there when she died?"

She watched as Arryn's brows furrowed, her nose flaring a bit.

Taking another cautious breath, Amelia continued pushing. "You were so young. Focus on that fear that you felt. Knowing what was about to happen. If you held a fireball that moment, one that could have saved her, how strong would it have been?"

At that moment, the blue sparks in Arryn's fireballs exploded, both of them turning a brilliant blue, and their core a bright white.

Amelia's hands were still close as a precaution, but she quickly yanked her hands back, a pain-filled hiss escaping her. She had no idea how Arryn could possibly hold that much heat.

"Holy shit," Cathillian gasped, taking a step back as shock rolled across his face.

"Arryn," Amelia said. "Open your eyes."

Arryn opened her eyes slowly, and then opened them wider. They were blacker than black, a deep obsidian. Amelia hadn't realized that color went so dark until that moment. Amelia could see the disbelief on Arryn's face.

"How?" Arryn asked.

"That's a lot of power you're using," Amelia said. "You might want to extinguish those. You don't want to waste your energy."

She watched as Arryn's eyes faded back to their original color, the fireballs disappearing as she did.

Arryn looked down at her hands a moment longer, seemingly just as amazed as Amelia. "How did I do that?"

Amelia shook her head, smiling. She felt intense pride in the girl, and she had no idea why. She barely knew her. But for some reason, she felt almost responsible for her. Like she was a lost child of Arcadia, one that she could've helped, but hadn't—yet. She sure as hell would now.

"I just wanted to teach you how to conjure a larger fireball. I thought the fireballs would get bigger, but they didn't. At least not much. They sure as hell got stronger, though."

"I don't know what to say," Arryn said, her eyes still wide.

"Say that you'll come to the Academy!' Amelia excitedly said. "We need someone strong like you. In fact, if you have even a fraction of that strength in nature magic, I'd love to have you and your friend here teach. It would give you guys some extra money to live on and bring excitement. I admit, the pay isn't the best, but it's there. I think it would do our students some good to learn something as pure as nature magic. What do you say?"

Cathillian laughed. "No offense, lady. I really appreciate the offer. But I'm not exactly what one would call 'good' in a structured environment. How I got this far as a warrior, I'll never know. It was definitely a lot of ass kicking. Not *me* kicking ass, but them kicking mine. I was quite the little bastard. All these years later, and all this sexiness, and I'm still just as free-spirited."

Arryn shook her head and sighed heavily as she looked at Cathillian. "I don't even know how to respond to that."

She turned to Amelia. "Obviously, I'm not as good at nature magic as he is. However, I have no money. Druids have no need for it. So, I'd be happy to teach the fundamentals of nature magic. Besides, anything they need to learn, I mastered years ago. It's the fancy shit I still can't figure out, but that's why I have my narcissistic friend here."

"And I'll just do what I do best," Cathillian said. "Wander around and explore. Besides, kinda curious to see what kind of girls they have in this place."

Arryn motioned to Cathillian as she kept her eyes on Amelia. "If you ordered your guards to kick the crap out of him, I *totally* wouldn't hold it against you. I promise I'll just look the other way. We can still be friends."

Amelia laughed hard at the girl's humor. She already liked Arryn and Cathillian and was excited to get to know them better. Given everything she'd seen in her mind and in her personality, she would be great to have around the city.

"Well, you'll probably be wanting to get settled in and check out the city. As I said, it's not much to look at right now. We have a lot to rebuild. But, I'm always up for ideas. If you ever need anything, you can come to me. And if you ever have any ideas, anything at all that might better the city, don't hesitate. I can use all the help I can get."

Arryn nodded. "Absolutely. I may not have been able to take part in the rebellion, but I can at least take part in the rebuild. Oh, and about that mental magic thing... You mentioned bad people being able to do it. Is there a way to keep them out?"

Amelia nodded. "I'm happy to hear the excitement about the rebuild! As for the mental stuff, I only know a little. There's a way to close your mind to others. It'll look suspicious to anyone—like me—who has good intentions, but it'll keep you safe from anyone bad."

"That's awesome! I've heard of that magic, but didn't really know anything about it. Maybe you can show me some time," Arryn said, smiling.

Amelia returned the smile with one of her own. "I can do that. Now, let me take you to your new home. I think you'll find it rather agreeable. During the process of putting our rebellion together, my friends and I spent quite a lot of time in the house. As far as I'm concerned, I can't think of anyone better to put in there."

Arryn smiled. "A house used for chaos? Yeah, I think that sounds like home."

NINETEEN

Amos had fallen asleep on the cold, stone floor since Talia's last visit. Between having been suspended for almost a whole day every day since she'd taken him as well as being tortured, he welcomed being chained to the base of the post and allowed sleep on the floor.

After all he'd been through, it was almost kind of her.

He had large burns across his back where she'd used her fire against him several times. Not quite badly enough to blister and potentially allow it to get infected and kill him, but certainly bad enough to make him scream in pain.

He enjoyed the cold stones on his raw back. It was the only relief he had, even though it hurt as badly as it helped.

The door opened, waking Amos with a jolt. It closed again, and his breaths increased as he listened for the footsteps.

Click.

Click.

Click.

Click.

Every step was incredibly slow. The pattern was different, though the sound was the same. He strained his eyes to focus in the low light, and he could see her there.

Staring at him.

Watching him without saying a word.

Her eyes were narrowed, her arms crossed over her chest as she mulled something over in her mind. It was all over her face. The demon-like woman had a lot to think about, and it was all about him.

"Talia," he said, his voice a whisper. "You've come back."

She nodded at first, still not saying a word as her eyes bore into his. "I did."

Her voice was different, the tone indifferent, distant even. She seemed lost in thought, but also like she couldn't care less.

"Are you here for another *talk*?" he asked, unable to stop the sound of hatred from leaking through, though he wished he had.

"No."

No. If she wasn't there to talk, then what *was* she there for? He didn't like that idea. The whole time he'd been there, he'd not been shy about saying he'd rather die than help her. In those few days, he hadn't managed to give her much of anything, but what little he had, she seemed happy enough with.

It had only been after she seared his back that he'd screamed out that Jackson had a group of people—students and teachers alike—that hated the Boulevard families and wanted them gone.

They may have been hateful people, but they were harmless enough. Rudeness was different than violence. He couldn't imagine what she planned to do, but from the look on her face at that moment, her current plans were far more absolute and far more threatening to him.

He didn't want to die.

Chills began at the follicles of his hair, jolting through his temples and then running down his spine to fan out over the rest of his body. In his situation, he'd gotten to know her mannerisms very well. Talia was not acting like herself.

"If you didn't come to talk, then what did you come for?" he asked, doing his best to sound at least a little confident. He sure as hell didn't feel it.

"I have a little trip that I have to go on. I'll be gone for a few days."

There was a pregnant pause in the air as she still stood there, staring him down. He swallowed hard.

"And?" he asked, trying to keep his breathing under control. "What does that mean for me?"

"Well, if I don't feed and water my pet, he'll probably die on me. Wouldn't you say?" Her tone was now blunt, cold. During her visits before, she'd been so animated, having delighted in watching him squirm with his fear of her, but now... Now, she was something else entirely.

"I would," he said, swallowing hard again. He began silently praying to the Matriarch that she would deliver him safely—somewhere... *anywhere*. Just away from Talia.

"Exactly." She sighed, placing her hands on her hips. "The question is how to do it. I suppose I should stop thinking about it and ask *you*..." She made her way over to him, kneeling by his side. She gently brushed her fingers across his face as her expression turned soft, her voice following suit. "How would you like for me to end your miserable existence here, Amos?"

There was no way around it. He knew there was no escaping. Both his arms and legs were bound, and he was far too weak to fight. He'd wasted too much energy fighting while she was gone, and she had *too* much skill in subduing someone with rope and chains.

"Please, just let me go. I'll leave Arcadia. I'll take my family and go," he pleaded.

She shook her head. "I'm sorry. I need you. I *need* you to die. You see, I have to be there for everyone. I have a part to play, and I can't do that without tragedy."

"You're killing me so you can be the hero when someone finds my body in some ditch? Your father was fucking crazy, lady—but I ain't *never* met anyone like you."

She smiled, running a gentle finger down his cheek again. "That's sweet of you to say. And yes, that's the idea. Also, it sets me up for later. See, if everyone's focusing on the fear of a maniac on the loose, they'll turn to me for help. I'll be the last person in the world they'd think of."

She lifted the skirt of her dress, pulling a knife from a small sheathe strapped to her thigh.

"My father tried to run the world with blunt force. Not with intelligence. That's why he failed. I won't."

"There'll always be someone there. For every bully, there's someone bigger and badder than they are waiting to take 'em down. You'll meet a terrible end. Mark my words. When you do bad things, they come back to haunt you."

Her mouth turned up at the corner, but it was full of sarcasm. "Is that why you're here? Mr. Assistant Hero of the Boulevard? You believe that you did something *so* good and righteous, yet here you are. With me. About to die. And you want to preach to me about things coming back around? If you're so good and I'm so terrible, where's your good fortune? Hmm?"

Amos sat in silence, staring at the exaggerated curiousness in her expression. He had no answer. At that moment, he'd never felt quite so forsaken by the light—whatever that might have been. Still, he refused to allow himself to be lowered to her level.

"My good fortune is in my death," he said finally.

Her brows furrowed as she snickered. "What—*the fuck*—is that supposed to mean?"

It was his turn to smile then. "You caught me at a disadvantage and captured me. You spent days weakening me to the point that I have no hope of fighting you. I'm not strong enough to take you down—not while alive."

She laughed, placing a hand on his chest. "You sure as shit won't be doing anything while dead, kid. Hate to break it to ya."

"My death won't be enough for you. You're gonna need a constant distraction to do what you wanna do. You *will* kill again. Eventually, someone will prove themselves to be a *real* problem for you. Someone stronger than you. And it'll all start with me. They'll connect the pieces, and when they do, all fingers will point to *you*. Believe me—when that moment comes, it'll be this very conversation that you remember when you're facing down your own fate."

Something flashed across her face, her eyes momentarily widening, but as quick as it was there, it vanished.

"I can promise you that no one, especially me, will remember you in a week. They'll be far too excited about the growth of the city. I hope you enjoy death. Wherever you go, I hope you meet my father there. I'm sure he'd *love* to continue what I've started there in the afterlife. An eternity of misery so you'll never forget either of us. Father *or* daughter."

Talia sat up then, her hand a blur as it whooshed across him. It took a moment before he felt the sharp sting in his throat, very quickly followed by the blood flowing in every direction to fill his mouth, his lungs, and puddle onto the floor.

His vision began to blur as he twisted and turned, desperate to close the gaping wound she'd created with the knife in her hand.

With his last few moments of consciousness, he watched as she pulled the bloodied knife to her lips and lick the blood away. She smiled. "Hmm… just like before. Tastes like failure. Farewell, pet," she said just before his eyes closed for the final time.

Arryn hadn't been sure what to expect when the Chancellor had walked in, but she was pleasantly surprised. The guards had been very kind, much to her surprise as well. They weren't anything like what they used to be.

She wondered how many of those men had come from the Boulevard. No noble would be able to fill that position. Their bodies were weak from being spoiled, and their attitudes would have reflected it. No, those men were used to being bullied and worked.

It made them humble.

The new Chancellor had been much the same. Someone with a kind heart, but with a strong spine as well.

Once they realized they were safe in the city, Arryn and Cathillian quickly wrote a letter to Elysia and attached it to Chaos to let her know they'd arrived safely, though there had been some complications in the forest.

They didn't want to tell her, but knew if they didn't and she found the lycanthrope bodies, they'd be screwed. Cathillian wrote he'd send Echo back with a letter once a week to update her. They hoped that would be sufficient to keep her away.

As they walked across the city, Arryn took in the different streets. The Boulevard, as Cathillian had mentioned, was completely destroyed. There were mounds and mounds of debris piled up just outside of the Boulevard.

She could see men carrying things out as they walked past. She shook her head, wondering how they must feel.

Were they bitter? Did they hate their lives right then?

Or were they excited for the future as Amelia had seemed to be? It was hard to say. Their expressions were unreadable from that distance.

The noble quarter, as expected, was largely untouched. The Academy still stood in all its glory, and most of the buildings on this side seemed to be unfazed. There was some damage to a few of them, but it looked to be more by hand than by machine like the Boulevard.

When Amelia stopped in front of a massive house—which had belonged at one point to a noble named Lord Girard—Arryn couldn't believe her eyes. It was huge. Way bigger even than the house she'd lived in when she was a child.

She desperately wanted to go see that one, but she worried what she'd find. Would it be vacant, or would there be some noble asshole living there? Would there be a happy family there?

It was something she didn't want to think about right then. All she wanted was to get comfortable. She would go exploring tomorrow.

"So, what do you think?" Amelia asked. "Nice huh?"

Cathillian stared at the house with wide eyes and an open mouth. Arryn almost laughed at him, but she found his astonishment rather amusing.

She reached up and closed his jaw. "Never seen anything like this before, have you?" she asked.

Cathillian shook his head. "No. Never. I can't wait to see the inside. I don't even have a clue of what to expect."

Arryn smiled at Cathillian. His happiness pulled her away from the worry about her new journey inside the city walls, replacing it with something more fun. She had no idea what the house looked like inside, but she wanted nothing more than to show him around.

Being a noble house, she knew it would have a shower. One thing she sorely missed. She couldn't help but laugh while thinking about what he would say about that.

"Do you remember me making the joke that I was the only one of the two of us that had a shower?"

His eyes suddenly light lit up. "Holy shit. Do you think that they have one here?"

Arryn did laugh that time. "Yeah, I'm pretty sure they have a shower in there."

Amelia walked them across the threshold, and Cathillian nearly tripped over his feet when he saw the inside.

All the ornate, beautifully crafted materials on furniture and curtains. The carved and stained wood of the extravagant furniture. Craftsmanship on the wood surrounding the doors. And the natural light from windows that shone in. Along the walls, he saw the magitech sconces that delivered light to the room.

Arryn could see the wonder all over his face as he looked from one thing to the next.

"This is amazing," Cathillian said, his voice barely a whisper.

"Be careful, druid," Arryn said. "I'm beginning to think you're about to trade in the Dark Forest for some old, dead noble's house."

Cathillian looked at her incredulously. "I wouldn't go and say that, but I could sure as hell use a vacation. Adventure, right?"

"This is the first time you've ever been out of the Dark Forest?" Amelia asked.

Cathillian nodded. "Yep." He looked around more, slipping further into the living room. "I've never seen anything like this."

Arryn stepped forward. "Well, if you're this excited about the marvel of modern furniture, just wait till ya see how we cook food. I'll give you a hint, it's indoors."

"No way!" he said. "They cook inside? How does the house not burn down?"

Amelia laughed. "I needed this. I'm so glad the two of you came to Arcadia. I'm gonna make sure that you two are very welcome. Now, let me show you around. This place has more than enough room for the two of you, and if you have visitors at any point in time, there's more than enough for them, too."

They walked through the house, moving from room to room. Amelia and Arryn took turns explaining things to Cathillian as they went.

He was like a child, seeing everything for the first time. Amelia was kind and patient, while Arryn took a more humorous approach. Making fun of him as often as she could.

As expected, Cathillian was overwhelmed with the whole idea of the shower. He couldn't wait to try it out. Arryn wasn't sure if she was more excited by being back in the city, or watching Cathillian do the walk-through in the house. It certainly had its moments.

"So, this position at the Academy," Arryn said. "What would be required? My parents taught me *some* magic, of course. My father used to talk about how the mechanics of magic worked and how the engineers study it, but he never taught me specifics. If you're not looking for any help with that, then I'm sure I'll be OK."

Amelia smiled. "It won't be anything strenuous on your part. Just the fundamentals. People like you and my friend Hannah, the girl that led the revolution—you don't use mechanics. You guys use passion. Emotion. Before, that school was full of spineless, coldhearted, spoiled brats. We had no other choice but to teach mechanics. But I can tell you now it doesn't make for good magic."

"And you think things have changed?" Arryn asked. "Do you think they're capable of learning in any other way? My knowledge is one hundred percent attributed to the wonderful men and women I grew up with. So, I can't be a judge on how people learn. But if you want me to teach what I know, then they'd have to be receptive to it."

Amelia gave a sad smile. "Unfortunately, I think in the past, it would've been impossible. But the students that we have now, they've lost so much, and they've felt so much pain, I think they now know passion and emotion. I think with a teacher like you, they'll be surprised at what they can learn."

Arryn thought that over for a moment, taking in the complete and total change in her life in such a short time.

She'd gone from waking up every morning in the forest and knowing she'd be going to sleep there as well, to now standing back in her home city and being interviewed for a position at the Academy where her parents once wanted her to attend.

"It does seem rather strange that I should be a teacher when I'm not even sure that I'd be a good student. If what you say is true, and the school teaches the mechanics of everything, I'm not sure I'll learn the way that I have in past."

Amelia smiled. "Then you'll be happy to know that you're in good hands. Take those classes, learn fundamentals, learn about the other students. Take your time to get to know the staff, your peers, and the basics, and I'll be your tutor. This is a wonderful opportunity for you, Arryn. Not only for you, but for the city as well. What do you say?"

"I think you should," Cathillian said. "Your goal wasn't to come here and sit on your ass doing nothing. You came here because you wanted to make a difference. This is how you do it. You wanted to learn at the Academy. You wanted to affect change. This is the perfect move for you. I think you should do it."

Arryn sighed for a moment before nodding. "Alright then, I'll do it."

TWENTY

As soon as *Amelia was* out the door, Cathillian began running around the house like a toddler.

"What's this thing?" he asked, pointing to a magitech light on the wall.

Arryn laughed. "That's a magitech light," she said. "There's a small stone in there with power channeled into it. They're motion sensitive. When you walk out of the room or sit down for a while, they go off."

"Wow," he said. He darted across the room. "What's this thing called again?"

"That's a wood stove. It's used for heat. You put wood into it and light it on fire, and it pumps heat throughout the house."

"No shit? That's awesome." He ran into the kitchen then. "Ooh! Show me this thing!"

Arryn followed the sound of his excited voice into the kitchen and over by the sink. Without saying a word, she walked over and lifted a lever. Water immediately began to pour from the faucet. They'd told him during the tour what it did, but she had yet to demonstrate.

His eyes widened. "That's magic."

Arryn held up a single finger, motioning for him to wait just a moment. She moved the lever on the sink, triggering the magitech heating, and within a few moments, steam began to pour out. Once again, his excitement took over as he put his hands under the hot water.

"OK," he said. "I lied. *That* is magic."

She smiled. "Actually, yes, it is. You still have yet to see how the shower works."

"Yeah! I saw that in the tour," he said.

She laughed. "Yes, you saw it, but you didn't get in it. Come with me, you overgrown child. I'll help you get it started. I'd hate for you to burn your dick off."

He gave her a wicked smile and winked. "I bet you would."

She rolled her eyes and punched him in the arm. "You're gross. You could *almost* be cute if you didn't think so highly of yourself."

"So, what you're saying is you think I'm sexy."

She wanted to smack the smirk off his face. "Matriarch have mercy on you when I sacrifice you. I'd *have* to sacrifice you because there's no way in hell she could deal with you otherwise. Now, shut up and come with me."

She led him upstairs to the bathroom and showed him how to work the magitech shower. She helped him adjust the temperature to his liking, and then left him alone to get undressed and relax. It'd been years since she'd had a shower—a proper shower anyway.

Waterfalls and rivers was the best she'd had. He was lucky that she thought so highly of him. Otherwise, she would've gotten in first.

She made her way downstairs and to the front door before stepping outside to stand on the front porch. She looked out at the streets, taking in the scenery.

It had been a very long time since she'd seen anything like it, and she wasn't sure if she ever would again if she went back to the forest.

As she looked around, pulling her cloak tighter around her because of the chill in the air, she became overwhelmed with emotion. For the first time in a long time, she let the tears silently fall without trying to control them.

She smiled as she looked out over the city, *her* city. Thinking about how proud her parents would be to see it liberated. To see the nobles and the Boulevard families moving together and working together.

It would be getting dark soon, so it was too late to go exploring. She told Amelia that she wanted a couple days to settle in before she started at the Academy. Amelia told her to take her time.

Most classes were out this week because of the cleanup with the factory, so the timing was perfect. Perhaps she'd make a pit stop there, maybe even taking Cathillian with her to see if they could help.

As Arryn stood there, looking out into the city, several guards ran through. Arryn knew the guards didn't run anywhere without an emergency. She momentarily looked back through the front door, wondering if Cathillian would be OK on his own.

He's a big boy, she thought. *It's not like he actually is a child, he just acts like one.*

Finally, she decided to follow the guards and see what was happening. She took off down the street as fast as she could. It didn't take long for her to catch up, though she tried to keep enough distance between her and them so they didn't yell at her for pursuing.

She wound through the streets and followed the guards into what used to be the Boulevard, letting them run through and keeping distance. As she got closer, she heard voices.

"He ain't been dead long," a male voice said.

That certainly caught her attention. She could hear several voices, but couldn't see who they belonged to. The felled buildings were at all different levels of destruction, some standing taller than others and hiding the men that were talking.

"Arryn?" a familiar voice said from behind her. "What are you doing here?"

Arryn turned to see Amelia running up. "Hi! I-I'm sorry. I saw a bunch of guards running this way and followed. What's happening?"

Amelia's brows furrowed. "I was told that a body was found down here. I'm here to identify it."

"I'm sorry," Arryn said. "I thought I heard one of them say something about someone being dead."

"Chancellor!" a tall man with dark hair called out.

"On my way, Andrew. Just a moment!" Amelia called back. "Why don't you head home? There's nothing you can do here. Unfortunately, whoever it is has already died."

Arryn thought for a moment. "I might not be able to bring them back, but I might be able to tell you how long they've been dead."

"Really?" Amelia asked, her expression reflecting shock. "OK, then. Come with me."

Arryn followed Amelia, swallowing hard as she did. What the hell did she just volunteer to do? *Why* had she volunteered to do it?

She didn't really want to see a dead body, but she *did* want to help. If the Chancellor was being called away, it certainly hadn't been natural causes that killed them.

They rounded a semi-crumbled corner of a building and found a young man roughly Arryn's age lying dead in the rubble. His eyes were wide open, his body a sickly pale color.

Even though he was long gone, Arryn could still feel what was left of his energy lingering, though it was nearly gone. Sometimes it took several hours for it to disappear completely.

"Arryn," Amelia said softly. "Are you alright? You don't have to do this, you know."

Arryn cleared her throat, absentmindedly straightening her clothing. "It's fine. I can do it."

She stepped forward, the confused men taking a step back as the Chancellor ushered her through. Arryn then knelt by his side.

"His name is Amos," Amelia said. Arryn looked up to see that her eyes were a bit glassy. It was obvious that she was fighting back tears. "His mother came to me, frightened that something bad had happened to him. Now, I get to relay the news that she was right. What do you see? Anything of use?"

Arryn looked down, placing her hands under some rocks to find the bare earth below. She then placed a hand on Amos' cold, still chest.

She connected herself to the small amount of lingering energy left in his body and also to the energy in the ground. It only took a moment for her to realize that something wasn't right.

"Actually... yes," Arryn said.

"What is it?" Amelia asked.

"Obviously, he's been murdered. It doesn't take a genius to figure that one out." She pushed a little harder, searching a larger area around the body with her magic. "But he wasn't murdered here."

"Are you sure? There's blood all over the rocks. There's plenty—" Amelia began, but Arryn shook her head, interrupting her as she made eye contact.

"No. There isn't. It's hard to explain, but I can feel what's left of his energy, but there isn't much. There's no matching energy in the earth around him, meaning the blood is only on the rocks. There wasn't enough to drain into the ground below. With a wound that big, he'd have bled out pretty fast. He's lost almost all of it, but the ground is dry."

Arryn pulled her hands away and stood, doing her best to avoid the dead stare in the man's eyes.

"So, someone dumped him here. Like trash?" Amelia's fingertips came to rest on her lips for a moment as she closed her eyes. It was clear to Arryn that she was trying to collect herself. The Chancellor took a deep breath before exhaling heavily. "OK. Guard, we're now looking for the original site of the murder."

"Now, it might be easier for you," Arryn said. "Him being killed here left the possibilities open to anyone in the entire city. Since he wasn't, you're probably looking indoors. Everyone is still a suspect, but the bloodstain left behind won't lie. Just look for that. If you find where he was murdered, then you've probably found the killer."

"Good point. Thank you for your help, Arryn," Amelia said. "Not even a full day here, and you're already making a difference."

Though it was only a simple little thing, her compliment, it meant a hell of a lot more to Arryn than what the Chancellor could ever know.

Marie stood with Samuel in front of a group of volunteers. Noble magicians. Unlawful magicians. Men, women, and teenagers from the Boulevard. Everyone gathered, a surprising group of fifty stood before them, ready to work. Each one of them united.

It brought a smile to Marie's face. It had taken a few days to get everything in order, but it was something she never thought she'd see in her time in Arcadia.

Marie stepped forward. "I'd like to personally thank each and every one of you for taking the time to come here and volunteer. You might think it's natural for you to be here, but I've seen how many people walked away from the city when they realized they'd have to work to get back to their peaceful lives. There are many things you could've done with your time, but instead, you chose to be here. So, thank you."

"I can promise ye this won't be easy work, lads and lasses," Samuel said. "I don't mean ta brag on meself, but I'm one of the hardest working bastards you'll ever meet. I expect the same outta the men and women I work with. All us laborers need ta stand back for a few minutes and let these magicians do their… whatever it is they do. Everybody got it?"

The crowd cheered, and Samuel stepped out of the way, the magicians all stepping forward.

Without another word, Marie turned her back to the people, her eyes going black as she stared at the massive destruction that was once the Arcadian factory. Others followed suit, coming to stand next to her, their eyes also turning black.

Marie focused, pushing everything away from her except the overwhelming sense of responsibility for the people standing around her. She allowed that to fuel her magic. She and everyone standing next to her lifted their hands, palms facing outward as they began to push their magic toward the rubble.

"Whoa!" Samuel said. "Brace yerselves, boys and girls. It's gonna feel like an earthquake."

The combined magic of over twenty people washed out over the sea of shattered glass, exploded containers, broken walls, and busted floors.

The ground began to quake, and Marie could hear glass breaking into smaller pieces and falling to the ground where it would be safely out of the way of hands. The clanging of smaller pieces of metal and wood rang out as they fell to the ground as well.

Marie was the first to put her arms down, her eyes fading back to their normal blue. Soon, all the other magicians followed suit. "I'm not sure that took care of all of it or not. But I'm sure it's a damn good start."

"Alright, men," Samuel said. "Let's get our arses in there and get ta work. Wear gloves. If ye come ta me with cuts on yer hands, and the gloves ain't bloody, I'm not gonna feel a damn bit sorry for ye."

Elysia stood in the middle of the trial pit, staring up at the wide-open sky. It had been a few days since Arryn and Cathillian had left, and she was already feeling it.

She thought back to what she'd seen Arryn do in her trial. It was remarkable, something she'd never seen. There were very few druids strong enough to conjure a storm.

Druids learned nature magic as a whole, never really specializing in anything other than what was needed to survive. Growing plants, cultivating the ground, making sure that the temperature of the ground was right for whatever they may have been growing was all they really needed.

Elysia had never taught Arryn how to conjure a storm, though the girl had seen Elysia do it a time or two when the heat had grown exponentially during the summer months. They hadn't seen a season like that in well over a decade, and rain was scarce. Crops would die if nothing was done.

So, Elysia had taken Arryn to the trial pit, where the skies were wide open, and the trees didn't block the sun. But even though Arryn had seen it, it didn't mean she should know how it was done. That was something that took Elysia a long time to learn and even longer to master.

"What troubles you?" the Chieftain asked as he wandered over.

Elysia looked up, startled. "I didn't even hear you walk up." She shook her head. "Nothing troubles me exactly. I just can't figure out how she knew how to do it. We never taught her the things she did."

The Chieftain smiled. "This again?"

"No, now, be nice," Elysia said. "I'm not worried. Chaos came back. They made it there unscathed, though there was a note. They were attacked by some lycanthropes on the way. It seems they took on four and lived to tell the tale. It was time to let them go, and that proves it. Still, I can't help but be fascinated by her. I'm just sorry I didn't see it sooner."

The sound of horse hooves running toward them echoed through the air. Before the horse even completely stopped, Maurice, another druid warrior, jumped off, running up to the Chieftain and Elysia.

He bowed and placed a closed fist over his heart. "Chieftain, Elysia."

"Whoa, Maurice," Elysia said, stepping forward, concern all over her beautiful face. "Calm down and tell us what's wrong."

Maurice held out his left hand, and for the first time, Elysia saw that he was holding something. Her eyes immediately lifted, locking on Maurice.

"Where did you find this?" she asked, her expression turning serious and voice grim.

"We found it just inside the barrier," Maurice replied.

Elysia's eyes narrowed. "*Inside* the barrier?"

Maurice nodded. "We were just as surprised, especially given just *how far* inside it was. It couldn't have been shot over the wall. There's no way they could have been able to get in, but they did."

"Take a group of ten men," the Chieftain ordered. "Take the fastest horses and scout the border. Inside and out. No one goes outside the barrier unless all of you are together. Take no chances. This was quite obviously a warning, so if you sense there's a trap, get inside. I refuse to lose anyone. Especially to the likes of them."

Maurice nodded and bowed.

"Make sure to take Nika with you," Elysia ordered.

Maurice nodded once again before turning to carry out the Chieftain's orders. Elysia looked down at the object in her hand, a solid black arrow. The wood was warped and charred, but still somehow strong.

She could feel the death inside the arrow's shaft. She knew without a doubt it had died from dark magic and not by normal means.

She looked at the Chieftain. "How is it possible they could've gotten through?"

The Chieftain shook his head. "The dark druids use magic we can't understand. It's darkness. Death. It's the exact opposite of ours. Our barrier should be able to keep them out, but if they had help from someone who understood our magic..." His lips pressed into a thin line as his brows lifted. She knew he was leading her to the answer, but she already knew what he thought.

Elysia's shoulders fell, along with her expression. "Oh, no. Jenna's brother, Aeris," she said, her mind turning back to when he'd left shortly after Arryn's arrival.

Having an outsider in the tribe had been too much—no matter how tragic Arryn's story was—and he'd taken off, betraying everyone in the process.

The Chieftain nodded. "Unfortunately, I think so. All this time, they've never been able to breach the wall. That's the only explanation I can think of."

Elysia's eyes narrowed as things unfolded for her. "Aeris has been gone for nearly ten years. He left just a few months after Arryn got here. Explain to me why this move would be made now?"

"What're you trying to say?" the Chieftain asked.

"Do you not recall how angry Jenna was when we allowed Laurel to go with the Arcadian's? Do you not recall how pissed off she was when Arryn won the Versuch? Her brother left because his parents raised him to believe our laws were absolute. There are *no* grey areas with them. There are *no* exceptions."

Elysia looked to the sky for a moment as she twisted the arrow in her fingers. "To them, rules are rules and to break them is treason. He left when he couldn't understand how we could take an Arcadian in. And now, his sister despises everyone here because we didn't treat Arryn like an outsider, but Jenna didn't seem to notice that we didn't treat Arryn as we would a native druid either. I think we need to have conversation with Jenna."

"Chieftain. My lady."

The Chieftain and Elysia turned, staring none other than Jenna's parents, Amara and Flynn, right in the face.

"What a coincidence…" Elysia began. "We were just about to come see you and your *lovely* daughter."

The husband and wife looked back and forth to one another, worry on their faces. They drop to their knees. "Please forgive us. We had no idea."

"No idea of what?" the Chieftain asked.

Flynn looked up. "Jenna came to us. She told us she'd seen Aeris. She sensed him outside the barrier and then went outside the Dark Forest. She asked us to go with her to see him."

Amara glanced over, tears in her eyes. "It's been ten years since I've seen my son. Ten years I've worried. Wondering if he was dead, alive, turned into whatever they are. I needed to see my baby."

"What came of this meeting?" the Chieftain asked, his eyes icy and his voice authoritative. The normally playful demeanor was long gone.

Flynn spoke. "We didn't think anything of it. He just kept saying he was OK. That everything is OK. That everything would *be* OK. We just thought that meant he was happy where he was, wherever that may be."

"And what makes you come to us now?" Elysia asked, doing her best to bite her tongue from saying things she truly wanted to say.

Amara was in a full sob now. Between painful gasps and wiping her nose, she said, "Jenna's missing now. We think she might've left with him."

Elysia turned to the Chieftain. "When a druid goes dark, their magic changes. There's a transition period, but he's well beyond that now. There's no way he could get through that barrier alone. Jenna went with him and must've been the one to let them inside. Our walls have been compromised."

The Chieftain looked to the husband and wife kneeling before them. "And what on Irth do you think that I should do with the two of you? I warned you about your hatred years ago. We didn't come to the woods because we hated *everyone else*. We came to the woods to live in *peace*. We came here to live a life where we were free of such things."

He paused for a moment, allowing his words to sink in before continuing, his voice growing even colder. "You brought your children up in our peaceful home, teaching terrible things like having enemies. Hatred. Personal gain. Do you see now why I warned you? Do you see now why I spoke out against you and teaching prejudices all those years ago? How many of our children have turned against us?"

The mother doubled over, loud, painful sobs escaping her. "Two." Her entire body shook with every painful cry. She inhaled deeply, forcing herself to sit back up. "Two druid children have turned against us."

"Yes," the Chieftain said, nodding and pointedly leaning over to look her directly in the eyes. "Two children have turned against us. What a coincidence they were both *yours*."

Amara broke down again as the Chieftain rose, this time completely inconsolable. Flynn wrapped his arms around her, pulling her in close. Elysia could hear his tears now, no doubt wondering what would become of them and their children if they were ever caught.

"Elysia," the Chieftain said, his voice stern. Elysia turned her head to face her father. "Things have changed. Gather every warrior. Move to the other two villages and gather them, too. We need to inspect every square inch of our barrier and reinforce it."

Elysia nodded. "Should we make it thicker?"

"Yes. Grab seedlings, and take water with you. Make sure everyone is rested up. You can heal yourself a little as you cast, but they can't. We need to regrow the wall, bigger and stronger than ever. I have a feeling this isn't the last we'll see of the dark druids."

"What about Arryn and Cathillian?" Elysia asked.

"They're safe where they are. They don't need to worry about this. They're just beginning their new lives, and while I have hope they won't stay there forever, I hope they don't return anytime soon."

TWENTY ONE

I t had taken a couple of days to get to Cella, but when Talia arrived, she found warm welcomes as soon as she reached the gate.

The Cella guard smiled, having remembered her visiting often when in need of supplies to take back to the farm she shared with her mother outside of town. She'd always been talented in the art of manipulation.

"Talia, is that you?" Paul, one of the guards, asked.

She smiled as she approached. "Yes! I've been away for quite some time. Well, I suppose not *too* long. I've been in Arcadia for a few weeks. I've accepted a position as the Dean of students there."

Paul's eyes lit up. "That's great! After all they went through, they need good people like you. Though, so do we. And you're definitely one of the finest." He winked with that last comment, and Talia faked a girlish smile.

"Aw, Paul, you sure know how to make this girl blush."

The man laughed, suddenly full of himself. It made Talia want to puke.

"So," Paul said, "other than flirtin' with me, what brings you to Cella? Isn't Arcadia gettin' back on its feet by now?"

"Actually," she replied, "it doesn't have much of anything. If I'm honest, I'm here brown nosing. I'm new to the city and my position, and I want to make a big difference. So, I came here to see if I might find a group of good men and women who would be willing to come back with me and lend a hand to Arcadia. I know she'd be very grateful for it."

Paul smiled. "With that pretty face of yours, I don't think you'll have problems of any kind getting anybody to do anything you want. Myself included. Count me in. Whatever you need, I'm yours if the Governor is good with me taking off."

Talia gave a wry smile, faking her interest in this large, sweaty man. "Anything, huh?" She winked. "Glad to hear it. Would you mind asking a few of your guard friends for the help? That would make me *very* happy."

He nodded, clearly lost in her charm. "Sure! I'd be happy to ask. I'm sure there are several guys I could round up."

"Are there a lot of rearick in town right now?" she asked. "Because I hoped to find more than a few. They work hard and have the backs for cutting trees. We can use all the help and all the resources we can get."

"Talk to our Governor. He's a good guy, and I'm betting he'd be willing to help out. How could he say no to you? He wouldn't want to lose trade with Arcadia, and it's already slowed down too much. We thought you guys were on the verge of being back on your feet. He never was a big fan of Adrien, but he traded with him because we needed the supplies. I'm sure that lady Chancellor of yours is much more agreeable."

"Oh, she is," Talia said with a fake smile. "She's just amazing."

He nodded. "Good. Glad to hear it. I'm sure you remember where it is, but if you head up the main road here and take a left, you'll find the Governor all the way down there, last house on the right. After all, the factories we have here are small. There's no way we could sustain ourselves and all the farmland around us without Arcadia."

Talia smiled. She was already looking forward to her trip. It seemed to be going well so far. As expected, the guards waved her through, and she made her way down the street, heading toward the Governor's house. Without a doubt, she knew she could convince the Governor to do anything that she wanted.

After all, most of the men in the Arcadian Valley were completely lost when it came to beautiful women. It wouldn't be hard for her to smile and flirt her way into whatever it was she wanted. Sometimes a woman's magic was far more effective than all the fireballs in the Academy.

She'd been traveling through town for about ten minutes when a woman stepped out from behind a building and directly into her path. "Hello, Dean," she said.

Talia's brows furrowed for a moment, immediately recognizing the woman. It was one of the three that she'd hired for teaching positions at the Academy. Scarlett. She was the one that had seemed rather off to her.

"Hello," Talia said. "Funny that I should run into you here. What can

I do for you?"

Scarlett smiled. "Oh, sweetheart. It's not what you can do for me. It's what *I* can do for *you*. I know exactly who you are, who your father was, and I've come to lend a hand."

The first couple of nights in old Girard's house was very different for Cathillian, strange but not at all unpleasant. The smells were the only bothersome thing for him.

Waking up to the smell of musty old house was a lot different— and far less satisfying—than waking to the clean scent of the Forest. He already missed that, but it was nothing.

He enjoyed learning about the different technologies they'd developed. So far, his favorite thing had been the shower. He took one every night before sleeping. The thought occurred to him that he had no idea how he'd learn to live without it again once he returned to the Forest.

Cathillian paced down the hall and slowly opened the door to Arryn's room. She was still sleeping. He stood there, watching her for a moment.

Ever since the morning in the Dark Forest when he'd had to wake her from a nightmare, he'd noticed she'd been having them more frequently.

Every night he heard her cry out, and every night he went to check on her, and every night she would wipe her tears, scowl at him, and then scold him—telling him she wasn't a baby that needed to be monitored.

The first night in Arcadia, he'd tried talking to her about them. "Why do you think you're having them?" he'd asked her.

She'd shrugged and clasped her hands together, not making eye contact. "It's the same one over and over," she'd said. "Maybe I'm trying to work something out in my head, how the hell should I know? They're just dreams. I mean—I'm back in Arcadia. That's probably why. Drop it. I'm fine."

And drop it he did. Instead of going in her room now, he always waited by her door when he heard her wake, listening for any sign she needed him.

But there never were.

It seemed to him that she was her most vulnerable in her sleep, though that didn't come as a surprise. That could be said for anyone.

Right then, however, she seemed to be sleeping peacefully. She needed it. Since the transition period was over, he planned to begin training her again. Hand-to-hand and magically.

But first... Cathillian had some exploring to do. It was mid-morning, and Arryn would probably wake soon, but he didn't want to wait around. He wrote a quick note on some parchment he found in the office next to his room and stuck it on the bedside table next to her. Then, he was off.

He pulled his long, blonde hair down over his ears to hide them. His clothing and taller-than-normal height was enough to draw attention. Though he was a lover of such treatment, there was a time and place for it, now wasn't it. Right now, he only wanted to explore.

He made his way down cobblestone streets, one after another, getting lost in the architecture and differences in style from one building to the next.

They were all very tall, mostly built of stone, though there were some wooden homes. He'd noticed most of the wooden homes were smaller, less fortunate. Those from what Arryn had called the Boulevard had all been made of wood.

Cheap to make and buy, he imagined.

He soon found his way back to the main road, walking through town toward what he assumed was the Capitol building. It was quite large, elaborate. Built entirely out of white stone, it looked regal and important above all the rest.

There were several people out walking this morning, relaxed, slow in pace just as he was. It seemed they were enjoying the sun and slightly warmer air. As he continued, he passed a rearick and a taller man that was still a few inches shorter than Cathillian with short, dark hair.

"We need ta get 'em ta move west. We can't risk another attack like that," the rearick said.

"No shit. We got lucky. Your friend, Ren, is a little crazy, though. No offense," the taller, dark-haired man said. "I'm pretty sure he'd go right back if he had the men to go with him."

"He ain't any better than any of the rest of us rearick, lad. All 'r mothers were a few nails shy when they built us. In other words, ain't none of us right."

"Samuel… I think that's the first thing you've said about your people that makes sense."

Samuel? Cathillian thought. All this had started because of a rearick named Samuel, and there stood one. It was too much to be a coincidence.

"Excuse me," Cathillian said, quickly crossing the street to meet the two men.

"Aye, lad," Samuel answered. "Are ye lost? Ye don't look like yer from around here."

Cathillian shook his head. "No, not lost, but I was wondering if you'd been in the Dark Forest lately."

The rearick's eyes widened a moment before he looked Cathillian over. "Ah! Now I see why ye look so lost, lad. Yer one of 'em. The druids, yeah?"

Cathillian nodded. "I am. In fact, I'm here because you talked to my friend and my mother along the Kalt. They saved you."

Samuel nodded. "Aye. They set me right. Ain't had a headache since. So, if yer here, are they?"

Cathillian brushed some hair back that had fallen into his face, careful not to uncover his ears. "Arryn is, the younger woman that you met. After she talked to you and found out Arcadia had been freed from Adrien, she wanted to come back."

"I'm glad ta hear ye both made it here alright. The Dark Forest is no picnic," Samuel said.

Cathillian laughed. "No, it isn't. We ran into four lycanthropes on our way out."

Samuel's eyes widened. "And the two of ye made it ta tell the tale? Damn, lad. That's impressive. We had a fight of 'r own recently. Remnant out by the Madlands."

"What the hell were you doing out by the Madlands?" Cathillian asked. "That's even more dangerous than trying to log in the Dark Forest!

And I wouldn't recommend trying that to anyone."

It was the taller man that spoke now. "Wood. Right now, that's more valuable than precious stones. We headed out there to convince the loggers we needed the help. Can't rebuild the city with nothin.'"

Samuel nodded. "That's when the bastards attacked. A dozen'r more. We managed ta get everyone out alive. Had it been a bigger group, we'd've died."

"Were there a lot of injuries?" Cathillian asked.

"Quite a few. Busted legs, large gashes from weapons. There're a few that might be getting some infections," the taller man said. "To survive a fight and then to die like that…" He shook his head.

"Eh, keep yer curses silent, lad," Samuel said. "They're fighters. Ye'll see."

"Maybe I can help," Cathillian said. "Take me there, and I'll heal what I can. Magic has its limits, but I can at least get each of them out of death's door a hell of a lot quicker. In fact, I think I can help solve several of your problems if you're interested."

The taller man's eyes brightened. "You can do that? I've always heard of the druids, but only bad shit. You don't seem so scary, not that I'd wanna take you in a fight. Not from the stories I've heard. Somthin's gotta be based on truth. The name's Andrew."

Andrew held out his hand, and it took Cathillian a moment to realize what the gesture was. He'd seen Arryn do it once. A handshake, she'd called it. A sign of peace, much like their own of placing their fists over their hearts. Cathillian took his hand and shook it.

"We appreciate the help, friend. Whatever you can offer," Andrew said.

The three men walked and chatted about their individual battles, discussing strategy on the way to the medical building. Cathillian's morning had been far more productive than he'd imagined. He couldn't wait to tell Arryn when he got back.

Arryn awoke to the sound of scratching talons on the footboard. Her eyes fluttered open, but it took a moment or two before she was able to focus. Rolling over on her back, she looked down to the end of the bed to see that Echo was perched there, tilting her head to the side as she studied Arryn.

"Where's Cathillian? Why aren't ya bothering him?"

The bird squawked in response, unfurling her wings for a moment before shaking her body and tucking them back in.

"Well, you're no help. And you better not shit on the floor. If you do, you're cleaning it up." Arryn got up and stretched before making her way out of the room, searching Cathillian's bedroom and the rest of the house, but coming up empty.

On one hand, his absence surprised her, assuming he'd be too uncomfortable to go out on his own or to leave her alone, but then she remembered it was Cathillian of all people. He couldn't sit still if his life depended on it.

She figured he must have decided to go ahead and explore instead of waiting all day for her to wake up. It was almost noon, so she couldn't really blame him. Lately, Arryn had been sleeping late. She wasn't sure why she slept so long, but since being back in Arcadia, it seemed that was all she could do.

After a change of clothes, she headed out the door so she, too, could explore the city. They'd been there for a couple of days, and she hadn't actually made her way out of the house yet.

With so many students and teachers absent from the Academy to help with the factory, she had no reason to begin her new job, so she just hung out at Girard's creepy old house.

The added wait time had been a blessing in disguise, allowing her to get used to being back in the city before leaping into socializing with everyone.

When she walked outside, she was greeted with warm air and beautiful sunshine. It was so nice outside there wasn't even a need for her cloak.

Every brick and every stone in every home looked familiar to her. She knew the streets like the back of her hand.

When she was young, she and her friends would run through them, playing and hiding from one another. She'd only gotten lost a couple times, but she always found her way back.

Wandering around and winding through them now reminded her of her childhood, bringing her back to those old memories. Right then, she was happy that Cathillian was nowhere to be found.

She had been exploring for nearly a half an hour when she stumbled across her old street. Though she had assumed she might come upon it at some point, it still came as a surprise due to not paying attention to where she was going—just walking and taking in the city.

That street in particular was built more for the middle class, those who weren't quite rich enough to own the stone homes, but not poor enough to belong on the Boulevard.

Each home was made of brick, yet each one looked very different. She swallowed hard as she turned toward the seemingly desolate road, willing herself to walk down.

All the homes seemed run down, possibly even vacant. Had no one been living in these homes? Or was it that these people had recently fled after the battle?

She saw the house where she often used to play when she was a child. Her friend Esther lived there with only her father, her mother having died in childbirth.

The more she walked, the more memories flooded her mind. Birthday parties, friends, pranks, and so much more filled her thoughts. There was a squawk that echoed off the exterior walls of the empty homes, one she knew from anywhere.

"Echo, what are you doing?"

"She led me here," Cathillian said.

Arryn sighed. There was no part of her that wanted Cathillian there, not right then.

There was a myriad of emotions running through her mind, and she needed to process them alone. She wanted to experience them and let them go. Get on with her life for good with her past planted firmly behind her.

To do that, she needed to have her moment to reflect in peace without the worry of someone seeing her, without wondering what they would think of her.

Even her best friend, Cathillian.

"Well, then she's more rat than eagle, I'd say," Arryn quipped.

"Ah, don't be like that. She was just worried about you. I left a window open for her before I left earlier so she could fly if she wanted. She came and found me and led me here. Speaking of which, what are you doing?"

Arryn's arms momentarily lifted at her sides before falling again. "I don't know. Something I probably shouldn't be. Something I'm not ready for you to be here for."

Cathillian looked around for a moment, taking a few steps forward. "Is this where you lived?"

Arryn couldn't help the mixed emotions that filled her chest or the blank expression on her face as she thought about answering that.

Finally, she nodded. "Two houses down from here on the left. This morning, I ventured out just wanting to explore—to see how the city had changed since I'd been gone. I think my memories led me here, not that it means I wanna go any further."

"Maybe it's time you should. You've been having those dreams. It might help you put aside whatever's crawling through your head at night. You aren't weak. You never have been. But ever since you met Samuel, your past life's been weighing on you harder than ever. I'll stay with you, or I'll leave. It's up to you."

Arryn turned, slowly bringing herself to face the house. After a few moments, she looked back to Cathillian. "I don't want you with me—but I also don't want you to go. I guess… I guess, you should go with me. Just in case. Besides, I'm sure it'll need broken into, and there's no one better at breaking in or breaking out of places than you are."

"Damn right!" he said, a reassuring smile on his face.

Arryn sighed again before turning and heading toward her old house. When they reached the door, just as she'd assumed, it was locked. Arryn stood to the side while Cathillian broke the lock to let them in.

A swell of emotion rose in Arryn's chest as her eyes took in the interior, but she managed to shove it away as she stepped inside. The magitech light hummed to life, and she wondered how they could've possibly lasted for the past ten years.

Everything was exactly the same. Nothing had changed.

The family portrait that had been painted over a decade ago still hung over the fireplace, her mother's art still hung on the walls around the living room, and all three of her father's uniquely crafted swords were still in the corner, leaning against the wall behind the door.

He'd left them there in case there was ever an emergency, but that had proven to be a mistake, an unfortunate place to leave them since he'd needed them upstairs that night.

As musty as Girard's house smelled, this home was far worse. There were cobwebs everywhere, but sheets were over the furniture. *Someone* had been there since they'd disappeared, someone that cared enough to preserve their things.

Arryn imagined if she pulled off the sheets, her family's furniture would still be in perfect condition underneath, though the original scent would be long gone, replaced with that of old, stale air.

She was silent for a long time as she walked through the bottom floor, taking everything in. The modest, yet well-done living room, the kitchen, the downstairs office; they even had a music room. Everything was exactly as it had been left.

She walked back through the living room, pausing to look at the family portrait. They'd sat for quite some time while the artist painted them. It was an expensive gift, but one that her mother had desperately wanted. They had only gotten it a few days before they were forced to flee.

"My mother begged for that," Arryn said, her voice barely above a whisper as she pointed to the painting. "I say begged, but really, my father couldn't deny her anything if he'd wanted to."

"It's beautiful," Cathillian said. "She looks exactly like I remember her. I'm sorry I never got to know her. But if she was anything like you, I'm sure I would've liked her a lot."

Arryn smiled. "She was far more. I am what I am because of her. Her strength made me who I am, which is why, even as I stand here, even as my heart breaks into thousands of pieces, I refuse to show it. I won't let her down."

"But you still need to process it," Cathillian said. "You've pushed it away for too long."

Arryn slowly nodded as she stared into her mother's eyes in the painting. "And that's the only reason why I let you push me in here. There's something I need to remember. My father told my mother something the night we left, and I need to figure out what that was."

Arryn turned away from the painting and made her way up the stairs, Cathillian following close behind. As she reached the top, she looked to her right only two doors down where her room once was. It only took a few steps to get there, her hand stalling on the knob for a moment before finally twisting it open.

She walked in and made her way across the room to her bed, sitting on it for a moment before finally laying down and staring at the cobweb covered ceiling before speaking.

"I was asleep when they came, the sound of them beating on the front door waking me in the middle of the night. Those dreams that you wake me from, they always start right here. This is exactly what I see."

Looking to the left, she saw the familiar flower vase, but there were no flowers inside. At some point, someone had removed them. Probably the same someone that had covered all the furniture with sheets. She sat up, looking past Cathillian to the door and then around her room.

"My father came in to wake me, but I was already awake from the guards pounding on the door downstairs. He told me we had to leave, and when I didn't move fast enough, he picked me up and carried me out of the room."

Arryn stood, taking one last look at her things while dusting herself off before making her way past Cathillian and out the door. He never said a word or asked a single question as she spoke, for which she was grateful.

Even while talking to him, it was easy to ignore his presence. Easy to lose herself in her thoughts as she walked and talked through her memories.

"The guards were in the process of breaking in while we were running down this hallway," she said as she led Cathillian down that very hall, coming to stop at another room. She twisted the knob and opened it, walking into the upstairs office.

She briefly looked around the room before continuing on. "We had bags packed and stashed away in here, ready to go in case something like this would happen. My father closed the door, but it did nothing to keep me from hearing them screaming downstairs. I could hear them coming for us, hear them directing each other on how to clear the bottom floor to make sure we weren't down there."

Arryn continued studying the room, taking in the mahogany desk and bookshelves that lined the room. As her eyes reached the window, she saw a familiar bag sitting there, covered in dust. It had been her mother's. The very emergency bag that Elayne had packed for their escape.

Arryn walked over and picked it up, setting it on the desk before opening it. Inside, she found her mother's clothing, some emergency supplies, and a canteen of water. Arryn thought back to that night, to all the confusion.

She laughed, but it wasn't happy or amused, having finally come to understand something. "She knew she wasn't going to survive that night." Arryn looked up to Cathillian, holding the canteen in her hand before placing it back in the bag. "My bag was right next to hers. There's no way she forgot it. She purposely didn't bring it."

"You're her daughter. You'd sacrifice yourself in a heartbeat if that meant saving the life of any other person you cared for."

She nodded as she thought his words over. "You're right. I sometimes doubt myself, but when I stop and think about it, I *would* die to protect anyone that I loved. I may not do it skillfully, or intelligently, or even valiantly, but I *would* do it. I'd take a sword to the gut to save your life."

"Aw! See? You *do* love me!" Cathillian said, placing his hand over his heart with a sarcastic smile. "Keep denying it all you want, though. I'll continue pretending that I believe it."

Arryn rolled her eyes, a smile threatening to spread across her lips. "I'd also do that for your mother—or your grandfather. You cocky prick. And thank you. I *will* keep denying it. Being mean to you is an excellent way to cure boredom."

Cathillian stepped closer, placing his hand over hers as it rested on the edge of the bag. "All that aside, you have a lot to give to this world, and I have a feeling you'll have plenty of chances to make her proud."

Arryn turned her hand over, giving Cathillian's a quick squeeze before letting go, not particularly enjoying the closeness, but not wanting to be rude and push him away either.

While she and Cathillian had always been close, somehow it felt like there had been a change in that in the last few weeks. A change that she didn't quite feel comfortable with given all she'd been through.

She stepped back and looked around the room and over to the window she'd jumped from that night. After opening it, she looked outside and down, seeing just how far she jumped with her mother. It was quite a long fall, but the straw that had been placed there—as well as her mother— had gone a long way to cushion the descent.

"I clung to this window, looking at my father and watching him speak to my mother, but with my racing heart and terrified thoughts, they drowned out anything that he said to her. I remember it perfectly, but I can't remember what he said because I didn't really hear it. I only saw his lips move."

She sighed as she thought back, hoping that physically being there would spark something. "There was something big he told her, the entire reason we were forced out of Arcadia. The entire reason he was taken. Even if it's pointless to know now because it would do no good, I need to find out what that was. If it was important enough for him to be threatened and then have his family attacked, then it was important enough for me to find out."

" Maybe Amelia could help. She mentioned having people you might talk to. That one—Doyle or whatever—was his closest friend. Maybe they'll find him, and he'll know what got him taken."

Arryn pulled back inside and closed the window before turning to Cathillian. "There's one thing that gives me hope above everything else."

"Yeah? What's that?" he asked.

"There's no blood anywhere in this room. I half expected to see large, red stains all over the floor in here from all those years ago, but there's none. That means he was alive when they took him. Maybe he still is."

Arryn jumped as Cathillian spun around toward the door, unsheathing his sword in one fluid motion as he did. When he stopped, Arryn saw the blade resting against the throat of a woman.

"Who the hell are you, and what do you want?" Cathillian asked, his voice suddenly cold.

The woman's eyes were wide, but without questioning it, Arryn knew it had nothing to do with the sword. Her focus was entirely on Arryn. Tears filled her eyes before spilling over onto her cheeks.

"I-It's... Impossible... Arryn?"

Arryn's brows furrowed as she looked the woman over, trying to figure out who she was. There was a long scar down the left side of her face, and it looked like it had been very deep, like it could've killed her when it happened.

"Who are you?" Arryn asked.

Cathillian slowly pulled the sword away, keeping it at the ready just in case. The woman fell to her knees, her jaw slightly parted as her eyes stayed locked on Arryn.

"I-I don't believe it," she said. "It's really you. All these years, I thought you were dead. I was a few years younger than you are now when you left, so I don't blame you for not recognizing me. I've changed quite a bit, too. Even with all that change, you still look just like her. My name is Celine. I'm Elayne's little sister—your aunt."

TWENTY TWO

Talia's trip to Cella had gone far better than expected. It had been very productive and enlightening. Not only did her visit with their Governor go over well, but her run in with Scarlett had been surprising, too.

Using her charm had gone a long way—just as she'd imagined it would. With only mild flirting, the Governor was more than willing to send men within three days of her leaving.

In fact, he agreed to send her a hundred men as long as Cella would get a discounted cost from the goods they purchased for the first three months. He'd originally wanted six, but Talia talked him down to three.

His other request was that his beloved son, Nathaniel, be allowed to travel to Arcadia and attend the Academy without fees. She wasn't exactly sure if those terms would piss Amelia off or not, but she imagined that any money coming in would be better than none, and the help would be worth the cost.

So—she agreed. And with Amelia's preference for access for all, how could she argue?

Still, that little meeting had only been for show. Her entire trip there was strictly to preserve and even grow her good name. Not even Mousy Marie had gotten a hundred men. Talia loved competition, but her real success was elsewhere.

Something had seemed off about Scarlett when Talia had met her at the school. An unknown but worrisome trait that she couldn't quite put her finger on. Scarlett was confident, strong, but so was the Chancellor. It didn't take that much to be a strong-willed woman.

This was different—darker. More seductive like Talia's confidence.

It was something Talia hadn't seen in the initial interview and that Scarlett had restrained during the tour, but it had been in full force there in Cella. Scarlett was no longer hiding anything.

She was a mystic.

Not a form of magic that Talia had much experience with personally, but Scarlett was much like Selah, the mystic leader that her father had once told her about, but altogether different.

Talia remembered the interaction as she traveled back to Arcadia, replaying it through her mind as she mulled over her level of interest in creating a friendship with someone she knew little about.

"You *are* the secret love child of the past Chancellor, Adrien, aren't you?" Scarlett had asked.

Talia's eyes had gone wide, unable to believe that the woman could have figured her out after having only met a single time. Talia's hand had shot out from under her light cloak, power resonating from it as she then swung it to the right, sending Scarlett flying into the wall of a building next to her.

She held the mystic there, pinned to the wall with Talia's telekinesis as she slowly walked forward, looking over her shoulders to make sure no one was around. "Who the *hell* are you?"

Scarlett swallowed nervously. "I'm a lot of things, but mainly an opportunist. I was curious to see what became of Arcadia, and I wanted to see exactly how strong their forces were. For having just reclaimed the city, they seem to be doing surprisingly well. Certainly not a foe I would want to cross. At least, not alone."

Talia narrowed her eyes. "*So* happy to hear it. Get to your point. If not… I have a free hand, and there's a sharp stone on the ground that's going to find its way into your heart."

Scarlett squirmed against Talia's hold, but it was no use. "I spent a few days in the city, studying everyone, looking for something that might help me take the city. Then I saw you—in the bar, hiding no less. You were quite—*tipsy* to say the least. Large pitcher of my people's brew if I'm not mistaken. Under the influence, your head was *very* easy to get into."

Talia knew all about the mystical arts. It was a subject her father had taught her at length about. He told her she should never let her guard down, always keep her mind hidden.

There had even been a way to sense when someone was looking in her thoughts, which she had done when Amelia had gotten a bit nosy during her interview.

Amelia, however, was a novice, so it was easy to think only of positive things since the Chancellor's power limited her only to the surface—not to deeper, hidden memories.

Talia had allowed her to only see the happy childhood she had with her mother on the farm and pure intentions in working for the Academy.

Her mother was a woman that Amelia had never seen before and therefore couldn't recognize. Permitting Amelia into her head enough to see those peaceful things had secured her position.

Apparently, Scarlett was just as good at hiding herself from the Chancellor, much to Talia's dismay.

"And what exactly do you plan to do with this information?" Talia had asked, her eyes narrowed and her nostrils slightly flared with obvious annoyance that bordered on rage. It was a thin line from one to the next with her. "I will warn you now, I do *not* take threats lightly."

The woman smiled. "Oh, I don't threaten. I come bearing gifts! Once I saw in your head, I applied for a position. You intrigued me. What you plan to do, you'll never do alone. Even *I* won't risk doing it alone. In fact, if that Chancellor of yours takes many more mystical lessons, we'll be screwed. She's been training with Julianne which means you—or better yet—*we* need to move a bit faster."

"Julianne's the master mystic now, is she not? Wouldn't that make Julianne *your* leader as well?" Talia had asked.

"There are many things you need to learn. But for now, I'll stick to the basics. You have an opening with that student of yours, Jackson. While I think you've started down a very positive road with him, I think we can quicken the trip. You need more than just one or two people on your side. All this *must* be done very delicately, very strategically. Understand?"

Talia had looked her over, lowering the mystic to the ground. Talia stared at the woman, wondering exactly what her game was. "I'll not be thrown off course. I *don't* know you. I sure as hell *don't* trust you. You'll not deter or overthrow me. You may have the mystical arts, but I can promise you I'm not someone you want as an enemy."

"I assure you I have no such intentions. We'll talk more later. For now, I believe you have business to attend to. I'll see you back in Arcadia, and we can continue our discussion there. Just keep this in mind," Scarlett had said before walking away.

Talia couldn't deny that she was getting more and more excited as time went on, thinking about what she might accomplish with help. She knew she would need it, but she never imagined it coming along quite like it had.

As she made her way back to the Arcadian gate, she wondered exactly what Scarlett had in mind with Jackson. Talia agreed there was a lot more that could be done with him, but her intention was to move slow, steady, making no mistakes.

Moving too quickly could have major repercussions. Still, whether she liked to admit it or not, Amos's words did stick with her just as he'd threatened they would.

Bastard.

She knew she needed to begin sooner rather than later or risk having her plans thwarted if someone found her out. She just hoped the mystic was true to her word and wouldn't be said downfall. Otherwise, she was in for a world of hurt.

As Talia crossed through the Arcadian gates, her trip seeming infinitely shorter with all she'd had to think about, she thought of the Chancellor. She'd need to talk to Amelia now that she'd returned and let her know exactly what had happened in Cella.

Things would move nicely for Talia once Amelia became overjoyed and very thankful. But, she wasn't quite in the mood to deal with the Chancellor quite yet, so she headed to her office first.

When she arrived, there was a visitor waiting for her—Scarlett.

"Why, Scarlett… I'm so happy to see you found the place," Talia said sarcastically.

Scarlett smiled. "It's nice to see you, too. I headed back as soon as we finished talking. I wanted to be here when you returned. How'd your trip go? Did you accomplish what you set out to do?"

Talia set her cloak down, throwing it over the back of her chair before sitting down herself. "It went fine, thank you. I got exactly what I needed. Now, about this conversation of ours. I assume that's why you're here."

"Indeed. So, I've been thinking… What do you suppose is the root of all evil or corruption?" Scarlett asked.

Talia looked at her incredulously. "How the *fuck* should I know? I don't break things down into good and evil. Only things that please or displease me. Planning pleases me. Being *alone* in my office pleases me. My father being destroyed by a bunch of whiny little bitches that couldn't be thankful for what they had and follow a few simple rules tends to piss me off a bit."

Scarlett smiled. "I see. Well, *I* believe the root of all corruption is power—or the promise of power, I guess I should say. No offense, but your father was very guilty of that. It's why these people rose up against him."

Talia rolled her eyes and sighed as she leaned back in her chair, rubbing the bridge of her nose. The conversation had only just begun, and she was already about to break the woman in two.

"Yes, I'm more than aware of why they went after him. While my father was a very smart man, he could be very stupid. He ruled with an iron fist, which got him in trouble and then got him killed. I don't care about power, all I care about is vengeance. Get to your longwinded point, mystic."

"My point is we have a greater chance of getting others to follow you if they believe there's a promise of power. They're less likely to agree if they think they're going be killed for their actions. We have to make them feel comfortable. Strong. They need more power." Scarlett stood and walked across the room to look out the window, peering down from the Dean's office to watch the students wander around the campus.

"Power *cannot* be granted. I'm sure even you know this, though you clearly don't know the details. Most people have no idea where magic originates from, but I do because the Founder taught my father. Magic comes from what the old ones called nanocytes, tiny machines in our blood. Every person is born with a *finite* amount of them and with a *finite* amount of the magical effects that they bring. We *cannot* give more power."

Scarlett turned to face Talia, giving a dark smile. "Exactly. But *they* don't know that. I also know the details, thanks to Selah—long before I went out on my own. Being what I am, I know the power of deception better than most. All we have to do is convince them you're powerful enough to grant them more power."

"What exactly did you have in mind?" Talia asked, still doing her best to restrain her annoyance.

Scarlett brushed a stray lock of hair out of her face before moving across the room to stand in front of Talia's desk. She leaned over and placed her hands flat on the wood.

"As you know, the mystics are master storytellers. There's one story that always stuck with me when I was just a girl. In the old days, there were people, remarkable people, who fed on the blood of others. That blood gave them the power of the gods. I think it's time we revive that legend."

Talia's eyes narrowed again as she seriously doubted the woman's sanity. "A placebo? Tricking them into believing they can harness the power from someone else's blood?"

Scarlett shrugged. "Like I said, the mind is a terrible and beautiful thing. It can allow the person great power, or it can cause them to worry themselves to death. You're smart. You hold the power in your hands to completely control each and every one of them. Promise them power, and they *will* come."

The idea was quite far-fetched to Talia, but she couldn't deny some truth in what the woman had told her. The mind certainly was a persuasive tool.

If her recruits believed they had access to more power, then they would be easier to mold. They would follow Talia anywhere she asked them to simply because she gave them the gift of more magic. Strength to defeat their own enemies.

After all, misery does love company.

TWENTY THREE

Arryn stared for a moment at the woman claiming to be her aunt, completely dumbfounded. She remembered Celine from when they were just kids, but it was still so very hard to believe it was her. Celine was only five years older than Arryn. She had just turned fifteen when Arryn and her parents went missing.

She looked into Celine's eyes, and she saw the same rich color that her mother had. The same high cheekbones. The same long, black hair. Arryn was filled with so much happiness at that moment that she was unable to stop herself from running across the room, collapsing on the floor in front of the woman, and wrapping her hands around her.

"I don't believe it," Arryn said. "I never imagined that Adrien would've left anyone else in our family alive. I thought he'd taken everyone."

The woman shook her head, pulling away before placing her hands on either side of Arryn's face. She smiled as tears rolled down her cheeks. "I don't believe it either. Word spread that your mother was dead after the Hunters brought her body back. They carried back the corpses of two of their men and said she was a traitor. I knew that wasn't true. And with Christopher missing, too... I knew something was wrong, but I was smart enough to keep my mouth shut."

"Do you have any idea what happened or what they were after?" Arryn asked.

Celine stood, extending her hand to Arryn to help her do the same. "I was about to ask you the same thing. The only information I was given was that my sister was a traitor, and her husband was taken for questioning. I was way too terrified to press the issue, but I got myself into a situation once and was told that he was executed."

"What happened? What kind of situation? And executed? Did you believe them?" Arryn was frantic as she asked question after question.

"I went to a bar and got drunk. I've always looked older than what I am, and noble bars don't really pay much attention anyway. I got way too drunk, and I stumbled up and began yelling at a guard. I told him I'd just buried my sister, and I needed to know what happened to her husband and her daughter. I just needed to know, no matter how bad it was."

Arryn's eyes widened. "And you didn't *die*? How the hell did you pull that off?"

Celine snorted. "I got lucky. He happened to be one of the few good guards in the city. Later, he ended up switching sides in the battle after he realized just how big of a piece of shit Adrien was, but he was killed. But he told me Christopher had been executed for treason, and my niece was dead. I knew that *he* believed that, but I never did. So, what the hell *did* happen?"

Arryn went into the story, telling her all about the couple of weeks that led up to them running, and the events of that night. Though Arryn had seen it all in her head a thousand times, Celine was seeing it for the very first time. Years of questions finally being answered.

Celine was clearly shocked by it all, and why wouldn't she be? It was an overwhelming story to Arryn whenever *she* told it, and she lived through it.

"It took a few weeks before I felt safe enough to come back to the house. The Arcadian Guard went through everything. This place had been completely destroyed. I cleaned it up and put it back the way I remembered it in hopes you guys would return. For a long time, I replaced the flowers in all the vases. Every week. But after the first full year, I realized you guys *weren't* coming back."

Arryn was moved by her aunt's actions when she still feared the worst. As sad as it was, it was nothing compared to the happiness that Arryn felt simply by having family around again. It had been an emotional day, but it had shown her much more hope.

"So, tell me, who's your *very* quiet friend?" Celine asked.

Arryn laughed.

And laughed.

And then she laughed some more.

She looked over to Cathillian, who was giving her a confused look.

"Why is that funny?" Celine asked.

Cathillian being seen as quiet was laughable at best. She calmed her hysterical laughing and wiped away the resulting tears from her face.

"Oh, damn. That was way funnier than it should've been. This is Cathillian, and he is in no way shape or form quiet. Ever. I mean, *ever*. Which is why I laughed so hard. He's only being quiet now out of respect. Because while I *do* give him a hard time, he's a good guy."

"I'm not exactly sure if I should be offended, flattered, or moved. Somehow, I feel a mixture of all three. Also, I hate you," Cathillian said. He turned to Celine. "I'm the one her mother saved in the Dark Forest all those years ago. Arryn and I grew up together, which is why she's so comfortable being cruel to such a gentle soul like me."

Celine smiled and nodded. "I'm happy you were able to find a family, one that clearly cared a lot for you. While I spent my days wishing that you were back here with me, I knew if you were still alive, then you were probably safe. You were certainly safer wherever you were than here."

"Where do you live now?" Arryn asked.

"I used to live at the end of the street, but these homes were abandoned after Adrien ordered all of them searched repeatedly for any evidence of treachery along with Christopher. We came back briefly, but after losing my mom, I couldn't stay there anymore."

Arryn's brows furrowed as she reached out to give Celine's arm a gentle squeeze. "I'm sorry. I don't remember much about my grandmother, which *totally* sucks."

Celine nodded. "You'd have loved her. Feisty as hell, just like your mom. After that, I went to go live with some friends. Seems that's what a lot of people are doing now, though I'm not sure why. There are more than enough houses to go around. Hell, the Boulevard families could live in the noble houses now. No one's around to tell them otherwise."

"I agree, but I don't think that's the problem. Amelia doesn't seem like the kind of person to just *forget* there are vacant homes—*nice* ones at that. If I had to guess, I'd have to say they're probably too proud, and I can't say I blame them. Change is hard for some people. We've been staying in Lord Girard's old house. You remember that huge bitch?"

"Seriously? I always wanted to go in there. Hmm. We won't be alone where I'm staying. How about I walk you home? We can hang out and catch up, and you can show me the house," Celine said.

Arryn nodded and smiled. "I'd love that. But first, I need to get that family portrait from over the fireplace. I wanna take it with me. There are family portraits all over, but that one is important."

"I'll grab it," Cathillian said with a smile. "You're too short."

Arryn rolled her eyes. "I'd punch you, but you're about to go and make yourself useful for once."

Even with the amusing insults, Arryn took the time to appreciate the moment. The moment that her life became even fuller, igniting an even bigger excitement for her new journey.

The group spent the whole evening catching up, or in Cathillian's case, getting to know the newcomer. Seeing Arryn so happy left a perpetual grin on his face. The next morning, he was up earlier than she was; he had things to do.

Because most of the loggers were out of commission with wounds, Cathillian thought it would be a perfect time to teach the men a little bit about replenishing what they take. Respecting the nature around them.

Over the last couple of days, Cathillian had visited the medical building and healed some of their wounds. Because so many were injured very badly, he couldn't use his full ability on any single person, so he performed small healings every day, doing what he could manage.

Still, it had gone a long way. The men with broken legs were up on makeshift crutches, and the ones with severe, deep wounds that had begun to fester were now up and walking around fever-free, though they still had a lot of residual pain.

Cathillian had a bag full of acorns. Many of which he had gathered from home and always had with him, but the rest he had taken from the base of the very few trees in the city. Cathillian explained how taking from the forest and not giving anything in return would eventually result in an imbalance, the forest thinning, and the loggers unable to do their work.

That was concerning for them, but their biggest fear—of course— was of another remnant attack.

They were too afraid to head back toward the forest bordering the Madlands.

It was too close, and too many of them had nearly died for the wood.

The pay wasn't even that good, certainly not good enough to risk death for.

This was yet another reason why Cathillian asked them to meet him just outside the city walls that morning. He planned to find at least one person in the group that had an affinity for nature magic and teach them the most basic skills—how to harvest plants.

Cathillian heard voices, and he looked up to see several men heading in his direction. The men that were unable to walk longer distances were on the backs of horses, no doubt helped up by their friends.

"Hey!" Cathillian shouted. "Glad to see you could make it."

It was Samuel that led the pack, hammer at his belt and a smile on his heavily bearded face. "Yer all right, lad. The way we figure it, if yer willin' ta teach, some of these rat bastards better be willin' ta learn."

"Besides, I think the men're finished with the borders. I doubt I can get any of 'em out there again if I tried," Ren said.

Cathillian laughed. "Well, no matter the reason, I plan to teach somebody something here today."

Cathillian reached into his pack and grabbed a handful of acorns. He handed one to each of the men and instructed them to go stand fifteen feet apart.

"Now, acorns are easy. We need to take the ground up a little—it should still be soft from the recent rain—and put the acorn in about two inches deep. As you do, do your best to completely clear mind. Focus on nothing except for the task in front of you."

Cathillian watched as the group did exactly as he asked. Each man planted his own acorn, taking their time and following each direction carefully. More than anything, he hoped that even one of them would show some kind of spark with nature. When it happened, Cathillian was quite a bit more than surprised to see who it was.

"Samuel," Cathillian said, an amused smile on his lips. "I have no idea how you're going to handle this, but would you come back here for a minute? I'd like to have a word with you."

There were a lot of amused "*ohs*" and groaning from the other guys, everyone making amusing snide comments about him getting in trouble with the teacher. Samuel mumbled *scheisse* and something about all of them being dicks as he made his way over to Cathillian.

"What is it, lad?" he asked.

Cathillian did his best not to laugh, knowing what the rearick was about to say. "Well, I have some good news. It seems that I've found my potential nature magic user."

Samuel's brows furrowed, his eyes narrowing as he stared up at Cathillian. "I'm gonna need ye ta think *real* hard about the next words about come outta yer mouth, lad."

Cathillian did laugh this time. "I'm sorry, Samuel, but it's true. Couldn't you feel it? I told everyone to clear their minds and focus because I wanted to see who naturally connected with the earth around them. There were a couple, but you were the strongest."

"Of course, I was because I'm good at anything I set out ta do. Doesn't mean I want any part of it," the shorter man said. "Magic's fer those who can't get along without it. Not fer me."

"If you look, where you planted your acorn, there are a few blades of grass trying to sprout through the dirt that you just planted."

Samuel rolled his eyes. "Boy, yer blind. I had ta tear up grass ta dig the hole. I put the same dirt back in. That's all that is."

Cathillian shook his head. "I thought so, too, at first, but I was wrong. Look for yourself. Yes, you'll see fully formed blades of grass that were already there, but you'll also see tiny, thin pieces growing from the bare spaces of dirt. In fact, I would have to say that if you pulled that acorn back out, you'd find a crack in it—maybe even a sprout."

Samuel looked back to the spot where he had been kneeling on the ground before looking back to Cathillian. "I ain't no magic user. Never have been; never will be. No interest in learnin' either. So, ye can find yerself a different one."

Cathillian nodded. "OK, OK. Just remember what I said. If you ever *do* want to learn, find me, and I'll teach you. It sure as hell isn't gonna hurt you to learn. In fact, you might save your own life or the life of others. Remember, you can heal people and animals."

Samuel waved a hand in the air, shaking his head. "Yeah, yeah. Still ain't carin', kid."

Samuel walked away, and Cathillian stayed quiet, allowing the man to return back to his station. It was time for Cathillian to put his little test in action.

"OK everyone, now I want you to lay your hands flat on the ground. Push everything out of your mind. As you well know, magic has its limits. Even for me, a druid. If you hope to give back to the forest everything you take from it—and you should—and you plan to have job security, then you need to learn to harvest and grow things for yourselves."

Cathillian watched, studying each of them as they laid their hands on the ground. Samuel waited until everyone closed their eyes before he backed away. It seemed to Cathillian that he was more afraid of learning magic than he was of fighting remnant.

But it didn't come as a surprise to him.

Samuel's people were naturally phobic of magic. It was thought that they had no magical abilities whatsoever, but he believed that it was more so that they had no desire.

Only one of the men other than Samuel showed any kind of real promise, while one other had at least some kind of connection, but that didn't stop Cathillian from trying.

"Next, I want you to feel the energy surrounding your hands. Part of that energy is yours. Feel for it, then, I want you to push it forward. Imagine that power is being channeled directly from your hands into the acorn itself."

Since Samuel had no plans on using his acorn, Cathillian decided to make his way over and commandeer it. He knelt, placing his hands on the ground around the loose dirt. He felt for his own energy and pushed forward, immediately feeling the acorn respond.

Within moments, the plant broke through the ground and began to grow even taller and thicker. In less than a minute it had grown to three feet tall and two and a half inches across at the base.

"Whoa," Andrew said from his left. "That's impressive."

"It is. And if each and every one of you take the time to learn this type of magic, you'll never run out of work. The forest will never run out of trees. We're gonna continue working on this, especially while most of you still can't work. In about three or four days all of you should be back to normal, and your trees should be sprouting nicely."

Cathillian realized he was being a hard teacher, but he had no idea how long he and Arryn would be in Arcadia, and he didn't want to leave them without knowing how to do these things.

If he did, it wouldn't take long before they came to the Dark Forest and tried to cut down trees. That, of course, would end up very bad for those men. He needed them to know how to harvest things safely. Like Arryn, he wanted to make a difference.

Amelia sat at home, sipping some of the aged mystics' brew that Julianne had brought her during her last visit. It had been quite a rough day, and there was a lot of forgetting to do—even if she *was* still supposed to be at work.

She called it an early day after another failed Doyle attempt. The only lead they had after this one was that he was overheard talking in private with a woman that was now traveling with him. Doyle was building a group of nobles to bring back to the city. She'd never let him get that far. He needed to be found.

Immediately.

Doyle hadn't been the only hard part of the day. She'd had to talk to Amos' mother. She had to break the news that her only son had been killed.

It felt like she'd failed Amos *and* his mother. She thought back to the moment when she informed Amos' mother what had happened. Tears welled in her eyes as she recalled the pained look on the woman's face as she told Amelia that it was all her fault.

After the battle, Amelia had paid many visits to many families, having to tell them their child, their sibling, or their parent had died protecting them—had died valiantly protecting the city and reclaiming what was theirs. That had been an honor—even if it was met with sadness. There'd been tears then, too, but they weren't senseless. Those tears had been shed for a good reason.

This was something different. There was no war. No battle. There was only a senseless tragedy.

Murder.

Some of the noble students had remained after the battle, a lot of them, in fact. It was possible that one of them had been guilty. She hadn't nosed into their minds quite like she had the teachers.

In the interview process, Amelia had been diligent in keeping an eye out for anything that she felt was off. She hadn't done that quite so harshly with the students. Perhaps if she had, Amos would still be alive.

She shook her head, blinking her eyes as she did. "Get yourself together, Amelia," she said. "There are other people who still need you."

Before she could officially call it a night, she still had at least one more thing to do.

She decided to take a quick shower and clean herself up, hoping the hot water would relax and sober her back into her normal self. Talia had sent word the day before that she had returned, and Amelia needed to go and greet her and tell her the news about Amos.

It seemed every time she visited Talia, she had both good and bad news. She hoped for once the visit could be pleasant, but problems would be a constant for a while.

It wasn't anything she couldn't handle, and she refused to let it get her down any more than what it already had. Besides, there was good news to be had. There would be a new nature magic teacher starting tomorrow, and that meant excitement, hope.

As Amelia made her way down the street from the Capitol building, she saw experienced Guard out training the new recruits. She'd hired another fifty men in hopes that nothing like what happened with Amos would happen again, but it would still take a while before they were fully trained. It seemed that it was easier to hire guards than to get help rebuilding the city.

Though, the Boulevard seemed to be coming along quite nicely.

She couldn't blame them for feeling selfish and seeking work outside the city after everything that happened to them, but if those feelings didn't change and people didn't start having more of a community mindset, then the city would never get back on its feet. All in all, she hoped it was only time they needed.

As Amelia made her way into the Academy, she couldn't help but notice how quiet it was. Most everyone was gone for the day, only a few—like the Dean herself—were left. She knocked on the office door, and Talia called for her to enter from the other side.

Talia had a broad smile on her face. "Amelia! It's so good to see you. I'm sorry I didn't go to you yesterday, but I was exhausted after the long trip. That being said, I come bearing big news. The trip was a success!"

That was certainly good to hear. Amelia immediately felt better upon hearing those words. "I can't wait to hear about it."

Talia gestured for Amelia to sit in one of the chairs in front of her desk. She moved some papers out of the way and sat down herself on the opposite side.

"So, as you know, I traveled to Cella. I went to talk to the Governor, who was very glad to see me. Lucky for us, it's a small city, and everyone knows everyone. I negotiated terms on behalf of Arcadia, and I hope that you'll be satisfied with what I came back with. I hope that's OK."

At first, Amelia wasn't sure how she felt about the Dean negotiating anything on her behalf. It wasn't until that moment she realized just how silly it was to allow Talia to go instead of going herself.

But, having thought about it, she realized Talia did have a better chance at gaining ground than she did, simply because of the relationship she shared with the smaller town. She relaxed and nodded, giving an encouraging smile to urge Talia to continue.

"The Governor agreed to send a hundred men to help us rebuild. They'll also bring supplies—though, I'm sure that won't be much. Most of the supplies they have come from us in the first place. Regardless, the hundred men will be a huge help. What he asked for in return was six months reduced cost on anything that they ordered from us, but I talked him down to three."

Amelia's eyes went wide for a moment as she thought about six months of making little from their biggest consumer, but Talia had corrected it. Three months would be difficult, but it was still money coming in. "That seems fair. Did he ask for anything else?"

Talia shifted in her seat leaning forward and placing her clasped hands on the desk in front of her. "He would also like for his son to attend the Academy free of charge."

Talia held up her hand when she saw Amelia was about to protest. Talia smiled.

"Trust me, I know doing anything for free right now is a big letdown. So, I told him yes to his son attending for free, only if he encouraged some of his non-Arcadian nobles to send their children to the Academy. He said those people would be happy to pay the tuition costs."

Amelia sighed in relief. "I hate charging large tuition costs at all. But with the Boulevard families being unable to pay anything, and the city being unable to tax anything because there's *nothing* to tax, we have no choice but to do income based pay structures here."

Talia smiled. "Everyone understands, Chancellor. Try not to worry about that."

Amelia nodded. "Once the city is up and running again, and everyone is working, everything will fall back in line. Tuition will be more regulated. Still, you did a wonderful job as an ambassador for Arcadia. I'm grateful. This'll go a long way. A hundred men. That was quite a feat."

Talia smiled and gave a curt nod. "Thank you, Amelia. I appreciate your kind words."

Amelia dreaded the next part. Talia had to know that one of her students had been murdered, and she was hesitant to start the uncomfortable conversation. "I'm terribly sorry to do this. I know I always have bad news every time I walk in this office, but I do, in fact, have terrible news."

Talia's face fell for a moment. "OK. I understand, though you never have to be afraid to come to me with anything. What is it?"

"I'm sure you remember me telling you about Amos."

Talia nodded. "Of course, I remember. How could I forget?"

Amelia shifted in her seat, coming to sit closer to the edge. "He was found dead on the Boulevard. At first, we thought he'd been killed there. But we were told by one of our newest teachers, a nature magic user, that he'd actually been killed somewhere else. She's been quite a help. With her, I think we might be able to find the one responsible."

There was a flash of something that crossed her face. Anger? Sadness? But it disappeared quickly.

"What? I… I don't understand. I have so many questions," Talia said, her brows furrowing as she leaned further into her desk.

Amelia nodded. "Understandably. Feel free to ask anything. I know this is probably very hard on you, too."

"Who's this new teacher? How would she know that he wasn't killed there? What if she could be involved? Seems suspicious to me. When you initially told me, I was certain he'd gone off on his own. At least, that's what I'd hoped. This is terrible."

Talia's eyes began to fill, a single tear escaping to run down each of her cheeks. She quickly wiped them away, clearing her throat and gathering herself.

Amelia felt terrible for the Dean. She knew Talia would take it hard, but Amelia had hoped that she wouldn't feel the guilt that she did.

"As for the new teacher… While you were gone, we had two visitors come. One was a druid from the Dark Forest, the other a former Arcadian turned druid. Her name is Arryn. When I saw her following the guards from the house she's staying in, she offered to help. I guess nature magic has a lot more to it than the obvious."

"I see," Talia said. "When will I get to meet this new teacher? Seems she might be quite handy to have around the city for something other than just teaching."

"Actually, tomorrow will be her first day. The students and teachers should be back, barring any issues that might arise today. The laborers are still working. It's slow, but when your men arrive, that'll change."

Talia forced a smile. "Well, I look forward to meeting her. The men should be here within two days." Talia looked down to her hands, fidgeting with her nails. "Seems like things are about to get *very* interesting around here."

Amelia thought it sounded like a strange thing to say, but she let it go. *Interesting* was probably a bit strong of an adjective, but productive certainly seemed like a good fit. She couldn't wait to see the progress, for the city to see progress, so spirits could be lifted.

Amelia thanked Talia and excused herself, heading back home. She wanted to get a good night's sleep before tomorrow. It's a brand-new day, and a brand-new opportunity for success.

TWENTY FOUR

Arryn made her way into the Academy, her anxiety rising with every step. She wasn't used to being up so early in the day anymore, a bad habit she'd vowed to fix. It was time to get her routine back—she'd missed it.

Cathillian had woken her early that morning so they could train, hoping it would calm her nerves. While it made her feel much more like herself, her jitters were still in full swing. Amelia would be there soon to give her the tour, a request that Arryn had made since she didn't know anyone else.

"Arryn!" Amelia said as Arryn walked through the door. "I'm happy that you made it OK. You're even early."

Arryn laughed. "My sleeping routine has been total *shit* since coming here; I'm just as surprised as you are."

Amelia smiled, reaching out and giving Arryn's arm a light squeeze. "Everything will start to feel more like home soon enough. It'll just take some time."

"I'm sure you're right. It's only been a few days. So, let's get this show on the road. I'm ready whenever you are," Arryn said.

Arryn followed Amelia through the many different halls of the Academy. There was a hall specifically dedicated to magic, where the other halls were for history, math, and other such things. The entire building was stunning, to say the least. It was far more than anything she'd imagined.

The longer Arryn walked the halls, and the more she pictured herself being a part of the Academy, the more comfortable she became. By the time she made it to the classroom, *her* classroom, she felt a bit more confident. Amelia stopped for a moment and turned to Arryn.

"I know this is all a lot to take in, but you'll acclimate in a couple of days I'm sure. Everyone here is very pleasant, and I think you're going to fit in beautifully. The Dean of Students, Talia, will be here soon to meet you."

Arryn took a deep breath and exhaled heavily, stealing herself before she walked in. "Thank you, Amelia. It's hard to think about where I started a couple of weeks ago and where I am now. Unbelievable really."

Amelia smiled. "It's certainly a great start, though." She reached out and placed a hand on Arryn's shoulder. "Are you ready?"

Arryn nodded, nervously fidgeting with her tunic. Amelia opened the door and led the way inside, Arryn close behind. Arryn was surprised to see just how full the class was, and now, all eyes were on her.

Everyone there was right around her age, give or take a year or two. She was in charge of teaching them, taking care of them, even being responsible for them, and they were her peers. Her eyes wandered from face to face, looking for anyone that seemed familiar to her, but there were none.

"Good morning, everyone!" Amelia said. "This is Arryn. I know this probably seems odd, given she's no older than a lot of you. For the first couple weeks, this class will be mandatory. I want each of you to give nature magic a chance and see if any of you have an affinity for it. After that, if you like it, you're more than welcome to stay."

A girl up front held up her hand before speaking out. "Hi. Emily. So, is it true that you're a druid? Rumor has it you're a druid."

Arryn cleared her throat, her eyes briefly cutting to Amelia before she stepped forward to speak. "Sort of. I was an Arcadian until I was nine years old, but after that, I grew up in the Dark Forest."

"Why would you choose to live there? Aren't the druids terrifying? Some of us met one during the revolution. I didn't, but from what I heard, she was weird as hell," Emily said.

Arryn knew Laurel very well. She was awesome, but definitely weird. "I know in Arcadia the druids are said to be scary and dangerous. The truth is, you'll *never* meet anyone with a purer heart than a druid. Living in the Forest, family took on a whole new meaning. Family isn't just important. Family is *everything*."

"So, they're just a bunch of pushovers?" one of the young men in the back asked.

"No, Shawn, you jackass," a man from the left side of the room said.

His words seemed hostile, but the two of them seemed comfortable with one another. He wasn't dressed quite as nicely as the rest, and she imagined that he was from the Boulevard. "You fought alongside Laurel. She was a badass. Kinda weird, like Emily said, but a badass."

Shawn looked just as confused as before. "*Uh...*"

The man from the left side of the room looked at Shawn incredulously. "Is this a joke? She was the one with the crazy squirrel she talked to! You clearly don't remember anything, do you?"

Shawn finally laughed. "Oh, yeah! Sorry, Tom. I totally forgot about her. She was pretty talented with a knife if I'm thinking right. Never mind, Arryn. Carry on."

Arryn laughed. "Druids are the best fighters I've ever seen. They spend every day of their lives training, cultivating the land, and growing their magic to make sure their borders are fortified and their food is plenty, but they also spend it playing. As hard as they work, and as hard as they train, they're just as loving and just as playful."

It amazed her how interested everyone was. They all sat straight forward, leaning into their desks as they listened to her every word. Then again, she couldn't blame them. She'd always been fascinated by the druids, too. The monsters of the Dark Forest.

"I wasn't born a druid, but I was raised one. My friend, Cathillian, was also asked to teach, but he politely declined. If you met him, you'd know why. Druids have the attention span of toddlers. Give 'em something shiny, and they're easily distracted." Everyone laughed, and she joined in. "I guess that's not *entirely* accurate. I say *they*, but really, I just meant *him*."

There was a knock at the door, and a guard stepped in, waving to Amelia. "Chancellor," he said.

Amelia nodded and stepped forward. "So, Arryn, why don't you tell the class what things you plan to teach them?" Amelia said before patting her on the back and stepping into the hall.

Arryn nodded, doing her best to think on her feet. She'd never taught anything except to the little ones in the tribe. She had no idea how to teach, let alone come up with a structured lesson plan.

That was one thing she and Cathillian had in common. Neither one of them did very well with structure, though Cathillian had somehow made that work during all his years of warrior training.

Arryn took a deep breath before beginning. "The first two weeks, we're going to focus on fundamentals. I know, fundamentals always make everything seem *so* exciting. But because some of you have been using physical magic your entire lives, you're actually at a *disadvantage*."

Everyone seemed very confused to hear this—the nobles especially.

"I realize you think knowing how to cast physical magic would put you ahead. It makes sense, but I promise you it's more of a hindrance than anything. Those from the Boulevard that have little to no knowledge of magic will have a much easier time grasping the basics because the two magics are different in every way. Creation and destruction."

Shifting her weight around, she leaned back on what was now her desk, sitting on the edge as she continued to fake knowing what she was doing as much as she could. Like Amelia said, after a few days, she'd feel right at home.

Right now, all she had to do was give them the same speeches that were given to her by Elysia—and there was no better teacher than her. Though, Cathillian came in at a close second.

There was a pause as the students looked to one another, but it was the Boulevard students that had caught her attention. The looks on their faces were tragic at best.

Those students knew exactly what true hunger felt like, and she knew it. The ability to harness the ability to create food to feed their families was priceless to them, and if they stuck around, she'd teach them exactly how to do it. She heavily doubted any of them would cut the class.

"I don't want you to think I'm an expert. I'm not. I didn't start until I was ten. I'm no better with nature magic than some of you are with physical magic. However, none of you know how to use nature magic. So, the way I see it, I can learn from you just as much as you can learn from me. I'll be in some of your other classes. So, don't be surprised when you see me around the school playing the part of student as well."

Talia had just finished up in her office and was making her way to what would now be the new nature magic room. Talia found it a little annoying, but it made the Chancellor happy, and whatever kept Amelia happy kept her away from Talia.

That was all that mattered to her.

She'd just turned down the hall that held that particular classroom when Scarlett darted out of an empty room.

"Heading to meet the new teacher?" Scarlett asked.

"*Fuck me!*" Talia jumped. She wasn't easy to frighten, but Scarlett had done so with ease. "What is the matter with you? You might see people coming, but I can't."

Scarlett smiled. "Sorry about that. I was just excited. I made it my mission to meet everyone that works here. I've met almost everyone, but I saved her for last. So… Are you gonna go meet the new teacher?"

Talia shook her head, irritated. "Seems that way. Not exactly sure how I feel about not being involved in the interview process. The way it sounded, there *wasn't* one."

"I asked around. I don't think there was. Amelia met her, liked her, and hired her on the spot. That doesn't exactly sit well with me either. You want me to loiter outside and see if I can get in her head?" Scarlett asked.

Talia kept walking, silent as she thought that over. "Well, I'm sure Amelia already took a look inside her head. I doubt there's anything to worry about."

"Ah, you mean like the way she looked in yours and found you harmless?" Scarlett quipped.

"Touché."

"Yeah. So, if it's all the same to you, I think I'm just gonna stand outside and nose around."

Talia nodded. "Thanks. Now that you've mentioned it, I don't want to take the chance either. I'm sure she's fine, but we needed to take a look at some point anyway. May as well make good on the opportunity we're given."

They walked the rest of the way in silence. When they finally reached the classroom, Talia told Scarlett to wait and do her investigating from outside the room. She opened the door, a large smile on her face as she did.

Talia watched as the beautiful young woman turned to face her, a smile on her face, though Talia could tell she seemed nervous. The newcomer took a few steps forward and extended her hand.

"Hi," the girl said, everyone whispering amongst themselves as Talia walked further in. She was shocked the girl had addressed her at all, especially in the middle of talking to her class. "I'm Arryn. You must be Talia. Happy to meet you. Looks like we'll be working together."

Talia extended her hand, taking Arryn's and giving it a light shake. She was about to respond when Scarlett's voice broke through her thoughts.

Caution, Talia… This girl will be your undoing. I can't look further now. Amelia's coming. Just watch your back with that one.

Talia swallowed hard as Amos' words came back. She struggled to keep her smile from faltering, though she was instantly filled with hatred of the girl.

Try as she might, she couldn't keep the worry and the anger of Arryn's presence from leaking darkness into her voice. "I'm Talia. It's *so* nice to meet you."

Amelia came into the room, a smile on her face, though it was forced. "Arryn, can I see you outside?" she whispered to Arryn before turning to the rest of the class. "Take an early lunch today, everyone. Introductions were all we had planned for today. Come back tomorrow ready to learn!"

"What's going on?" Arryn asked.

Amelia said nothing as she led Arryn down the hall, out of earshot of any students wandering by.

"I thought I was teaching a full class today," Arryn said.

Amelia turned, waving her hands in front of her as she looked around. "Do you remember me telling you we were hunting someone?"

Arryn nodded. "I do. Doyle, or something like that. He was a friend of Adrien's."

"Yes. It hasn't gone well, and I'm sorry, but I'll have to keep this brief. The Hunters have tracked him down to a noble house about twenty miles outside of the city. There's a group hiding there."

Arryn's eyes widened. "Oh, hell. Are they planning to come back for the city?"

Amelia sighed. "Yeah. We're almost sure of it. Doyle isn't that smart, so he's being led by someone else. There's no proof, but he's an idiot. Anyway, we have no idea what we're up against. I'm telling you this for two reasons. One—I promised you the shot to talk to him once we find him. But I'll be honest; there is a bigger reason."

Arryn pursed her lips. "You're scared someone is going to get hurt, and you wanna make sure you have a healer on hand."

Amelia nodded. "Yes. I'm sorry, but I have no idea what's going to happen, who's there, how strong they are, or anything else. I can't even promise we'll get him out alive, so I don't want to give you hope, but this is a better chance than any. So, what do ya say?"

Arryn stood silent for a moment, thinking it over. "I get to possibly beat the shit out of Adrien's best bitch and protect the city from possibly getting attacked?"

"Yep. That's the short version," Amelia replied.

Arryn smiled. "Next time, just tell me to get my shit because we're leaving."

TWENTY FIVE

Before leaving the city, *Arryn* and Amelia stopped to get Cathillian. Arryn knew if her primary purpose for going was healing, she wasn't going to be nearly as much use as him.

More than anything, all she wanted was information, but the possibility of getting to do damage to someone that was so close to the man her parents died to take down—well, she couldn't pass that up.

Amelia, Cathillian, Arryn, and ten other guards left Arcadia on horseback. Amelia wanted to take more, but Cathillian had warned her it was a perfect opportunity for whatever Doyle was planning.

He was worried about the possibility that Doyle had allowed himself to be found for the sole purpose of leaving the city unprotected while they pursued him.

Arryn wasn't worried, though she was cautious. She had a feeling they were getting ready to walk into something terrifying, but she knew it would be well worth it.

The house Doyle was staying in was a few hours outside the city. Only a single Hunter had returned to warn Amelia, the rest having fanned out around the perimeter at a safe distance where they couldn't be seen, but close enough to see any activity if those inside tried to leave.

It had taken a few hours, but Amelia was sure they were coming up on it.

"While I'd like to pretend I'm a battle genius," Amelia said. "I'd have to say you guys are probably a little better at this than I am. We need a plan."

It was hard to talk or hear over the loud hooves, but they couldn't stop their pace. Not yet.

"We need to get close enough you can use your mental magic, and I can use my nature magic to sense how many people are in the house. We need to know what we're up against," Cathillian said.

"If anyone in there is sensitive to mental magic like I am, we'll give ourselves away," Arryn said.

"She's right," Amelia said.

"OK then," Cathillian said. "Well, I have another plan. Arryn, you'll come with me. Amelia, order your men to spread out around the building."

From there, they rode in silence. As they saw the building coming up in the distance, Arryn found a few Arcadian men hiding in the tall grass and watching for any movement. Amelia signaled for everyone to stop, and they all slowed their horses.

"Have you seen or heard anything?" Amelia asked, getting off her horse and kneeling next to a couple of the men on the ground.

One of the guards shook his head. "Nothing outside the house, but we see movement inside. We think there are at least twenty people in there."

Arryn heard that number and cringed. She'd been training for a long time, and she'd trained with others besides just Cathillian. Still, even after all that and after passing the trials, she'd never faced a human enemy. This would be her first time.

And it scared the hell out of her.

Then, as she stared forward, thinking of all the people inside the house that were plotting against her city, threatening to undo all the good that had just been done, a dark smile spread across her face.

The chance that had been robbed from her when Elysia and the Chieftain had decided not to tell her about the Founder coming was now right in front of her. On a much smaller scale, but there it was. Her excitement grew, and suddenly, she couldn't wait to get in there.

"Cathillian, what's your plan?" Arryn asked. "I'm ready to go. I wanna do this."

Cathillian shook his head. "This isn't like sparring, Arryn. This is battle. We took on those lycanthropes, but they're straightforward. No tricks. These are magic users."

"I'm ready!" Arryn said. "Call me a bitch or something to piss me off real good and send me in." She smiled, but she was only partially joking.

"Arryn," Amelia said. "Don't go in fireballs blazing. If you do, you'll exhaust yourself very quickly. It's dangerous. Do what you can do—as much as you can do—physically before you resort to magic. Whatever happens, though, don't let them use their magic on you."

Arryn nodded. "Noted. Now, let's go save our city."

Cathillian shook his head again, sighing as he did. "If you get killed, I swear to the gods, I *will* find a way to bring your ass back, and then I'll kill you again. I'll do it repeatedly until I run out of energy and can't do it anymore."

"Well, what if you ran out of energy after you kill me? Then I'll have to stay dead since you won't have the energy to bring me back."

Cathillian smiled, his left brow rising. "Then I guess you shouldn't piss me off and take the chance, huh?"

"Damn. What a bitch," Arryn said.

Cathillian winked. "OK, Arryn, follow me. Do exactly as I say. Amelia, give the men their orders."

Cathillian rose into a crouch, running as low as he could, Arryn following close behind, doing the same. They came to a stop about two hundred feet away from the front of the house, each of them kneeling to the ground.

Cathillian looked to Arryn. "Place your hands flat on the ground. We're gonna give Amelia just a couple minutes, and then we're gonna announce ourselves."

"Announce ourselves? How are we gonna do that?"

An almost evil, yet playful smile spread across Cathillian's lips. "I think I'm gonna split that bitch in two, but I might not have that much power."

"Please tell me you're talking about the house," Arryn quipped.

Cathillian laughed. "I'm gonna shake the house, let 'em know we're here. I'd say one big ass tree should do the trick. As soon as it starts, they're gonna start running out the door, scattering in different directions. Amelia's men will be able to step in then. I want you to stay back as much as possible and don't be afraid to use that bow."

With a brief nod, Arryn turned forward, watching the house. She was ready.

After almost ten minutes, Amelia ran up behind them, causing them to jump because of how quiet she'd been. "They're all ready. I have no idea what you're planning, so I just told them to watch for the sign. I figured they'd know when they saw it."

Arryn snorted. "Oh, they'll know it all right."

Cathillian faced forward, placing his hands on the ground in front of him.

Arryn could feel Cathillian casting next to her, his energy connecting with the ground below him, urging it to move.

She remembered back to the dark forest barrier. This felt exactly like the magic he cast then. So, she decided to repeat what she'd learned.

As Arryn began to push, Cathillian spoke next to her. "Save your energy if you can. I don't want you to push too hard, too fast. You'll weaken yourself."

"Uh... What exactly are you doing again?" Amelia asked. When no one answered, she just said, "OK, then. I'll just sit here and watch, I guess."

"Me, too, apparently," Arryn said sarcastically, clearly not happy about Cathillian stopping her fun.

Arryn saw Cathillian dig his fingertips into the dirt as his magic pushed through his palms and raced through the ground toward the house.

The ground shook, breaking open just in front of the house, traveling underneath. From that distance, it was hard to hear, but the sound of broken glass rang out as the building shook.

Just as Cathillian had predicted, screams erupted as almost thirty people ran out of the house—all adult men and women.

"No one else is in the house; I checked," Amelia said.

"Crush it?" Arryn asked with a smile on her face. "We don't want them to be able to run back in and force us to go in after 'em."

"I've got it," Cathillian said. "The tree is through the floor, and everyone's out.

"Holy shit," Amelia said. "I see him. That's Doyle, I can see him from here! Yes! Crush it! Keep 'em out in the open."

"Hell yes!" Arryn said excitedly, no longer caring about Cathillian's macho request.

Arryn grinned before leaning over, pushing her magic forward into the ground. She began to push harder and harder, urging the magic to carry forward while digging her fingertips into the ground as she did.

Within seconds, the sounds of the house breaking and tearing apart echoed through the sky as a massive tree ripped through the roof, the entire building crumbling before them.

"Go! Now!" Amelia shouted to her men.

Cathillian looked to Arryn. "Holy... shit. Well, now—I wasn't expecting you to pull that off."

"That's what you get for doubting me. Also, instructions are great, but no one is making me out to be a delicate flower. In case you hadn't noticed, I don't need to be protected all the time. I'll always need your help, but I'm not a little girl anymore."

He smiled. "Sorry I doubted ya. Maybe you could be a rose. They're all thorny, you know."

"I seriously thought you said something else there for a second," she said with a relieved sigh.

He laughed. "Well, that, too. How are you feeling? We just used a lot of magic."

She shrugged. "It was a lot, but so far, I feel fine. I doubt I could do that again, though."

Cathillian shook his head. "You shouldn't have to. Just do what you do best. Get your bow and take 'em out from a distance. If they don't cast magic, use non-lethal shots. But if they try attacking in any way, well, you know what to do."

Arryn nodded. "And if they get too close—" she started.

"Kick their asses like you kick mine," Cathillian said, giving her a wink. "Or you could just insult them to death. That also works great."

Before Arryn could insult him again, Cathillian ran off. Arryn shook her head as she readied her bow, excited to find the man that might be able to tell her what happened to her father.

Amelia ran for her men, making sure everyone was fighting and safe.

Grabbing the sword she had lashed to her hip, Amelia found her first target and ran for him. They circled one another, each eyeing up their opponent. Finally, the man spoke. "How did you find us?"

Amelia kept her sword out at the ready. While his shook slightly, hers was as steady as a rock. "We kept the name *Hunters* for a reason," Amelia said.

The man laughed. "Well, you just saved us a trip. We were coming for you anyway, and now that you're here, we're gonna finish you and your little minions off before putting the city back the way it belongs."

The man arced his free arm over his chest, but he didn't have the chance to pull it away before an arrow whistled right past Amelia's head and went through his heart.

Amelia jumped, her own heart suddenly racing as she turned to see Arryn more than a hundred feet away with her bow raised. She doubted that Arryn could see her expression, but if she could, she would see just how shocked Amelia was.

Arryn was a *damn* good shot.

Shaking it off, Amelia left the man's corpse and went for the next one. Now that it had been confirmed that everyone here wasn't just harboring a fugitive, but had been prepared to kill them to bring back Adrien's ways, Amelia felt perfectly justified in taking each and every one of the bastards out.

A fireball hit the ground next to her, and she turned to see a woman in her late twenties standing there. She had another fireball in hand, ready to launch. Shoving the tip of her sword in the ground, Amelia stepped forward, readying herself for the attack.

The woman smiled as she pulled her arm back before throwing the fireball. Amelia recognized her as one of her former students. She remembered teaching that girl just how to form a proper fireball.

And here she was... trying to kill her.

Without hesitation, Amelia's arm whipped to the side, the fireball veering off course and hitting what was left of the toppled house.

It immediately burst into flames, unfortunately giving each physical magic user in the area the ability to pull from that fire without using as much of their own magic to create their own.

Amelia didn't plan to give this woman the chance.

She lifted her hand, palm facing up as her sword levitated from the ground. She then swung her arm again, the blade flying through the air and impaling the woman in the stomach.

Not wanting to burn all of her energy conjuring fireballs, and not yet having the best aim while throwing knives or blades of any kind, the minuscule amount of power it took to send the sword seemed the best course of action.

As the woman fell to the ground, Amelia ran up, pulled the sword from her stomach, and drove it through her heart.

Now, time to find Doyle.

Cathillian had already dispatched five people, hoping he wouldn't kill the one Amelia had promised to Arryn.

In his peripheral vision, Cathillian saw a sword swinging in his direction. Without hesitation, Cathillian lifted his arm, catching the blade with his powerful wooden bracer made from the powerful Heilig tree.

As expected, the sword did nothing to the wood, failing to make even a single scratch.

He swung his sword, knocking the Arcadian's blade away to the right, as he spun left, slicing out to the side. The man screamed as the blade cut through his thigh, bringing him down to the ground. Cathillian then wrapped his arm around the man's throat and, with a swift jerk, he ended the fight.

As Cathillian turned to run to the next person, a large fireball hit him directly in the chest, throwing him back to the ground. He tried to inhale, but his chest was burned so badly it felt like the oxygen was being pulled right out of him.

A woman came to stand over him, laughing as she looked down at him with wild eyes. "Hmm. Pointed ears. A druid, huh? You're not anything like I expected."

Cathillian flattened his hands on the ground, feeling for the energy all around him as he pulled it into himself, the woman oblivious to what was happening right in front of her eyes.

A mountain of a man had spotted Arryn and was now running directly for her, but that wasn't her biggest worry.

Someone was standing overtop of Cathillian while another was coming up on him from behind. She'd seen the fireball hit him, but she could sense his energy now. He was healing himself.

Looking at the man that was coming for her, and then over to the one coming up on Cathillian, she made her decision.

Arryn nocked an arrow, letting it loose and shooting the man coming for Cathillian through the throat, effectively dropping him to the ground.

Then, she turned to the man running for her before dropping her bow to the ground and using her foot to kick her staff into the air. She caught it before swinging it around and jabbing him hard right in the stomach.

As he doubled over, she drove her knee into his face, sending him stumbling back. Not one for wasting time, she took a few steps forward and swung her staff, striking him hard across the head and taking him down.

Taking a deep breath to steel herself, she stepped forward and brought her foot down hard on his neck, ending him.

She looked back to check on Cathillian as she heard a feminine scream rip through the air. Vines had burst from the ground, wrapping around the woman's limbs before Cathillian waved his hand, throwing her across the field.

Her screams abruptly stopped when she hit the ground.

Another scream called out, and fear chilled her from head to toe. She knew that voice. Arryn's heart jumped as she turned to see a man run Amelia through the gut with the sword.

Amelia stood, doubled over with her hands wrapped around the blade of a sword, her mouth hanging open as tears ran down her cheeks from the pain, blood bubbling on her lips.

"You shouldn't have come for me," Doyle said. "Should've known better."

"Killing me won't solve anything. The city's stronger than ever. You'll never win." Amelia spat at him, the blood dotting his face.

Doyle yanked the sword free of her stomach and punched her hard in the face, sending her to her knees. Amelia could hardly move as blood pooled in her hands. If it weren't so permanent, she would almost see dying at the hands of Adrien's kiss-ass funny. But since it would mean *actually* letting that happen, she didn't.

The wind began to pick up, bringing with it the stench of death and causing the fire in the distance to grow. Amelia thought she heard a rumble, but she couldn't be certain.

She couldn't believe anything she thought right then, knowing that the blood loss was about to make her delirious, if it hadn't already.

"You have *no* idea what's going on in your city, do you?" Doyle asked. "Do you *really* think I'm the only one?"

"Bullshit!" Amelia choked out. "The city has been cleaned of assholes like you."

Doyle laughed, the sound was surprisingly cold and confident. She'd met Doyle a thousand times, and he'd always been a pathetic piece of shit.

Adrien's death must have broken something in him. She'd always assumed he was subservient out of fear, not out of actually caring for the man, but she'd been wrong.

"Adrien had me deliver a letter before he died. That's how I got out of the city before you bastards ever showed up. He had someone outside the city, you clueless bitch. I don't know the woman's name—not that I'd tell you anyway—but I've seen her. I never opened the letter, out of loyalty, but I know she's in your city, and she's coming for you."

"Lies!" Amelia shouted. "Lies from a desperate man."

He laughed again and then shrugged. "Who's the desperate one bleeding out in front of me? You won't live to find out who the enemy is. She's going to rip that city apart, one Boulevard bitch after another. It's a shame you won't live to see all of those traitors die."

The sky suddenly began to darken as Doyle raised his sword, that rumbling very close now. Amelia cringed, knowing she had no way to defend herself as her vision grew cloudy, the blood loss taking its final toll.

She looked to the sky as it quickly turned grey—and then black.

"Arryn! No!" Amelia heard Cathillian scream.

Arryn stood there, tears filling her eyes as she saw Amelia on her knees. She could feel her energy waning, and instead of forcing her into swift action, it stopped her in her tracks.

This woman, who had not only welcomed her into the city, but had liberated it, was about to give her life to protect it—just like her mother had.

Amelia had trusted her. Had even brought Arryn along on this mission because she'd placed so much faith in her, that she believed Arryn would be able to keep everyone safe, everyone alive.

Amelia had wanted to give her a chance to fulfill the promise she'd made to her parents, while also having the opportunity to learn what had happened to them.

Suddenly, everything drained out of Arryn, her brows furrowing and her teeth grinding as her jaw tightened.

Everything except for rage, guilt, and a searing hatred for the man standing over Amelia.

Thunder cracked overhead, lightning webbing across the sky as she began walking forward. Her eyes locked on her target. She kept her hands out to her side, the tip of her staff dragging along the ground as she headed in his direction.

"Arryn! No!" she heard Cathillian scream.

But it was of no use.

That man had his sword over his head now, ready to finish Amelia. Ready to end the woman who had given her so much hope. She couldn't save her mother, but she *could* save Amelia.

No...

She *would*.

Out of Arryn's peripheral, she saw two men charging for her. Not breaking her stride, she only briefly looked at them as she lifted her staff to the sky, a lightning bolt crashing down to the ground and striking within a few feet of them.

Screaming, they both turned and ran in the other direction.

Amelia's attacker looked over as he saw the flash of lightning, and then Arryn's attackers fleeing for their lives. His eyes widened as they locked on her, bringing a smile to her face.

Arryn thrust her staff forward, throwing him back away from Amelia.

She could hear shouting, people screaming her name, but it meant nothing. She couldn't actually understand their words.

The man stood, arcing his hands over his chest. Arryn planted her staff in the ground, preparing to do the same thing, but he screamed as a blade pierced his stomach, bring him to the ground.

Where did it come from?

No... It doesn't matter...

Arryn placed her arms over her chest, but she very quickly found herself on her back, Amelia throwing herself on top of her, head resting on Arryn's chest, her hand on Arryn's face.

"Stop! Arryn, you have to stop. That's Doyle! He knows things," Amelia said, her voice weak.

Arryn gasped, like it was the first breath she'd ever taken. Suddenly, she was hyperaware of everything around her. Her eyes looked up to the sky, the black clouds dispersing as her power waned. She felt exhausted. Almost unable to will her body to move at all.

Arryn heard a grunt followed by a crunching sound. But she couldn't see anything. She'd become very aware that Amelia was beginning to feel very heavy on her chest.

Arryn saw Cathillian kneeling next to them before he rolled Amelia off her. "Everything's gonna be OK," he said.

Arryn could feel the energy that Cathillian was pulling on as he healed Amelia. Arryn felt a tear slide down her cheek, grateful that Amelia would make it.

"Doyle," Arryn said, trying to sit up before falling back on the ground again.

"Who?" Cathillian asked.

Dread suddenly filled Arryn. "Him, the man that I was just fighting. The one that nearly killed Amelia. She said that was Doyle. He could tell me about my father."

Over the roar of the fire in the distance, over the sounds of the thunder retreating in the sky, over the pain of her pounding headache, and the fatigue draining her body, Arryn could hear the hard swallow.

A sigh escaped her, her chest aching with what she knew was coming. "Cathillian?" Arryn said.

"Arryn... I'm sorry. I... He's dead."

Arryn wanted to break into tears, but she couldn't. There was no energy left. So instead, she did the only thing that she could do.

She gave in to the magical drain and allowed herself to fall unconscious.

EPILOGUE

It had nearly been a week, and Arryn slept most of it. Cathillian had been to see Amelia several times, and she'd slept almost as long.

Today was Arryn's first day back to school and Amelia's first day back to the Capitol building. No matter how much they liked one another before, there was a bond forged between the two now that couldn't be broken.

They'd saved one another's lives.

Had it not been for Arryn, Doyle would have succeeded in killing Amelia. But that life debt had immediately been repaid when Amelia had used what was left of her strength to kick Arryn's legs out from under her, climbing on top of her and holding her tight to bring her back from the darkness.

Had it not been for that, it was hard to say just what kind of magic Arryn would have conjured in her rage, and it would have taken every last bit of energy she had, potentially killing her.

When Arryn walked in the front door, Cathillian was standing there waiting on her. Her expression was clouded with confusion as she closed the door, staring off into nothingness.

"Not exactly sure how to take your grand entrance," Cathillian said. "Did you have a good day or a bad one?"

Arryn slowly crossed the living room, flopping down on the couch across from the fireplace. She sat back and shook her head. "The day was fine. Actually—it was better than fine. I'm exhausted. Still not myself, but it was great. Teaching was something that I never in my life imagined myself doing, but it's a lot of fun."

Cathillian came to sit down next to her, curiosity all over his face. "OK? All that sounds awesome. So, what's with the fucked-up expression? Did something happen?"

Arryn slowly nodded. "It's about the Dean of Students."

Cathillian sat there, staring at her, obviously waiting for more, but Arryn's head was too cluttered to process that. Finally, he said, "I swear to the gods, if you don't look at me and stay focused while we talk, I'm going to slap you back into reality. You seem so lost right now. Full sentences, woman."

Arryn smiled as she changed her position, putting her feet up on the couch and turning to face him. "I'm sorry. It's just—have you ever met anyone that seemed so nice, but there was something there that you just can't explain?"

"What do you mean?" Cathillian asked.

"Talia. The Dean. Her voice was even, calm, and she sounds sweet.

She seems excited to have me there, and there's no reason for me to doubt her. Amelia only has good things to say about her, and the students even seemed excited to see her."

Cathillian nodded. "But?"

"*But* when I shook her hand the day that I met her, and when I crossed her today, I don't know... I can't explain it, but something just wasn't right. I felt *sick*. There's something so familiar about her, but I just... I just can't place it. All I know is I don't like her. I just have a bad feeling about her I guess. Ugh... I shouldn't even worry about this. I still need to meet Amelia and go over everything with her."

Echo hopped her way through the living room, bringing herself to perch on the arm of the couch by Cathillian. He scratched at her chest before turning back to Arryn. "Well, the good news is that it's not like she knows. As long as you were nice and friendly to her, I see no reason for you to worry about it. Just be nice, but be vigilant. You know what Mom says. Always trust your gut."

Arryn gave a sarcastic laugh. "Yeah, except trusting my gut means continuing to hate my new boss. I just can't shake it. I feel like something's there, but there's no reason to."

"If you don't like her, there's probably a reason. I'm not saying don't give her a chance, in fact, I think you should. Seems like you might be giving her a hard time without really knowing her, but I think it's important to hold onto that feeling until you know why it's there. Nature magic allows you to sense things. Don't ignore it."

"I'm sure you're right. I've never really had a superior and real structure before, so maybe she just makes me nervous. I mean, I've known Jenna my whole life, and she never gave me a bad feeling, and she's a real bitch." They both laughed.

"Yeah, see? It'll be fine. Just stay vigilant but be kind," he said.

Arryn nodded. "Yeah. Like you said, it's not like she knows I don't like her. There isn't any awkwardness there. As long as I keep to myself and I'm nice, there shouldn't be a problem." She sighed. "I think I'm gonna go upstairs. I'm exhausted."

With that, Arryn took herself upstairs for a hot shower. She wanted to lie down and go to bed early that night. Celine had spent a lot of time there since they found one another—especially after the fight with Doyle.

Arryn was grateful to have her, but also grateful to be able to take the night for herself. A night to process just how much her life had changed, and just how much more would come.

It also gave her time to sort out her feelings about Talia.

She wondered if she could talk to Amelia about the mental stuff. Maybe it would come in handy. At the very least, maybe she could learn how to keep her mind closed to others.

The thought of Talia being in her head made her sick. Despite what she'd told Cathillian, that bad feeling ran deeper than she cared to explain.

It chilled her to the bone.

Something was *not* right about that woman, and she seemed to be the *only* person that saw it...

As Scarlett walked across the school grounds to leave for the day, she heard loud voices. *Several* loud voices. She made her way around the side of the building to find a group of four male students surrounding Jackson. From the looks of things, they were all Boulevard students. Scarlett took a few steps back, making sure she was out of sight.

As she listened to them, she quickly realized they all believed that Jackson had something to do with Amos' disappearance *and* his untimely death. Every time Jackson tried to defend his innocence, the other students would scream at him, telling him that if he wasn't such a piece of shit that had spent so much time bullying them, they wouldn't think such things.

Scarlett thought this over for a few moments, wondering exactly how she could turn this in her favor. It didn't take long for an idea to snake its way into her mind.

She focused on the four boys that surrounded Jackson, picking out the one whose emotions stood out the strongest.

"I swear, I didn't have anything to do with it!" Jackson said, his voice quivering a bit. "I might not like you guys, but I wouldn't hurt anyone."

We'll see about that, Scarlett thought.

"It doesn't matter!" the largest of the four yelled. "We're part of this school just like you are. We fought to be here. Because of us, you don't have to live under Adrien's thumb anymore. You get the benefits, too, but you still hate us. You still pick on us. Well, now you know what it feels like to be bullied by a group you feel is stronger than you."

Ugh. Fuck, this is boring. Let's see if we can make this a bit more interesting.

Scarlett focused in on the boys, connecting her mind with theirs. Doing such a thing with so many was risky, but she wouldn't need to for long. All she had to do was convince them that Jackson was about to attack, which was easy enough to do.

She willed each of them to see Jackson pull his fist back. In reality, the now-unfortunate young man was standing still, hoping to solve the problem without violence—but that hope was lost as the others defended themselves against an assault that never happened. The four boys jumped into action, the largest one moving first to punch Jackson in the jaw. It was a free-for-all then as all of them piled on top of Jackson hitting and kicking him.

Scarlett gave it just a moment, letting Jackson feel the full force of his fear of them, his rage at being helpless against them before intervening. She ran around the building yelling at them to get their attention. The four boys quickly jumped up, Jackson left severely beaten on the ground. As she approached, she could tell that Jackson would be just fine. As anticipated, they hadn't done too much damage. Nothing seemed broken except for some bones in his face, but she didn't care either way. Nothing the school's new little druid, Arryn, couldn't handle.

"What the *hell* is going on here?" Scarlett asked, rage in her voice.

What a week. It was one that Talia knew would weigh on her for a while. Her plan had just hit its first snag.

Arryn.

The girl seemed very sweet, but Scarlett suggested otherwise. She said the girl had some secrets that needed further investigating. One thing was certain, though.

The girl was an enemy of Adrien. Not an angry bystander like the rest of them.

She'd wanted to rise up and take him down herself. It was blatantly obvious that she was no follower. If given the reason to be, Arryn could and *would* be a huge thorn in Talia's side.

But it wasn't like *Arryn* knew that Talia knew that.

All Talia had to do was smile and continue with her work. Do good things and look good in the process. Arryn was young and naïve. It wouldn't take much to keep her happy. Talia sighed as she reminded herself that she was in control. There would only be a problem if she created one herself by being too paranoid.

Talia was just about to head out the door to go home when Scarlett walked through, Jackson's arm wrapped around her shoulders as she helped him stand.

The Dean's eyes went wide as she looked at two of them. "What the hell happened here? Who did this?"

Jackson coughed, and blood spurted from his nose and mouth all over the floor. It would have disgusted Talia if she hadn't been so caught off guard.

"It was a group of Boulevard bastards," he said, his voice hoarse and weak.

"They had him on the ground beating the hell out of him. I stopped them, but obviously it was too late," Scarlett said out loud, quickly followed by telepathy. *Use this opportunity. It's too convenient not to. Now is the time. Turn him.*

The mystic was right. It was exactly what she'd needed, but she felt completely unprepared for it. Talia walked over and placed her hand under his chin, examining his face. "This is horrible. Jackson, I had no idea that something like this would happen."

Jackson suddenly found strength in his voice and vented. "I did! I've been trying to tell everyone! Those bastards are terrible people. It's not about them being poor. It's how they were raised. All I wanted was to talk it out. I tried to be civil with them. Yes, I have my problems with them, but I still tried to do it without violence. They can't be trusted! Do you see now? Something *has* to be done. It *has* to be. Otherwise, this will just keep happening."

"But what can we do? I can punish them. Give me their names, and tomorrow I'll bring them in here, and I'll expel them. You have my word," Talia said, faking the deepest level of concern in her voice and expression that she could manage.

"No!" Jackson said forcefully. "That's not going to work! They're just going to continue. Do you really think that being kicked out of school is going to stop them from taking an entire lifetime of hatred out on the nobles? No. They have to be stopped."

"Oh, Jackson," Talia said. "You're the first student to give me a real chance around here. I hate to see you hurting like this. I don't know... Maybe those Boulevard kids aren't as good as they seem. I suppose you're right, but what could I possibly do? I'm the Dean. I have to remain neutral."

Jackson's eyes lit up with hope. "Please! Please help us. I'm not the only one. I told you about them before, in my letter. But it's more than that. We have a tight group—meetings and everything. We use it to safely talk to one another, but really, we've been hoping and praying to find a way to get things back to normal. We didn't like Adrien any more than anyone else, but he made those rules for a reason. It doesn't change the fact that he was right. This Academy has been ruined, and so has the city. If anyone can help, it's you. Please. I'm begging you. We would never breathe a word of this to anyone! I swear on my life."

Talia pulled him into a hug, sealing the young man's fate. His body shuddered against her as he began to cry—completely broken, completely battered, completely vulnerable.

At that moment, he was completely hers. She looked over to Scarlett, grateful that the woman had stumbled across the fight. It had been the perfect time to turn him.

A dark smile spread across Talia's lips as she looked over to her new partner, a smile that rivaled Scarlett's.

"Jackson, I think you're right. I think it's time for me to meet your friends. I think it's time for some *big* changes around here."

— FINIS —

Author Notes

CANDY CRUM

Written July 18th, 2017

Sitting here, thinking about what to say to the readers and how to properly introduce myself, I can't even believe I'm here. It's surreal to me. I began this crazy ride with Michael's group as an editor, and now here I am.

When I was told about how amazing his fans were, how dedicated, and how excited they are to read all things KGU, it was a dream come true to work to create something worthy of him and of his fans. You guys are epic, and the opportunity to be able to do this is monumental.

So, since this is the first time (but hopefully the first of many) you're reading anything about me, I'll introduce myself so you know exactly who I am and why I think this and all of you are so bad ass.

I began writing *eight* years ago. I started my first book (*The Eternal Gift*) in April of '09 and finished it in September of '09. It was NEVER supposed to be published—I didn't even know that was possible! And I wrote it all while going to nursing school full time, working full time as a Certified Nursing Assistant (CNA) in a long-term care facility, with two *very* little boys (only twenty months apart at one and two years old), and with my husband several states away in basic training.

It was one hell of a ride, and I'm still shocked that I didn't rip my own face off at some point out of exhaustion and confusion. I think writing was a huge coping mechanism for me. It started with reading. Because even with all that, I read one book every single day—until I started writing. And as I said before, that book was just for fun. In fact, I only ever planned to write it for my co-workers. I didn't know self-publishing was a thing, but I soon would.

Things were action-packed back then when it came to my hectic schedule, and I hadn't considered doing anything except write, print, and bind those chapters every week for my friends, but eventually, I got brave enough to publish a few chapters online back in 2010, and my entire world changed.

People were constantly asking for more, so I wrote more and more and posted a lot until I stumbled upon other people doing even more than that. I made a few friends and then…

I learned a few things.

The next couple of years I spent writing The Eternal Series, and the characters inside became my fictional children. The universe was so big that it allowed me to create so many wonderful characters—vampires, werewolves, immortals, succubi, and more—full of rich pasts and trials of their own.

Every one of them powerful in their own way, and every one of them near and dear to me. Later, I'd realize just how fun it was to expand on the universe.

Now, eight years later, here I am. I'm one husband lighter, fifteen books heavier, and the with the absolute best group of writers (now friends, whether we've met in person or not—totally sounds creepy) that I've ever had the pleasure of knowing.

Eight months ago, because of an amazing author and friend—Bonnie R. Paulson—I stumbled upon Michael and all the amazing people that I now have the joy of working with.

On top of learning a shit-ton of amazing things, I go through every day with at least a couple of dick jokes, *more* if I'm editing for Chris and Lee, and isn't that what makes the world go 'round?

I certainly think it *helps* at times.

[Edit - add by Michael - *Absolutely*!]

My boys are now nine and eleven, and my youngest, Matthew, just finished his first children's book—which he wrote on my laptop sitting next to me while I sat at my desktop—which is very sweetly named *The Legendary Kitten Adventures*. No clue when it will finally be published, but we are working on it together, and it's so much fun.

I had to *force* that child to read (the book I chose was *The War of the Worlds*), and once he finished it, he was hooked. While I found it very amusing, given that very same thing happened to me, only with *20,000 Leagues Under the Sea,* I couldn't have been prouder of him.

Now, being a full-time author, I get to watch him grow every day. I get to watch him grow his imagination and develop his stories.

My oldest son, Brandon, has an imagination that I'm convinced is bigger than that of anyone I know, but he isn't the book writing type—

though, I'm still working on it. Anyone that can create over a hundred unique monsters in a single year with each one having their own unique name and super power *needs* to tell stories! So, I'm hopeful, but he's welcome to keep it to drawing if he likes.

He's a sweet boy with an evil genius mind for stories, and I love it. Maybe one of these days, my boys will grow up and be able to write in the Eternal Universe and create creatures of their own.

How awesome would that be?

For right now, my goal is to continue to inspire them as I have been. It's every parent's dream to be an inspiration to their kids, and I've achieved that. They think I'm cool—because they're weird and are still too young to know better, but I hope that never fades.

They are my life and to have the opportunity to not miss out on their lives is a blessing. My goal in publishing has always been one thing: make a life for my family. And now, because of Michael Anderle, his genius brain, this amazing Universe, and all the crazy awesome fans, I stand a chance of doing that. So, again, thank you! Because this is absolutely a dream come true.

There is another person that I owe a big thank you to. Several, actually, but I want to start with Michael York. I've had several jobs and several employers/superiors, and I never learned a thing from any of them except how *not* to treat people.

I started working for Mike about six months after my divorce, and I'd never had anyone push me quite so hard. He never let me give up or take no for an answer, and he pushed me to realize that I was a much different person than I thought I was. I was stronger and more capable than I'd ever thought possible of doing anything in the world that I wanted.

Because of his initial pushing and my ever-growing desire to succeed, I made goals every day at work, and I smashed them. It made me so motivated *inside* of work that it carried over to my home life, and I began writing more and more all the time. Instead of telling me to focus more on my job (a Sales Rep at an authorized Verizon retailer), he let me write my books in my down time and always asked what he could do to help.

I doubt many people take the time to stop and thank him—because I'm well aware I'm not the only person he's tried to inspire with his positive attitude and hilarious yet wildly inappropriate sense of humor—so I wanted to make sure that he knew. Friends like that don't come around often.

I'd also like take time to thank Scott Paul (author T.S. Paul) for being a badass and believing in me and helping me along my journey. Michael Anderle—you are my hero, even if you don't wanna take credit because you're an awesome guy. You're the shit, and I'll always be grateful to you for letting me write in your world. Chris and Lee—you guys are the best and helped this entire project grow into something amazing. It's hard to believe this all started with editing a few awesome books (the Age of Magic books) and turned into this.

The time is finally here! *Cheers!*

As I'm writing this, I'm sitting on the first third of the words finished in the second book, and it has even more action and fun things to look forward to. The next book is full of madness, so as excited as I am to write it, I hope you guys are just as excited to read it.

Thank you again for all the warm comments and reviews. All this is still unreal to me, and I'm just damned happy to be part of it.

–Candy

Author Notes

MICHAEL ANDERLE

Written July 19th, 2017

It is always something special for me to write this first paragraph of the Author Notes. Which goes like this… *THANK YOU! Not only did you read the whole story, but NOW, you are reading the Author Notes as well.*

I just got finished reading (and editing) Candy's author notes. I'd like to say I didn't edit much, but I did take out a few exclamation points.

Why? Because when Candy gets excited, and emotional, she whips out those "!'s" and she flings them throughout the author notes like she was giving out candy at Halloween.

So, I HAVE to tell you just how much you guys mean to her. I know she tried (through the aforementioned incredibly excessive use of exclamation points) to try to express her appreciation, and I think she accomplished it so well. She is a sweet woman who has been a huge help in the 20BooksTo50k group and then got yanked into the Kurtherian Group (LMBPN Publishing) due to her association with CM (Chris) Raymond and LE (Lee) Barbant.

So, she was editing their stories, and when it came time for Chris and Lee and myself to open up the opportunity to write for you, they asked her if she would enjoy writing a series?

And, it just isn't easy to do this.

For one, she had to be willing to review, re-read, and decide if moving to a Kurtherian voice was something she would be willing to do? (Some authors say they will, but when it comes time to make it happen, aren't willing to do it.)

She said yes.

Then, the rubber hit the road and the writing, and re-writing, and 'oh holy crap, I have to rip ALL of that out of the story?' happens.

Then the whole episodes of working with our cover artist, and the challenges that come along with it (have to grow up, grasshopper) happens. Here in LMBPN, we are a family, but that doesn't mean we aren't ....mmmm.... not demanding really, but very focused on providing stories that marry our collaborators voices with mine and provide the entertainment, and just kick-assery of characters we all grow and love.

It causes a few of our authors to step into a whole new world, and Candy jumped into the pool with both feet and came up bubbling with laughter. She is SUCH a hoot in the group (and really, she does love those jokes from Chris and Lee.) Here is a secret I've mentioned a few times lately. I think most female authors are WAY less concerned about things being PC (or correct in any way) than a lot of ladies I see played on TV.

It seems I'm the one who has been embarrassed when I've had to suggest anything sexually clarifying in our conversations.

For example, on the cover for Quest For Magic with Martha Carr (July 31st, 2017 - the new Oriceran Universe) I had to tell her that the cover artist had not done something … correct … with our main characters breasts.

Martha had to suffer through me stammering out that Leira's left breast seemed to be squished over to the middle of her chest. My face was *FLAMING* red as I stuttered through that. Then, Martha had to take that information and talk with the artist (another guy) and work with him to fix the issue.

Apparently, I think their original clarification took less time for me to explain to Martha my concerns.

Then, I related that story to Sarah Boyce (another Oriceran group writer) and she agreed. Indie Female Publishers were VERY pragmatic and generally didn't care about things that I stumble over explaining. Hell, Ell Leigh Clarke is the one who makes sure the covers for her books sizzle.

So, when Candy Crum (which is her real name, not a pen name) is speaking about the joking around with Chris and Lee, I get it. Sense of humor is a wonderful thing, and girls can be just as humored as guys about stuff I'd be embarrassed to say at times.

Yeah, this is coming from me, right? With some of the stuff I put into the Bethany Anne stories I can only imagine some of you are thinking 'WTF?' I curse like a sailor in real life, I don't share too much other stuff IRL (in real life) as I put into my stories.

Damn, these author notes are freaking *rambling*.

Once upon a time, we had just one female author writing in The Kurtherian Gambit (Natalie Grey). Now, LMPBN Publishing (The

Kurtherian Gambit, The Oriceran Universe and minority partner on Allazar Universe) will have the following ladie's stories out or coming soon and I couldn't be happier.

1) Natalie Grey (The Kurtherian Gambit - Trials and Tribulation Series - Paranormal / Sci-fi)

2) Ell Leigh Clarke (The Kurtherian Gambit - The Ascension Myth Series - Age of Expansion)

3) Candy Crum (The Kurtherian Gambit - Tales of the Feisty Druid series - Age of Magic)

4) Martha Carr (The Oriceran Universe (Co-Creator) - The Leira Chronicles - Urban Fantasy)

5) Sarah (SM) Boyce - (The Oriceran Universe - The Fairhaven Chronicles - Urban Fantasy)

6) Amy Hopkins (The Kurtherian Gambit - A New Dawn - Age of Magic)

7) Amy DuBoff (The Kurtherian Gambit - Uprise Saga - Age of Expansion)

8) Abby-Lynn Knorr (The Oriceran Universe - The Kacy Chronicles - Urban Fantasy)

9) JL Hendricks (The Kurtherian Gambit - Series to be Named - Age of Expansion)

10) Holly Dodd (The Kurtherian Gambit - Chronicles of the Queen's Rangers - TKG)

11) Sarah Noffke (The Oriceran Universe - Soul Stone Mage Series - Urban Fantasy)

12) Hayley Lawson (The Kurtherian Gambit - Series to be Named -
Age of Madness)

Chrishaun Keller-Hanna Publisher / Author (Tales of Allazar among
MANY others)

–Michael

For a chance to see ALL of Candy's different Book Series

Check out her website below!

Website: www.candycrumbooks.com

Michael Anderle Social:

Website: www.kurtherianbooks.com

Email List: www.kurtherianbooks.com/email-list

Facebook Here: www.facebook.com/TheKurtherianGambitBooks